OUR SWEET GUILLOTINE

MARY GRAY

MONSTER IVY
PUBLISHING

OUR SWEET GUILLOTINE
Copyright © 2017 by Mary Gray

http://www.marygraybooks.com

This book is fiction. All of the characters, organizations, and events portrayed in this novel are either products of the author's imagination or are used fictitiously.

Cover Design by Cammie Larsen

ISBN (Mobi): 978-0-9987426-0-1
ISBN (ePub): 978-0-9987426-1-8
ISBN (Paperback): 978-0-9987426-2-5
ISBN (Hardback): 978-0-9987426-3-2
ISBN (Audio): 978-0-9987426-4-9

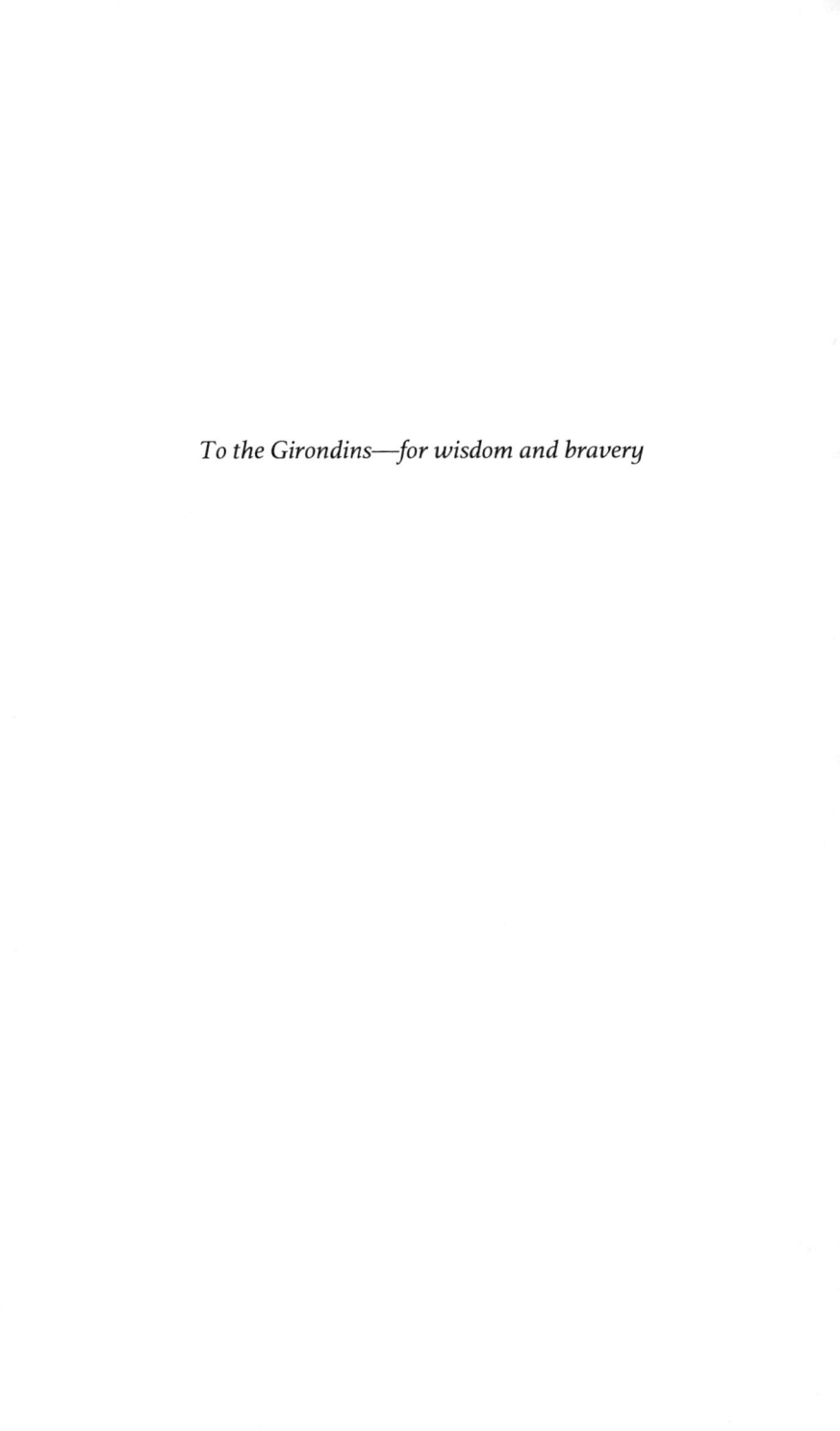

To the Girondins—for wisdom and bravery

1

TEMPESTE

ONLY THE NOBLES have the luxury of losing their heads.

That's the way it used to be, anyway. Now, the crowd twists and turns like maggots packed inside a dead mule's body. And I cannot help but smile, for at last we have our weapon that offers death with the softest of caresses for rich and poor alike.

Our sweet Killing Machine.

The sun's rays splash against the high blade suspended between twin red posts, and I lick the sweat from my upper lip, greedily. *He is going to die. A stranger, true enough, but he is set to die the way you should have, Maman. We've done it. We have our painless Killing Machine.*

Because I've no doubt stolen from, cut, or maimed at least a dozen townspeople in this square, I duck my head, careful not to make eye contact with a single soul in the Place de Greve. The last thing I need is another squabble with a fish wife or cobbler over a mangy trout or shoe they didn't need anyway.

I wind past boys tossing buttons and black-robed clergy clutching rosary beads. It isn't until I've veered around a cart full of potatoes and a slew of toy soldiers scattered on the ground that a pit rises in my stomach. *It's supposed to be you enjoying this tender mercy. Where you never writhe and sway and gasp for breath—please, God, make it stop. Stop stop stop, I am screaming for mercy.*

"Tempeste?"

Unwittingly, I spin at the sound of my name. Before I can hide my stringy hair and dirt-stained face, I lock eyes with a girl I've known for half a decade.

Charlotte, my friend. *My enemy.*

I could muse over the time we spent together transcribing scrolls at the convent, or the fact that we swapped secrets in the dead of night when we should have been sleeping, but the heat of what she did crawls like a hungry parasite through my body. She tattled—tattled like a rat— which only ended up hurting the kindest of souls I have ever known and my one true ally.

Choosing to be as stoic as Charlotte, I lift my chin, taking in her carefully manicured curls. Curls, I might add, which I had managed with a fine pair of scissors to obliterate while she was sleeping.

"I see your hair grew back well enough," I say almost sweetly.

Charlotte doesn't bat an eyelash. "And I see you've taken a fall since the convent."

So I haven't bathed except for the icy cold fingers of a stream, and my dress has become so thin and torn that one can see my skin through the sleeves. Well, with Charlotte's lavender gown and matching feather bonnet, she might as well be a peacock strutting about during mating season.

Regardless, I cannot help wondering why she is in Paris at all. She always planned on returning home to rectify a harm done to her family. But to ask why she's here instead of there would denote that I actually care, that I haven't forgotten her painful past which has been seared like a brand into my memory.

I dig into the folds of my dress to rub my thumb over the cool paring knife I stole from an apple vendor earlier this week. Not because I feel the need to defend myself against Charlotte, but because finding a weapon is what one should do when one feels uneasy.

A group of children scamper past, their dark shoes *click-click-clacking* against the cobblestones, and an old woman crows as she plants a black soldier's hat on her own head. These laughs, these drums, each and every out-of-tune drunkard singing is enough to make me want to run from the lot of them, shrieking. Where are my corners, my dark alleyways, my tunnels far, far below ground? Oh, to enjoy the savory sound of nothing but a furry little rat gnawing on a bone ever so quietly.

"Who might this be?" a young man asks, stepping up to Charlotte in her purple travesty.

To be clear, I had not realized that Charlotte was in fact with a gentleman. But of course she is. She's always on the hunt for the male species. His long, narrow nose and face mirrors the shape of *mon papa*'s, but his dark, wind-swept hair and splash of blue energy in his gaze suggest that he might be somewhat interesting. The red cravat dangling from his neck implies he's a commoner, but the way he holds himself and the careful articulation of his words means he's enjoyed a higher schooling.

A member of the bourgeois, just like *mon papa*. Just like I'm supposed to be.

The young man quirks a brow as he studies my clothing, so I level him with my gaze. "I've decided to save a few *sous* in lieu of my outfitting."

He laughs, carefree and throaty. "So I see," he says far too cheerily, like he believes there's a God, but I've long decided that if there is, he doesn't reside in this city.

I expect Charlotte to assign me an insult before pulling the young man away, but instead she cordially extends a ring-clad hand, which mystifies me. "Tempeste, meet my —meet Louis."

Before I have time to dissect why my former friend is actually being civil, Louis thrusts out his hand.

"It's Saint-Just." He winks, correcting Charlotte. "No one actually calls me Louis."

Tentatively, I accept Saint-Just's hand, my chapped fingers betraying what the elements have done to me. It's only the briefest of moments that I enjoy the smooth feel of the ruffles of his sleeve before I remember what "gentlemen" tend to do to girls like me, and I jerk my hand away.

"Tempeste," Charlotte says, laughing at my blunder, "is from another lifetime. If my memory serves me, I would say she's in the throes of rebelling."

I spread my teeth to arrange my lips into a smile but find myself grimacing instead. Who is she to say that she still knows me? It's been a year since I left the convent for the second time. People change, and daily. Am I still disenfranchised with *mon papa*? True. *Do I want to stick a pitchfork in his eye? Oui*. But that doesn't mean—

"Did someone say something about rebelling?" Saint-Just's olive-toned skin contrasts with his blinding white teeth. Only his dark blue eyes are not on Charlotte's. They're on me. Scouring. Like he, too, can unfold my darkest secrets, my carefully tucked away memories. "And whom might you be rebelling from, mademoiselle? If you don't mind my asking."

Automatically, I look to Charlotte, remembering the

long nights we discussed my falling out with *mon papa*. How he had the power to stop Maman's execution, but Papa claimed that admitting our connection to Maman would, heaven forbid, soil our name.

Who am I rebelling from? I take a deep breath, burying my partial madness the way I always do when I speak. I offer Charlotte's friend the most sincere answer I can. "Someone close to me."

Saint-Just frowns, transforming his otherwise pleasant face. "You hate him?"

I fight the urge to shout a few obscenities. "If we weren't related, I'd shove an apple in his trap and pig-roast him already."

Saint-Just lifts his face to the sky, shaking. At first I think he might be suffering from convulsions, but then I see the smile tearing open his oval face. He's laughing at me. "You have suffered," he says, calming his breathing, "but to make a point. Tell me, Tempeste, do you miss your mama, *ta maman,* so terribly?"

Heat flares like a wildfire inside me. How—how could Charlotte tell him about Maman? Can no one see that she needed our protection, that her life was *far* more important than Papa's need to ensure whom I would marry?

"You are a prodigy," Saint-Just is saying, but I could drop-kick him in the knees. "I believe in a proactive people, and you are the very essence of what many of us are trying to be. You choose to abandon the comforts of home to honor her life. To put it quite simply, Tempeste, you inspire me."

Anger? It deflates like one of those silly hot air balloons I sometimes see flying over the city. How long has it been since someone has understood why I left in the first place? Has anyone ever understood?

All I can do is stare at him, stupidly.

Training one wary eye on me, Saint-Just gingerly takes my hand in his own, and feeling the cool material of his bone-made ring against my fingers, I force myself not to dash away like a spooked rabbit.

"Before you return to your papa," Saint-Just says softly, "think of what difference you can make." He squeezes my fingers, which buzz like a colony of bees. "Settle a score. Fulfill a debt." My heart ricochets against my rib cage. "Make a difference."

As soon as he releases my hand, everything spins wildly. A fountain a few paces off and the blur of blue, red, and white flags flutter in my periphery. My, if Charlotte hasn't met a young man with a little more substance than knee breeches and cuff-links.

But he is right. He speaks so clearly. What improvements in the world have I made these past few years? I've stood up for my convictions and refused *mon papa's* expensive gowns and jewelry, but beyond that—nothing. Might I live in such a way that my words, my actions might reflect who Maman, if she were still alive, would be?

Cheers break out from the crowd, and the final tumbrel is just now approaching. In the back of my mind, I know that it's him—the young executioner who caused Maman so much pain that day—and as quick as a flash, I can see her red dress falling so low that her breasts are fully exposed, and how he tried to snap her neck so that her hanging was quick and painless but *he misses time and again and she cannot breathe and my chest is screaming for oxygen because she's lifting her shoulders like it might help! help! she isn't breathing.*

His dark hooded eyes survey the square, like a hawk sniffing out a foundling. It's been months since I've watched him from the shadows, imagining ways to help him "slip" and fall prey to the Killing Machine. But a score of soldiers already flank the bottom of the stairs, guarding against overzealous onlookers, muskets ready.

Is it possible? To "settle a score, fulfill a debt, make a difference"? What about now? I'm licking my lips. I itch to act quickly.

The ghoul jumps from the front of the cart to tie the horse's reins to a lamppost in the square. He's actually close enough for me to spot a dimple working in his cheek, which —how can he be smiling? Doesn't he consider the life he will soon take? My teeth are grinding so hard that a tendon in my neck pops loudly. I'll grab him by the hair, lay out the times I've watched him force a prisoner to drink an entire bucketful of water as the poor wretch sputtered, drowning. *Maybe I'll do that to you,* I'll say, *only with your* maman *watching.* I'll remind him of the time he took a club to a brittle old man tied to a wheel and smashed apart his bones like they were bits of glass in need of pulverizing. *What if I smash apart* your *bones, bourreau? Make a necklace out of the most fetching pieces for your grandparents?*

It's like I've just been launched atop the highest mountain overlooking the widest valley. The sun is fair; the sky is clear. Even the poppies are in bloom, which always have me sneezing. Now, what is it Saint-Just just said?

Settle a score. Fulfill a debt. Make a difference.

I have found my trajectory.

Gripping my knife, I fly past a braying goat, through a wad of children sticking a rodent's head into a toy Killing Machine, and pause only when the tumbrel is at my feet. *This this is it.* I run my thumb along the edge of the blade, drawing blood just to know the sharp sensation he'll soon be feeling. Should I go for a foot or gouge out an eye so that he resembles a pirate, giving him nothing to work for but treasure and whiskey?

As he nudges the prisoner forward, I tense to plant my knife just below the wrist so that he can never again execute another innocent person, but as I lift my arm a fraction of an inch, the strangest thing happens.

My resolve weakens. Literally, I freeze.

Why is it so hard to hurt this one? I am not one to shy away from enacting justice. He deserves this action far more than the butcher whose nose I helped relocate when he refused me his last scrap of meat.

But the bourreau's already walking past me—his shoulders back, his chin held high, marked off by twin sideburns —and it amazes me that he doesn't notice my indecision, that he doesn't even know my name.

So I gather all the recesses of saliva in my mouth and spit upon the fiend.

It is far less impressive than blood spurting from his hand like a geyser, or crimson droplets running down his nose, peacefully. Even so, my chest swells with pride, for my saliva has found its mark: prime center upon his dimpled cheek.

Slowly, as though he's suffered from a heavy dosage of brain softening, the young executioner bows his head to me. I expect him to growl, *Piss off, hussy.* Instead, he raises two round, sorrowful eyes—doe eyes. I grit my teeth as he says, "*Je suis désolé pour tous vos soucis.*" I am sorry for your pain.

He doesn't even bother to wipe the spit with his sleeve, but keeps it there like a damned metal or trophy. These imperious, narcissistic Frenchies. They assume every feminine gesture symbolizes a girl's love for them in some way. His hooded eyes turn downward like he's truly suffering, and his broad shoulders slump like all he wants to do is mock me. Anger twists in my stomach because he's not supposed to feign an apology.

We're supposed to fight, have a brawl, sever a limb or something. But now all I know is my heart is flopped sideways like a dead fish tossed out of the sea. And as I look past the white bonnets, red caps, the black soldiers' hats clogging the square, my eyes snag on a red cravat and a pale lavender gown—Saint-Just and Charlotte beaming at me.

I should be proud that I have finally made my point (albeit, not quite as dramatically as I first dreamed) but the brute pretended to know who I was, pretended to feel guilty! He's one of those crows that pecked and pecked and *wouldn't stop pecking at Maman's eyes—two black holes swallowing.*

The crowd's chatter quickens; a soldier's found his drum and has begun pounding. As I look high at our weapon with its white, flowered wreath, my pulse slams in my neck, strangling me.

Everything is quiet. The hairs on my arms stand up straight like infantry. I should be running to Charlotte and Saint-Just, bracing for the rich sound of metal sliding on metal before the blade severs head from spine. But I do not get to cheer nor gloat nor bray for our new grand weapon; nor do I get to enjoy the speed at which my heart is racing. For all I can hear is the short, candid reproof of my one true ally.

Do not hold onto your anger, Tempeste.

But without my anger, dear friend, I have nothing.

2

GABRIEL

LORD, have mercy. For I have trained these past six months for this moment, but I am far from ready. Four or five stairs like the Hotel de Ville? Try fourteen. Fourteen steps I must magically walk this man up the scaffold. As if my eyes actually work, as if they do not tell me an object lies in one place when it actually lies in another. If only I were more capable, more whole and faultless like Henri. But he is on the battlefront with the Prussians and Austrians. And I am here, and Père is here, ready to pull the rope for the Killing Machine.

With the crowd chirping like hungry vultures and the afternoon heat pulling sweat from my brow, all I can think about is that girl. The mad one who spat upon me earlier with pain stabbing her eyes and premature crow's feet. Her face and gown have grown filthy, and the muck on her boots and dirt under her fingernails proves she fends for herself, something few of us can claim in the bourgeois or aristocracy.

I deserve what she did to me.

I deserve a lot more, honestly.

But I'm reaching the scaffold stairs, and I'm praying

again to calm my nerves because I have always reached out to Providence. Just like the rest of the Sanson family. We've faithfully discharged our duties for generations, and the sacred standard for superior work cannot end with the youngest son. We have an obligation to be the blunt instrument for the Assembly. Before that, for our King. France whoops and laughs because all are set to die equally. And I'll prove to *mon père* that he was right to put his faith in me.

Only, instead of finding my much needed confidence, I find the Patient's rank body odor—rancid onions and turnips—which has me coughing.

"Don't I smell pretty?" the Patient cackles.

I take in his crusted eyebrows and soot-stained face, sorry I couldn't offer him a chance to bathe earlier. There's nothing to do now, though, but try to lighten his no doubt downtrodden heart with a little joviality. "Skip your rose petal bath this morning?"

The Patient laughs, appreciating my jest, before closing his mouth over his yellowed teeth. "I suppose I did." His wrinkled eyes light with humor before it fades.

He's about to die. We share a final jab, and now he's preparing himself. I cannot help but be quiet, too. I hadn't needed to extract a confession from this one, *Dieu merci.* Now I can allow him to say his final prayers before he falls away from consciousness completely.

Measuring the height of the first step with the toe of my shoe, I discover it's about two and a half times the height of my boot. If I look, it will only confuse me. So, keeping my vision straight ahead, I lift my foot slowly before lifting the other.

And like the ticks of a pocket-watch, we are climbing.

Halfway up, the man moves his bound hands to the side, and—wait—why is he reaching behind him? Now the stairs are spinning. The world is nothing but a brown, smudged sea. I close my eyes to isolate the feel of my bottom foot on the stair, but all at once the steps are far too small. It's like I'm mounting the miniature steps of a doll's house. So I grip the Patient's arm, not to pull him down, but because dizziness is tolling through me.

I swipe at the air, not wanting to pull the Patient backward. I wish I knew something more about him, like the names of his children or his Christian name, when the old man does something unprecedented: he sticks out his leg, bracing me.

It's kind of him, but it's embarrassing. It takes me a moment to slow my pulse and rampant heartbeats, but the old fool has me solidly on the wooden staircase. With a breath of relief, up is up and down is down again.

Merci, Seigneur. Merci!

While *mon père* would never allow me or any of his other assistants to publicly thank a Patient, I give the old man what credit I can. "I will ask God to have that rose petal bath waiting for you."

The Patient nods, tears glistening on his leathern face.

Somehow we cover the length of the remaining stairs, and once at the top, the Patient's shining eyes find me. "There's a letter in my pocket."

Looking down at the man's mud-stained cotton tunic and worn trousers, I find the ripped pocket he had moved his hands toward before. "You were reaching for it?"

"I am sorry it startled you."

I frown. I tend to be thrown off by the smallest distractions because of my eye deficiency; next thing I know, I'll be screaming like a little girl when a butterfly flies past me. So I forge a lie that could explain my behavior. "I had thought you were reaching for a weapon."

And yet the man did just save me from falling in front of the entire city. I reach over to fish the letter out of his pocket, but he's a foot—three?—wide and one of the other assistants are already nudging him forward. Père will have my head, but I'm suddenly calling out in my baritone voice, "Wait!"

The other younger, scrubby-haired assistants look to one another like they might grab me instead and lay me below the Killing Machine, but they haven't my seniority. *Mon pére* only hired them because they were the best he could afford in these trying times, so I cover the wooden steps between us and fumble around for the letter before *mon père* yells for me to let it be. My fingers squish inside the damp pocket's fabric before they close around a wad of parchment.

"This?" I pull out a piece of folded paper, praying the man doesn't expect me to read it now, as our time is thinning.

Tears fill the old man's eyes. His Adam's apple bounces and rises in his skinny, parched throat as he swallows painfully. "Press it to my cheek, won't you?"

A head of cabbage smacks me on the shoulder, and I'm gritting my teeth, for they have such little patience. Can they not see his final wish is trivial in the grand scope of things? It would be wrong to refuse to help the poor wretch. So I raise my hand near his scruffy face, unsure where it will land exactly.

Miracle of all miracles, my knuckles hit stubble as parchment washes over cheekbone. The Patient closes his eyes, basking in the blessing, and I'm reminded of the small allowances I've always given others like him when no one is watching. The extra drinks of water, the lifting of spikes so that they do less damage to their feet.

He barely has time to feel the moment before *mon père's*

other assistants are shoving him forward like he's a piece of wood that needs to be added to the fireplace. He nearly topples, they grab him so fiercely. But I grasp him by the coal-stained tunic and right his footing. He presses his chapped lips into a thin smile of a line, and I wish I could do more. Find out if the Assembly is truly justified in ordering his execution today.

The scrawny assistants strap the old man's bony frame to the platform, and I'm clamping my mouth shut to prevent myself from saying something dull-witted. He was *un criminal*. If I do not believe this, there's no way I can stand by and wait.

The straps wrap around his wrists like snakes constricting round a sapling, and before my heart can strum three more heartbeats, his head's lying on the other side of the wooden brace. Metal slides against metal. *Plunk!* And just like all our trials with the corpses and sheep, his head drops into the leathern basket, akin to the drop of a mere coin. He does not struggle for breath like my Patients who hung on the gallows. And he does not burn nor wail. Père needn't hack and hack with a sword because he can't get his aim just right, causing him to slice a jawline sideways before decapitating.

So I bite the inside of my cheek hard enough to taste blood, something I often taste at these killings. Blue, red, and white flags flap like the twang in my conscience. I didn't even know this Patient. The Assembly said he plundered a carriage and killed three, but it's like someone's chiseled away at my heart—or chiseled where it's supposed to be. And, just like Père warned, no one's cheering. A man and woman in matching striped bakers' aprons simply stare as if, for the first time, they're viewing a Baroque masterpiece of Poussin. But this is no piece of art. The Assembly had instructed us to create the contraption because the people begged for greater equality, but when it comes down to the killing part, they simply scratch their heads. Like they're hoping for a little more song and dance. Another melee.

A wrinkled woman with gray scraggly hair and several missing teeth crows, "The gallows gave us justice." Disgusted, she tosses stitching needles at the window-riddled Hotel de Ville, where the Assembly with their powdered wigs and black heeled shoes are watching us. But what if it were *her* son, her brother, we just killed today?

A man yanks off his red cap and mumbles, "Give us back our wooden gallows." He dons the same scraggly gray hair as the woman, and they move forward, eyes wild, like they mean to snatch up what's left of the Patient. But can they not see what's left of him's already being hewn into the cart down below, like a sack of grain?

Perhaps the people wish for me to hold up the Patient's head. Punt it like a ball across the square, but that is not what we do anymore. We do not dramatize executions, per the request of the people and the Assembly.

A throng of children in dirty little jackets push their way through the adults—all wearing the tricolor ribbon on their lapels—parroting, "Give us back our wooden gallows! Give us back! Give us back! Give us back our wooden gallows!"

Louder cries pepper throughout the crowd, and I want to give them a collective shaking. Do they not remember how a hanging could go so wrong? How it felt when the Patient was their aunt or child or friend or cousin? The people say they want equal deaths, and yet their thirst is unnerving.

For some reason I cannot explain, I find myself searching for the girl. The one who spat upon me earlier. I have to know how she's reacting to things.

Another cabbage whips through the air, and a ball of yarn rolls not a foot away from me. My gaze snags on the lone girl with the smudged face and wild black hair.

Tears run down her cheeks.

An older man approaches her—a man in a white wig and long, narrow face—and the girl throws her lithe form into his taller figure. There's something tender between them, which I cannot help but watch. The man takes the girl's small head in his hands, and the softness in his touch suggests he might be the girl's *père*. But then her sobs grow even more loudly, and she's pounding her *père*'s chest, the buttons on his greatcoat rattling. She's making such a spectacle that priests and monks and children are peering at them like they're a display of blasphemy. An old woman sits on a nearby bench and watches, head tilted, imparting a silent judgment while her needles click.

Eventually, the girl quiets with a hiccup, which echoes across the tall multi-windowed Hotel de Ville. Others join the old woman in her knitting, needles in hand, bent forward, listening.

The girl's *père* tries to pull her away, but when she doesn't move, he murmurs, embarrassed, "It will be all right, Tempeste."

Tempeste. An unusual name.

Without even looking up to meet her *père*'s gaze, the girl says, her words bouncing off the dung-filled cobblestones, "They do not appreciate it."

"Sorry?" Even now, the man's voice is filled with patience.

The girl holds out a shaking hand to the people. "They do not appreciate our Killing Machine."

As an impatient woman tosses an apple core at the pair

and the chanting children scamper for a baker rolling out treats, my heart seizes.

How?

I take in her stringy hair, the memory of her spitting on me still as sharp as the Machine's diagonal blade. How is it that she of all people has plucked from my heart exactly what I'm thinking? I had thought her to be a lunatic—or lonely—but now I have to take an extra step on the level surface of the scaffold. Sweat breaks out on my neck as my heart constricts in horror.

Never in my life have I been so fascinated by a girl.

I must not let it happen. She has not the refinement nor grace for which I have been looking. Furthermore, if she ever knew the extent to which I've been forced to do my work, she would never fall for me. The well-kept man with the white hair and silk cravat would not, under any circumstance, consider the son of a "bourreau" an eligible suitor. Bourreaus—the derogatory name for executioners, which connotes we are soiled and filthy—only end up with people of their own station, other families in the business of killing.

Murmurs arise from the crowd. A flock of pigeons flap, and as if the incident between the girl and her *père* never happened, cries bubble up.

"Give us back!"

"Give us back!"

"Give us back our gallows!"

I try making eye contact with the girl to give her a sympathetic look or something equally as pathetic. But she's walking the other way, arm in arm with her white-haired *père*, and I cannot help wondering how, in a town of over six hundred thousand, I will find her outside the blood-lust of the Place de Greve.

3

TEMPESTE

ÉLISE'S PINK and green china clinks loudly from the other side of the door as I lounge in bed, unable to fall back asleep —especially with that awful *tap-tap-tap* of Papa's cane. Must he hover so incessantly?

Last night, how many times did the floorboards squeak when he levitated near my door because I accidentally cried out in my dreams? The gall, to twist the metallic, clanking handle. But, thankfully, he remained on the other side, for I have drawn a stark line in the mud and dirt between where he belongs and where he'll happen upon his black sheep.

It has been a great long while since I've fancied a trip to the home of *mon papa*. It took the splendor of that machine and then the crowd's insidious response to coax me. I have grown tired of park benches, though. Simply required a softer bed. I'll still *settle a score, fulfill a debt, make a difference,* as Saint-Just said—I simply required a silk-sheeted reprieve.

Still, I do not like the suffocating guilt crawling into my gut as Papa tentatively knocks for the thirteenth time since the crack of dawn, for I know he expected me to return to him when I first ran away. He knew I didn't enjoy being hungry; he saw the way, when tired, I used to crawl into my canopied bed, clutching my dolly. But that is not me anymore. Isolation and abnegation of possessions are the metal of my armory.

He's knocking again and *merde!* I'm tossing aside my patterned quilt and bedsheets. "Yes yes yes, I am here. You're the one who brought me."

The door squeaks open as Papa balances a tray in one hand, his haunted face taking in my halo of hair I've artfully arranged in tufts about my shoulders and neckline. It's so snarled, so masterfully odious, he stifles a sob, and that flare of guilt rushes through me.

Face ever so lined, Papa says, "*Bonjour.*"

I am the one to blame for the shake of his voice, but Papa tightens his hand round his silver tray, and he's raising his chin. I am rather proud of his inner resolve to face me.

He hobbles across the purple dyed rug to my fine mahogany end table and carefully sets down my tray. "I brought you some tea." He laces his voice with false security, so I eye the muffins, which are tipped sideways. Ah, the cook always makes them uneven. The mixture of dough and crustiness and lemony zing!

I grapple for one, treacherously bringing it to my teeth, because it's been a great long while since I've consumed such a fine pastry. But the yellow breading is just what I remember, and I'm devouring it like a roasted porcupine. And I'm squishing its meaty flesh, stuffing it between molars and canine teeth.

Papa sucks in a breath, and I glance up. His patient eyes are watering. So I drop the muffin to my lap and dab what's left of it with my dirtied fingernails and lick them clean.

Looking down at his knobby knees, Papa says in his low, delicate way, "I suppose you found some sleep?"

I glance at the mirror above my burnished chest of drawers, but the dark circles under my eyes haven't faded in the least. So I roll my eyes, turning to the side so that I might gaze through the window—at the neighbor's red, blue, and white flag flapping.

As if to gain my attention, Papa hobbles to the window, too. He shouldn't feel the need to tiptoe round me, though he's pulling aside the heavy velvet curtains. Soon the wind will cut my face, and I'm not ready for the elements yet. I cry, "Stop, stop it, stop, please!"

He flinches, but I do not want him to see my inner weakness, so I allow a yellow bird to snag our attention—one which nearly flies through the latticed window pane. "You may leave it closed." He is not a housemaid, so I affix an, "If you please."

I try not to think of the day, four years ago, when Papa sought me in my friends' homes, crying out my name. Force myself not to remember the falsehood I spread that I'd returned to my quarters' closet and was hiding inside, munching on pastries. I do not dwell on the fact that he roamed every avenue, every dark alleyway with that old twisted cane, frightening his new prim wife, Élise. For he never gave up the hunt of finding me.

I am not a sentimental soul, though, so I cut him with my bitterest gaze. "Maman would have given *anything* to die the way that man did yesterday." Her botched hanging is our shared worst memory. He must be reminded of why I first ran away.

For the fiftieth time, I say, "Why did you never try to clear her name?"

Because she never wanted me to. I can practically hear his words as his knobby fingers twist his cane. Like the answers are there in his mind, if he would but *feed* them to me.

What happened, precisely?

How could he let her die in that fashion?

Why was protecting our reputation worth her very life?

Tossing my quilt to the wooden floor as if it's covered in lice, I descend like a stately queen. "Even now," I glower, "you will not explain." And I'm pacing, practically feeling the red veins of my eyes scouring the wallpapered walls, like they might hold some hidden clue I missed when I searched them in earlier days.

I look to the stack of books I once perused when I was of a healthier mind—ah, Rousseau! Voltaire! I flit out a hand, mentally pushing them away. "To think that I thought coming here would change things." I reach a shaky hand toward my open closet, because I mustn't be tempted by the books Papa and I studied. Retrieving a cloak—one he special-ordered for me years ago with the help of Élise—I snatch a pair of too-small wooden shoes that will have to work for my feet. And I'm making ultimatums, because this is my talent, instead of banging out a silly tune on the piano forte.

"Here is what we'll do." I slam the closet door shut like I'm shooting a blunderbuss rifle, which is glorious with its flared muzzle; one can hear it as far away as Nice. "I will visit you on holidays." I heave. "And you will see me in crowds, witnessing every execution."

Papa brings a dainty hand to the side of his elongated face. "Why would you go back to that life, Tempeste? Altering what the papers said would change nothing!"

"The papers?" One of his precious lies has leaked. "What do the papers have to do with anything?"

The papers must hold a secret truth, for his eyes, which are usually so calm, so gray, are splitting at the seams, and I'm onto something. He stopped receiving the paper when

Maman went to prison—true! Why hadn't I picked up on this anomaly?

Grabbing him by the collar, I shake. "Papa—" I cannot help the spittle from flying from my lips to his cheek "—talk to me!"

Like a war-torn battleground, a fight commences on his face. *To tell me, or continue lying?* Why is there a battle in the first place? Doesn't he wish for me to avoid the weevils in my food and the cold, sewage-filled streets? Does he like seeing lice crawling over the grease in his daughter's hair, or does he want his daughter back? I might even forgive him if he explained.

My arms—my fingers—are shaking so badly, I am sure I will collapse in a heap. So tenderly, ever so tenderly, *mon papa* lays his physician's hands on my shaking fist.

"This is not the life you should be living, *mon cherie.*"

I jerk my hand away because that's what he called me when I was small, and that's the name he used when he started talking about me finding a good—reputable!—husband for my wedding day. As if something like that matters when Maman isn't even alive.

He's stifling a sob, true, but this is the way it has to be, for I am exactly one-half Colette de la Croix and one-half Joseph-Ignace Guillotine. Doesn't matter that Maman was a prostitute. Doesn't matter that she lived the lowliest way.

"I will find out what you mean." I lick my lips, which are calloused from all my licking, but because of that muffin are now sugary. "Papers. Papers..." I fumble with the heavy twisted hood of my too-large robe. It shall be a trial, but I shall learn to run in the thing.

Cinching the robe with a drawstring around my waist, I pretend not to see the inner turmoil in *mon papa's* gaunt face. He's tempted to lure me with a bath—with perfumed rose leaves—plead for me to stay. He'll pull down my largest tome of Voltaire, and offer to debate the working class' stolen rights. But I mustn't let myself become distracted. Must avenge Maman's name.

"In the *meantime*." My eyes are the electric currents Benjamin Franklin used to keep his kites in flight. "I shall watch you at each and every execution by your beloved new weapon." Talk to me.

"But it isn't mine!" Papa cries in his impossibly low voice, his brittle eyes watering. It's painful to see him cry, for I know he first proposed the weapon because he wanted painless deaths for all criminals. But he would never want to be tied to it by name.

Steadying myself on the smooth wall-papered walls and ignoring the purple rug and canopied bed that are supposed to be mine, I flinch only slightly when he warns, "Vengeance will only bring you pain."

I stomp to the door like one of those savages across the sea, hairbrush on my dressing table rattling. "Every time I see the blade fall," I say, slicing my hand through the air, "every time I hear the *plunk* of someone's head hitting the basket, I'll remember how you, the great and almighty Joseph-Ignace, spoke so enthusiastically about granting equal rights for everybody."

"And we are doing that! Your maman would be so proud, Tempeste!"

"But when it came time for Maman, *my* family," I say, skewering him with my blackest gaze, "you said nothing."

4

GABRIEL

"You tripped." *Mon père*'s axe whistles as he swings it high in the air, severing a thick log in two. "And you helped a Patient."

I hang my head in shame, wishing there was something else I could say. I may or may not have given an apple this morning to a Patient, too, while Père greeted an inspector from the Assembly. I could point out that I've drowned my regrets in prayer, and that I've practiced walking the steps of the scaffold three times per day, but this job of ours is like an albatross hanging round my neck. I wish to support his work, but I would do anything to get away.

"I could gather more straw, more quicklime."

Père chops another piece.

Père, the Master Executioner of Paris, is a well-respected man. Rather, he used to be. Now, commoners have begun drawing him as this ogre with his hooded eyes, and instead of his finely tailored clothes, as a toothless hag in a monk's robe. He may not be wealthy (God knows the meager salary the Assembly offers has been a blow, indeed) but the necessity for our trade has been dwindling. Before, an execution meant aiming the sword with an utmost precision or hanging a Patient at the proper height for snapping the neck quickly. Now, my *grandmère* could easily pull the rope for our new Killing Machine.

Shoving away from the cool shade of our pillory, I try to make amends once more. "I shouldn't have insisted that I walk the Patient up the scaffold."

Père glances up from his executioner's axe, his dark eyes chastening me.

"And I am sorry I helped the Patient gain access to his letter." I don't mention the apple with the Patient this morning. Less is infinitely more sometimes.

Père shakes his head, his short dark curls flopping. Like atonement means doing additional tactics I haven't even dreamed. "The Assembly's inspector said we must improve what we are doing." He supports the hilt of his axe in a bed of scraggly weeds. "To satisfy the people of Paris, it seems we are not ready to abandon the old ways." He winces as he says this. "We must give them a show unlike what they've ever seen."

His arms flex, and my stomach churns like the butter my friend, Carvell, had been churning when we last met to discuss farming.

I thought the inspector would tell us we're not digging the holes for the bodies deep enough, or that we needed a few additional screws in the scaffold, not to dramatize our executions like before. If we're to go back to our former theatrics, what is the point of our "egalitarian" Killing Machine?

Our family knows all too well how the people cried for Patients' entrails to be cut out before them; for blood to splatter their faces as they held out their hands, dancing. They love drama, bask in the misery—unless it's their loved ones about to meet the Lord early.

I watch the dark smoke float from our chimney to the stratus clouds hovering over our family's sinister dwelling where Mère and Grandmère have shut themselves away. Broken shutters and a ruined well greet any and all visitors. We've had to skimp on firewood, too, burning leaves to get the fire going.

"I have an idea," Père says, his voice husky. "You aren't going to like it, but I'm afraid it's what we need."

This is the forewarning Père always gives before instructing me to inflict more pain on a Patient strapped to a wheel. *Club him on the fingernails,* he'd say. *They give up more quickly.* Or, *blind-fold them before you stick their feet in the boot. They cooperate better when they can't see the spikes coming.* Sometimes, after I put his instructions into practice, I vomit whatever I just ate.

Knowing Père is not in truth a dishonorable man—he teaches his children to serve the Lord, our king, and now the Assembly—I carefully watch him as he strides to the wood he just finished chopping.

"Once the head drops into the leathern basket," he says, grabbing one of the halves of wood, "I want you to hold it high for everyone to see." He lifts it high above his head, demonstrating.

I stare at the lump in Père's meaty hand. "Surely, that's not what that awful inspector means."

"Be civil with it."

"Oh, so you want me to cradle it, then."

"Don't be a nitwit." Père tosses the wood to the dirt. "You'll hold it by the hair of the head. And I know you'll do it, because you always do whatever our family needs."

I glower at the bales of hay stacked to the side, because it's true. I have always prioritized the needs of our family. But severed heads tend to blink and grimace, which will undoubtedly have the crowd shrieking with delight. With all this talk of "high minded" liberation, what sort of a France are we fighting for, anyway?

Amidst all of this, a tiny voice cries, *What if you simply walk away? Leave Paris. Accept that marshy land Carvell is offering.*

But I cannot muck up the reputation of my family. Abandoning them would be to soil not only them, but my other relatives, for we are not the only Sansons who are executioners. My cousins, my uncles, rely on me.

In a perfect world, I would simply ask *mon père* if I could leave like Henri, but Henri left knowing he would return and that I'd be here to support Père in every way. Further, I encouraged Henri to go. There's such a softness about him, and both Père and I felt fighting in a battlefield like he wanted was just what he needed to face my family's duties. He does not possess the hardness, the acting skill I draw on when I perform in front of the crowds.

My brother returns as often as he can, and when he does, all three of us play music, tell stories, and drink. Henri has a talent for raising our spirits even while sharing tidbits about how the Austrians and Prussians might overpower our forces. We try not to hope that there might be a return of the monarchy someday, for such thoughts are treasonous and we wouldn't wish to be accused of not embracing liberty.

Oui, in a perfect world, I would find land far away from the stench of the city. Purchase that farming land from Carvell and raise my own sheep. But I haven't enough money. If I did, I'd plant cabbage and zucchini, and maybe, just maybe, I could convince a certain young girl to come see me. Tempeste.

In *mon père*'s home hangs an old portrait of Mary Magdalene, La Magdalena, which depicts her kneeling at an altar of weaved wheat. In her eyes, she holds this hope and adoration for her Lord while clasping her hands together to pray. It's the exact same look Tempeste held in her eyes whilst looking at our Killing Machine in the Place de Greve the other day. They both seek deliverance. To be saved from their trespasses or unknown histories. Mary, surrounded with a crucifix, a skull, an empty bowl, and a book of opened scripture now inevitably reminds me—every single time I walk past that portrait—of Tempeste. The sharp cheekbones, the pointed chin. But the nose that is rounder, proving she can be soft when needed. The skin, smooth. Ivory. Her curls drizzling down her barren shoulders like silken string. She's a bit nude, Mary—in the portrait, I mean —but that was, er, by all intents and purposes the style of art in the sixteenth century.

Bending down to grapple for a piece of wood to assuage the blush flaring up my neck and cheeks, I force myself to think of the task at hand. Of my family being pigeon-holed into fighting for a profession we hate. *Mon père* didn't choose it. None of my ancestors did. But leaving means death, exile, or imprisonment, so here we remain.

Inevitably, my fingers connect with a host of slivers, as I've again mucked up my aim. But the son of the Master Executioner of Paris does not cry out in shock or complain. *Evidemment pas.* He lends the support, no matter how difficult, his père needs. Even when he thinks of digging up land and cultivating the rich, fertilized dirt with pumpkin seeds.

So I raise the chunk of wood high in the air, mimicking

the heads that inspector of ours thinks the people want. He is right, but I cannot pretend to be happy about it. I think on my brother's steadfast faith and pledge, as always, "You know I will do whatever you need."

5

TEMPESTE

MADNESS IS LIVING inside of me.

And the only way to vanquish it is by finding those responsible for Maman's death and dropping them to their knees. The executioner? Guilty. But he's nothing more than a piss ant who should eat horse feces all the rest of his days. No one actually believes Maman was capable of killing. So I will find whoever sent her to the gallows and rearrange their limbs the way the gravediggers do when they drop dead men's bones into the catacombs.

You think I'm bluffing.

Why did I return to *mon papa*'s house in the first place? Because even I have my limits of sleeping in the cold; of waking up bound, naked, bloodied. I thought I knew what it meant to live on the streets, but no one told me there would be people who would pick me up, drug me with laudanum while sleeping, and stick me in the worst alleyways. I have yet to know who the bastards are, but when I do, they'll wish they'd picked a different prey.

To survive, I've had to be creative. For a while, I paid a

deserter to teach me how to wield a blade, and when my skill improved, I paid him a little extra to pounce on me while I slept. My reflexes have improved, but I still haven't been able to catch who keeps taking me.

It's why my bed in Papa's house was so tempting. Those feather-made pillows give me the best dreams. Sometimes, as I close my eyes, I think a certain man is lurking, readying himself to do unmentionable things, and I flee, half awake, to another alleyway. Stretch out on a bench half covered with acorns and larvae, but I need to sleep, and other alleyways can be terrifying.

Even so, I'm a nomad; my feet move even before I'm fully awake. How can I live with a *papa* who refuses to tell me the name of the person who sent Maman to the gallows? Who refuses to explain anything?

So, I skulk through the smoke-infested city, grateful for the smooth, warm cloak wrapped around my arms which drags a little too long at my feet. For the first time in a great long while, though, I am not cold. I have hope. Research gives me a purpose, and I have a gift for rifling through old papers and other documents. *Papers,* Papa had said. Maman's killer must be in the newspapers in some way. And I know exactly where to look, for Papa often spoke of the place when he served as a representative of the Assembly.

The Palais de Justice houses titles of land ownership, nobility, and contracts for weddings. Every noteworthy document of which one could dream. And luckily, the Palais de Justice is not far from Papa's home—only a few blocks due north.

I need only scamper over the stony bridge, the Pont Notre Dame, and breathe in the fishy scent of the Seine to land on the Île de la Cité, the central island of the city. The majority of Paris' Gothic buildings reside here, and with all the gargoyles perched high atop buildings, both of our claws long and blackened, I cannot help feeling like yet another one of them—only hewn from the rock. Liberated. Poor things.

I'm just ducking beneath a rod strewn with washing when a gravelly woman's voice calls out, "*There* you are!"

I spin to find a fish wife pointing a butcher's knife at me. With the stray hairs dangling from her chin, I immediately recognize her. As it happens, I pillaged a fish head from her just last week.

The fish wife's rolled sleeves reveal arms wider than my whole person. Even so, I delicately hold out my hands in innocence. "It was rancid anyway."

She must have known that I'd have a falsehood ready, for she marches toward me like she'd like to sell my limbs as piecemeal at the next market, so I round—right into a woman carrying a parasol. This woman's bonnet of ostrich plumes provides little barrier, but her bustle? That's an entirely different story.

The fish wife grabs for me only for the museum-sized bustle to block us. Lucky me! And the prim and proper woman's crying out while smacking the fish wife with her umbrella.

The exchange is as good as any opera, until a carriage, a sparkly, finely crafted carriage, nearly flattens me.

I jump back, quick as a finch. But the fish wife has finally gotten round that bustle. She's madder than an ox, and half as pretty, so I spin for my only option.

I've never caught a ride from a carriage. The idea looks most precarious, indeed, but I sprint and jump to grab hold like my life depends on it. It does, if I'm not to be locked up in the Conciergerie.

I'm just able to grasp one of the gold ornaments dotting the top of the coach's body when the fish wife's sword swipes my left leg, but she only grazes me.

I'm an oversized icicle hanging on a brittle pinecone. Pretty! Fresh red paint tickles my nose, and as I press my cheek into the window, someone knocks the glass, startling me. I all but lose my grip on the ornament, but I dig my fingers into the metal until my fingernails bleed. I stare at the turnip of a man inside—rouged cheeks, powdered curls. He's obviously a noble, but how much longer will he dare to flaunt that revolting little fact to me?

His lips contort. The mole next to his squishy mouth bounces. And I gaze at him, because, as the carriage wheels past a blasé cusp of hedges, there's nothing to do but leer.

The wind whips through my midnight hair as we roll past sign-posts, windows, doors, and multi-colored awnings. I'm reminded of the time I scaled a cathedral so done up in ornamental grotesques that I named each and every one of the darlings. Maximilien. Claude. Philippe! I watched the sun peel open the sky, pinks and reds flaring like the ribbons Papa used to purchase for me.

Snap! The driver's whip has found me. My shoulders scream with pain. And the rouged mole-man's smacking his door into my legs. My hand's slick. At any moment, I'll be falling. And then it's like I'm in the woods; a river gurgles; birds *tweet-tweet.* For the horseshoe-shaped Palais de Justice lies like a warm hug about me. I drop, roll just like the deserter taught me, and it is not hard to ignore the driver when he shouts an assortment of obscenities.

The oldest cathedral in Paris, the Saint Chapelle, with its one, three, five windows looms over the Palais. The windows are monster eyes, their pointed tops poisoned darts, ready to strike me.

My abductors could be inside. They could be anywhere, really. But I am on a mission, not here to study the cathedral's wiry tower, nor think on how the nuns tried to control me.

I should rendezvous with my one true ally before attempting to sneak inside the Palais, but for the first time in a great long while, I have answers ripe for the plucking. Sneaking inside won't be easy, for the Palais de Justice is blocked off by an iron fence double my height and done up with so much gold, I want to dismantle the thing. I could scale it, but one of the dozen or so blue coated National Guardsmen patrolling the grounds would catch me. I could grab a passing monsieur, force him to tell the guards that we need to get inside—we're *to be married!* But that would mean allowing a stranger to touch me.

A lone oak tree guards the fencing, and I'm just about to scuttle up its branches and drop silently to the other side when the black and gold gate creaks wide open.

Bless the virgin Mary!

A sturdy girl carrying white lilies strolls toward the fence where a National Guardsmen is waiting. Her escort's dolled up in suit tails and pumps. Her hair is curled with such precision, they must be about to marry. I shouldn't interfere, but I won't find a better opportunity.

I yank the bouquet from the bride's gloved fingers, the flowers' sweet scent washing over me. The guard tries blocking me with his bayonet, but I toss the flowers in his face just as the deserter taught me.

His bayonet strikes the metal fence. *Clink!* and I pull the wrought-iron gate closed behind me.

The latch closes securely as I lock eyes with the bride, who doesn't seem too upset by my antics, thankfully. "You've helped a girl on your wedding day." I beam at her just as a cane taps my shoulder through the fencing.

It's Papa. His face is so whitewashed, I should offer him smelling salts, suggest he might rest his feet. But that's not who I am anymore, and he's reaching for my arm, so I jerk back, because he will not stop me.

His oval face twists in disappointment. In pain. Like when I declared I would never accept his new wife, Élise. "Tempeste, do not go in there. Please!"

A pair of portly guards are marching closer, their blue and white uniforms with the fancy buttons and fringe only galling. "You think I can just forget how Maman was stolen from me?"

Papa's hand trembles as he tries to raise his chestnut cane. "Doing this will only bring you pain."

One of the guards swipes for my hair, so I duck into a thin cusp of hazelnut trees as *mon papa* shrieks. Another guard runs through the gate to question Papa about my break-in, but Papa shall be fine. He's Joseph-Ignace Guillotine.

A third guard's veering round a shroud of flags jutting to the smoggy sky, so I wait and jab him in the throat with my elbow when he's least expecting it before slipping his musket from his shoulder. I must learn the accuser of Maman, else I lose whatever tenuous grip I have on sanity.

I lock eyes on Father's, which have never looked older or more gray. My conscience pangs, but I must set my sights on my current mission:

To avenge Maman!

Four guards down, nine to go. Easy as pilfering sardines.

∼

*I*t is well-past dark when I'm able to sneak back outside the Palais. I hadn't thought it would take all day to find the papers, nor convince the clerk to show me the ones with the proper dates. But it all worked out well in the end. She'll wake up from blacking out shortly.

I've found the newspaper article of which I know Papa had been speaking, for it refers to Maman specifically, and it's the proper date. Hopefully Élise has helped Papa find those smelling salts he uses in emergencies.

The paper's as hot as coals inside my pocket, rustling. I want to frame the words; *burn* their blasphemy. But I haven't waited this long to avenge Maman's death only to jump to the wrong conclusion. The publisher of the paper might not be the man responsible for Maman's killing. So, I need to discuss matters with my one true ally. Talk to her objectively.

The Madelonnettes Convent might be the plainest building in the city. Brown, square, boring. It's served as the locale for many offerings: prostitute reformatory, the destination for girls of disorderly conduct—sent there by the king. Mostly now, though, it is the home for sisters. Nuns, like Sister Josephine.

I'm eager to find out if the Assembly's still pressuring her to denounce what she believes, but I must first skitter past a group of glassy-eyed beggars dotting the street. It's not uncommon for our city's homeless to lie outside the convent's walls. Where else are they more likely to wear down a passerby's conscience? Perhaps I can share a treat— if Sister Josephine does what she always does and offers one to me.

Once at the door—a side one near where Sister

Josephine sleeps—I knock the secret knock we've long arranged. *Slow. Slow. Quick, quick, quick,* though Voltaire ridiculed secrets like these. The great Philosophe wasn't infallible, so it seems. My breathing slows, and my pulse evens, for I am about to see the one person who truly understands me. It is hard to forget the multitude of times she's offered me food or mended an over-worn stocking. Born with a clubbed foot and an upper lip that doesn't close properly, Sister Josephine understands what it's like to endure hardship. She extends kindness to anyone she sees suffering. Once she offered shelter to a woman who purposely drowned her own baby; she fed a man who ripped apart his friend's stomach with a scythe. She even watches out for a boy who tried burning down a reformatory.

But that's what Sister Josephine does—she offers succor to "the least of these." I once asked her why she didn't just do what all the other nuns do—pray, read—and she told me that Paris has a great need for people who are willing to ease its suffering. At first, I thought she was ridiculous for even trying—millions of people starve in our streets—but she says, to God, we are all beggars. It is rather difficult to hate someone who loves every soul she meets.

As the door creaks open, my own own body is tensing, but I can hear the familiar *tap-tap-tap* of her gnarled cane before her vocal chords scratch, "Tempeste?"

A spoon rattles in a bowl she's readied for me. From the corner of my eye, one of the beggars watches. He's skinnier than even me, so I wrap my hands over Sister Josephine's brittle fingers and murmur, "*Merci.*"

It won't take long to deliver the bowl to the man. The trick will be convincing him to share his treat.

A stray dog with matted fur and a bleeding tail trails me

as I approach the beggar. The man's dead eyes barely brighten as he watches me hold out the bowl.

I survey the collection of beggars, all draped in rags and reeking like a latrine. One possesses a rattle in his cough. Another twists a ratted powdered wig between his knees. I would help them. I would help them all if I had the means. But I do not have the resources. It's one of the few times I wish I had *mon papa*'s money. But there's no going back to that life, so it's not worth mentioning.

Shoving the bowl toward the most emaciated one, I murmur, "Share, and I won't take out an eye."

The man spreads his yellow teeth in a grin that says, *Sure, harpy.* So I pull the paring knife out of my pocket, toss it in the air, and let it flip three times before catching the handle, just like the deserter taught me. I level him with my gaze. "*Oui?*"

The man tenses, but he still needs some convincing, so I flick the blade against his bearded cheek—not hard enough to draw blood, but when his eyes widen, I know he grasps my meaning. I hover a beat. I'm a governess schooling her protégé. And it isn't long before the fool's shoving scoopfuls of porridge into his scratched, jaundiced face. He's about to take another greedy bite when he catches my eye and, mid-bite, stops himself. He shoves the bowl at a boy missing half his fingers.

When the boy opens his leathery mouth to eat more than his share, my protégé leans forward and snatches the bowl away. He shoves it at the next beggar.

I force myself not to smile. "You will return the bowl to me."

I let the lot feel my eyes, hot, on the entire ring before turning and trotting away.

It seems that a slop of porridge spilled over my fingers, so I allow the dog to lick them clean. His warm, slippery tongue makes me smile, so I rub his crusted-over ears as his poor frayed tail wags fiercely.

When I make it back to Sister Josephine, she's stretching her gummy smile at me. I hate it when she thinks I'm redeemable, so I snarl, "I only did that because you were watching."

She promptly bends down and raises another bowl, viewing me with her all-seeing eye. It makes me all prickly.

"You were testing me?"

She shrugs, but there's no happenstance with Sister Josephine. Charlotte and I learned long ago that she can be as calculating as me. But this is how our relationship goes. She tries to instill me with goodness, and I forget to be my vile self for a moment, which then makes her believe I'm worth teaching.

It's exhausting, really.

My stomach growls, so I snatch up the bowl, its bitter odor wafting over me. I pretend not to see the weevils lodged inside, nor mind the too-hard pieces of grain. The spoon's scraping and I've found the bottom of the bowl sooner than I intended. Throat thick with sludge, I wipe my face with the back of my sleeve, all too well remembering the time she gave me a *different* bowl of grain.

I'd broken a few of the convent's rules—back-talking, refusing to do my chores or pray—when Mother Superior said I'd learn my lesson if she took away my supper and locked me in my room for a few days. When Sister Josephine snuck me a bowl of porridge, Mother Superior gave her fifteen lashings. I told Sister Josephine that I would make Mother Superior pay. Sister Josephine warned me that our Lord and Savior would not retaliate, but *turn, turn, turn the other—*

I will not think on it. The concept makes my eyeballs bleed.

I couldn't let it go; it simply wasn't a part of me. So I got ahold of that corded whip and cut it to pieces with a shovel before hand-delivering it to Mother Superior with a note that read, "Imagine what I could do to your liver."

It was only a day later that I discovered it was Charlotte who told Mother Superior of Sister Josephine's choice to feed me. *Charlotte. The tattling little rat who was once my friend, but will never be again, not even if she begged.*

Now, though, Sister Josephine's moving her cracked lips, but no sound comes from her throat. Cancer of the throat, she once told me. The veins in her neck pulse; her smooth wrinkles beckon me. So I lean in to make out what she's saying, my own thoughts slipping away until I shove the newspaper into her withered face. "He claimed Maman tried ripping off her accuser's ear with her teeth. He's lying."

Sister Josephine's silver eyes seem to grow in intensity. She looks down at the wadded-up paper, stiff as an ionic column to any building.

"Her attacker," I say, trying not to screech, "this Jean-Paul Marat claimed she tried to strangle him with the bed sheet." My arm shakes. "He called her *deranged!*" The lunatic's words pulse like a whirlwind inside of me.

Something crinkles, and I know it's not my paper, because the sound is farther away. Straightaway, I find the culprit—her veiny hand's stuffing something back inside her wool habit. I catch a glimpse, only a glimpse of parchment, and like a viper, I snatch up her hand. "What were you going to show me?"

Her wrist is small and thin; sometimes I forget she is so

weak. My fingers twitch to snatch the paper from her grip, but like a sinkhole, her eyes swallow me.

She croaks, "Perhaps another day."

My own newspaper is ash; it's disintegrating. I crumple its thin pages in my hands and stick it in my pocket so it's out of the way. She was going to tell me something.

I am on a rue; my road stretches out uncertainly. There's a swatch of thorns, but I will cut them down, find out what secrets she's keeping from me. The writer of my paper, Jean-Paul Marat, is the leader of the lowest part of the working class, or *sans-culottes*, the most bloodthirsty hierarchy in the city. His little paper goads these *sans-culottes* to stick heads on pikes. Eat the hearts of anyone wealthy!

He's the animal who should be suffering.

And I know it's wrong, I *know* I'm one of the devil's brigade, but I'm reaching out and yanking the paper from Sister Josephine's clutches because I have to see.

Between our aged hands, it's tearing.

Sister Josephine cries out—in fear? protest?—and even now my crusty heart twinges with guilt, but I must read what she found, what she wanted to share with me.

I unfold the note quickly, staring down at the mess of words sprawled like weeds. The banner is the same banner as the paper I have in my hand, and I'm smiling in victory. "Friend of the People," it says, by Jean-Paul Marat. Only it's dated today.

I scan his introduction, always a call to arms for the *sans-culottes* and disparaging of the nobility; his little newspaper is the most highly circulated in the city, but not everyone gives credence to his brays. After my research today, I found that many claim he "embellishes" stories. So why would the Assembly execute a woman based on what he has to say?

A conspiracy. I could light a fire with my animosity.

He goes on and on and on. His pen is so vulgar, so filthy. The emaciated, bearded beggar I shared my porridge with sets his emptied bowl on the porch next to me with a *clank* just as my eyes trip across the next line:

Guillotine to be rightful name of Killing Machine.

My breath grows *hot! green!* That cannot be right, for "Guillotine" is *mon papa*'s name, not the name of the Killing Machine.

"No." My breath is toxic—arsenic!—choking me.

"Your papa brought this to me."

But Papa would never want his name remembered this way. "No," I say again, because he should be remembered for wanting to abolish the death penalty. Here again, this Jean-Paul Marat is slandering my family.

"He's worried about you, Tempeste. Knows you believe you are two halves of your parents in your own body. But, my dear," she says, licking her papery lips, "your parents' identities are polarizing."

I cannot *hear* what she has to say. The Killing Machine was supposed to be called the National Razor, Red Widow, Silent Mill, The Hungry Lady. The thirsty *sans-culottes* make up names and songs about the contraption daily.

My stomach twists like it's beneath the blade of a cutlass. Sister Josephine's gnarled finger taps the bottom of the page, so I read the final phrase:

And so, may the good doctor always be remembered for the thousands of lives his little machine will soon be slaughtering.

These words—they're inhumane. How could he paint Papa as the one to blame? I know how our city works. Someone *will* blame him for their brother, sister, cousin, child for being sent to this wretched machine.

Sister Josephine's brittle fingers close around my wrist.

Her fingers are so calloused it's like being caught in a sandbar.

"When he showed me this," she says, "I knew I had to be the one to show you, Tempeste, else your body would rip in twain."

I want to jerk my hand away, but doing so would be unfair to Sister Josephine, she who wrapped my wounds in bandages when no one would help me. "To tell me to do nothing?"

"To remind you to consider your actions, child. Pray."

Does she think *prayer* at this time will help me? Lighting candles and strolling about the convent? Those measures would accomplish nothing.

But then she's speaking again, and I'm wrapped in the cool shadow of her voice. She loves me as she says, "It is obvious that Marat is targeting your family, but consider coming inside. I have more things to explain."

Does she not see that this is the clue for which I've been hunting? I couldn't ignore these articles now if someone were to tempt me with macaroons—figs from Toulouse!— which I love more than Papa's muffins with the lemony zing.

She wants to help, but where I must go, she cannot help me.

If I were a kind soul, I would throw my arms around Sister Josephine's tiny, frail shoulders for sharing this article with me today. I would be careful not to touch the welts covering her back, only breathe in her musky scent of dust and sulfur from all that candle lighting.

She is but a withered tree.

My withered tree.

I reach out to show her that I mean only love for my friend, my one true ally. I'm nearly touching the black veil near her face, and my throat is made of rocks as I back away. "*Merci*," I tell her, despite the fear shining in her gaze. Despite the fact *mon papa* felt that he could stop me. But she and he both know I must do everything in my power to redeem Maman's—and now Papa's!—holy name.

6

GABRIEL

PÈRE TUCKS a letter into his green greatcoat as we stop outside the Palais de l'Égalité, the biggest collection of shops and cafes in the city. The sun dips below the Halle aux Blés, the tall, wide grain silo, and leaves twitter across our path like we've had a normal day. Like hunting down three escaped counterfeiters en route to their execution shouldn't require a drink.

Ladders lean against windows where shopkeepers hope to find the money to paint peeling awnings or replace broken windowpanes. Atop one dolloped terrace, a violinist is practicing a concerto. Might that be Mozart or Nardini?

"I'll tie the horses," I tell Père, knowing his mind is still on the correspondence he tucked away.

"I'll find us a table," Père murmurs as I round the cart to help him, but he waves a strong, gloved hand away. It will be a great long while until Master Sanson, a formidable bear by any standards, needs my assistance, but I always offer. I want to, honestly.

It's taken some time, but we've gotten back to our usual ease. I've walked the Patients up the scaffold without any more incidents and held up their heads, making the crowd laugh and giggle at my charade.

Père needn't know of my eavesdropping on farmers, hungry to know of how they expect their crops to do next spring, or of the bets I placed on one sheepherder, that he'll sell more wool than any of the others. He needn't know of my consultation with a money lender to see if he could loan me the money to purchase Carvell's land. The money lender turned me down, anyway.

As Père stalks toward the Palais de l'Égalité, he pauses mid-step to pull the letter from his pocket and shake it at me. "They threaten to take away our citizenship," he says in his hoarsest voice. "They do not like our former allegiance with the king."

I stare at Père's hooded eyes, the veins bulging from his neck from our recent physical activity. No one would truly threaten the Master Executioner of Paris, would they? Not even the Assembly. Without citizenship, we would no longer be allowed to hold land. Vote. *Mon père* would not be able to support his family.

I reach for the paper, but miss—obviously—so I appreciate it when Père explains, "They like what you're doing with the heads, but they claim anyone could do what we're doing."

"That's not—" I drop my hand. There's no skill in our vocation anymore. Our expertise is going to waste. And now I feel even worse for consorting with that money lender earlier today.

"The ease with which the Guillotine works—" Père scrubs his hands over his ruddy face—"I fear they'll use it injudiciously."

Now, because of our machine, a hundred souls—guilty or not—could be executed in a single day.

Henri would know what to do. Crack a perfectly timed joke or something, but it shall be months before the next time he's on leave. Our ancestors would have ideas for how to respond, but our ancestors have gone where most ancestors go—to the grave.

Père pulls out a second sheet from his breast pocket, and it takes me a moment, peering in the waning night, to see what's written—names. Name upon name is listed on the paper, and this sordid list is all the Patients we're soon to be executing. Mostly counterfeiters, but a few are even members of the aristocracy. "Fifteen? They think we can house fifteen? The most we've ever held is three."

Père shoves both papers in his greatcoat with a grunt. He squares his meaty shoulders, and if I were the Assembly, I would quake. "I've asked for Henri to come home to help with the family duties, but apparently he would be dishonorably discharged for leaving." Muscles pop and flare along his jawline.

"Surely they can't threaten us with de-citizening."

Père takes a swing at a nearby oak tree, its leaves and branches trembling. "They love the symbol we possess—to the people we are most menacing—but to cinch the noose around our necks, they mean to increase our workload. There is no escape."

I stare at the green pocket where Père just hid his messages. "Surely the Assembly can't prove all these people are guilty."

"Charles—Henri." He fights for my name. "Gabriel, son. That is not our job. We do not question how or why the Assembly convicts someone of a crime. We merely carry out the sentence."

The strain in *mon père*'s voice is evidence enough that he's struggling. He doesn't wish to execute innocent men. He has a hard enough time sleeping with the lives he's taken already.

"The Girondins are making progress," I offer. "Maybe they'll soon release our king and queen. That would certainly limit the number of counterfeiters and aristocrats actually found guilty."

Père shakes his head, his dark curls rustling beneath his top hat, and I'm reminded that in any other life, he'd be a performer on the stage. The lover of some tryst. A forbidden consort. I suppose he is, in a way.

Shoulders hunched, and not so much as marching but dragging, Père finds his way to the Palais de l'Égalité. It terrifies me that he's losing that prowl of his, one which he has been famous for decades.

I could write to Henri, but what else would he say? *Work harder. Lighten his mood with good music and proper food.*

Like the lull of a ritardando, I can feel the slow of my dreams. I should plan what to do, but is it even worth fighting for when we are killing possibly innocent beings?

My lips try to whistle a simple refrain—I do not know, to boost my spirits, like Henri—but the tune feels all wrong, and this particular one I composed to help my family. I feel as though I'm a hamster on a wheel, running, and running, never to progress, never to get gain.

I've only thoroughly botched the first few stanzas, and turned to follow *mon père* inside, when a shadowy figure in an oversized cloak darts right past my nose.

Her hair's as dark as the tar I pour on my uncooperative Patients, and the cloak's so long that she has to lift it to run.

My chest trips.

Oh bloody hell. Not now.

Bloody, bloody.

I can still hear the way her *père* said her name in the

Place de Greve. *Tempeste.* My chest twists, and my hands are already turning clammy. But *mon père* needs me. Bloody, bloody.

Part of me wants to call out. Say something foolish like, *Wait!* but the last time we met, she spit upon me. I needn't draw attention to myself now. And *mon père* is waiting for me.

"Hello, handsome," a woman's voice says, smoother than drizzled honey.

I round to find a mademoiselle rising from an abandoned bench on the street. Her dress plunges so low that there's little left to the imagination, and she's actually quite fetching with her smooth skin and tiny waist.

She sidles up next to me, gliding her fingers down my great-coat's sleeves. *"You,"* she purrs, "can have me for free."

I fumble as I attempt to tie the horse's reins. Prostitutes are plentiful enough in Paris, but I am not typically accosted by ones this fetching. Her warm, sweet breath is licorice on a string.

"Carvell wanted me to give you a message. He has another buyer—so you'll have to act by the end of the week."

I glance past a row of box elders to be sure *mon père* isn't listening. Perhaps Carvell has heard that I'm second-guessing my dream. He promised to show me how to raise chickens. Goats, he vowed, are most easy to raise. If only I could scrape together more money.

When I miss the post to tie the horse's reins, the prostitute chuckles softly. "Of course, now that I've delivered my message, you're welcome to do *other* things to me."

I rifle through my pockets for spare change, because I must pay her off so she'll know I'm not interested in other things. But she must tell Carvell I would like to work something out if there's any way. But my family...

I consider scribbling down a message, but I haven't a pen, and her painted lips are stretching into a smile most beguiling. She misunderstands my meaning, so when my hand closes round a cold, fat piece of silver, I toss her the *livre*. "Get yourself something from the cafe. I'll speak to Carvell." See if I can extend his deadline. Perhaps he has another stretch of land he can offer me? But first—bloody, bloody. I must track Tempeste.

The woman narrows her thin eyebrows, and the specter that makes up Tempeste is just now disappearing round a copse of fishermen dragging their nets from the *quais*. I may never see her again.

I must follow her, even if Père wishes to bludgeon me.

The woman whimpers. So I turn toward her, taking in her smooth bone structure; symmetrical. Lovely. Her curves? They're more ideal than any I've ever seen. Her musky scent of jasmine is the kind of smell most men would kill for.

Even so, I take the voluptuous woman by the shoulders, telling her what I always tell the women who choose to work this way. "*Vous êtes tout à fait charmant.* You are quite delightful."

Her gaze drops; even her shoulders are drooping. Rejection can be hard to take. So, carefully, I lift her thin fingers and press my lips to her knuckles just to show her that I mean it in the fondest possible way. Her fingers are coarse; selling her body is not the only job she's tried to support herself on these streets.

The mademoiselle presses her fingers to where my lips just grazed, and I know my gesture is not something she typically receives. Perhaps I've somehow brightened her day.

Even so, I know that I shall not be content until I've talked to Tempeste. See if it's just in my head, or if she really does resemble that painting. Even if this means I shall owe *mon père* extra prayers and chores for weeks. Because a simple girl has never made me so diseased. So I stride past the fishermen laying out their fish to bleach on wooden crates, knowing I am being foolhardy.

Foolhardy indeed.

7

TEMPESTE

WITH HAIR DROOPED and fuzzed as frayed yarn, I move past a pigeon of a girl sifting through the pockets of a drunken National Guardsman. He's sprawled on the street, unconscious and lanky. I never know what to make of the child when I see her—I've spotted her half a dozen times, at least —but I have to give her credit for braving a National Guardsman's unconscious body. She could sit with a tin cup waiting for the *sous* most don't bother offering, but she is doing what she can. It is hard not to be fond of the half-starved foundling.

But the Guardsman's fingers are twitching—he's obviously waking—and the stupid girl's too busy counting her coins, so I clock him on the head with the heel of my boot, because we girls need to stick together if we're to survive the devils in this country.

I skirt past a pool of piss and a crow pecking at a rodent's body, feeling only slightly guilty that I ran away from Papa and now Sister Josephine. But hiding secrets and offering *prayer* will never be enough to soothe my pain.

It isn't until I've rounded a slew of empty bottles from

the dairy and a copse of hazelnut trees that I arrive at a green awning on a red brick building.

Friend of the People, the awning screams.

I spit on the trash-infested street. *Friend*, indeed. While it took me longer than expected to find the newspaperman's office—he's moved a few times—an old, unsuspecting *sans-culotte* woman explained the way. Now I've got him under my thumb, and he can scream for bloody mercy.

After all the hours I've poured over his articles, scoured black word after black word, I can't help feeling a little upset with myself that it's taken me four entire years to find him. Writing those lies has no doubt made him wealthy, boosted his readership so high that the *sans-culottes* use his paper to wipe themselves in the privy.

I know what I'll be using, anyway.

Grabbing the cool metal handle, I jerk the door toward me, only for the chain on the other side to clang like the trumpet's blast of the enemy. *Merde!* No doubt, someone's heard me, but when I glance about the darkened alleyway and swaying hazelnut trees, no one lurches forward. And when a street lantern highlights a loose paving stone, my heart's barely had the chance to rap three more beats before I'm grabbing the stone and hurling it through the office door's sidelight window. Because Marat needs to pay for what he did to my family.

The sound of the breaking glass is like a sonnet, and my, it's been too long since I felt like reading.

The resulting hole is still too small to fit my arm through, though if I had a cannon, I'd wheel it up and light the fuse already. But I do not have a cannon nor a musket nor a six-barreled pistol, which I have long been coveting, so I grab a slew of pebbles and fling them at the hole so hard that my wrist pops painfully. I finish the job with a clever swing of my foot, glass crunching beneath my wooden shoe.

By now, the hole's big enough to reach through, so I snake my arm past the glass' jagged teeth and grapple for the chain's latching. All I find is the door's cool wood grain. So instead I wrap my elbow with the soft fibers of my cloak and knock out the final shards of glass before lumbering through.

My petticoat tears, but that's no matter. It's the sound of Maman and her friends' corpses singing from their graves. The newspapers I've been studying crackle in my pockets, and it's a joyous anthem to return them home, where they, like an aberration, came to be.

Looking at Marat's office is like peering through one of Papa's dirty microscopes at an organism from the sea. Dust clogs the room, not unlike the pollen I used to find on my room's window in the morning. But I've put *mon papa*'s padded life behind me. And I must think on what the great Philosophes would say. Plutarch, Rousseau, Voltaire—they would plead for vengeance. It's my greatest form of liberty.

As the wooden floor stretches across the room, the smell of ink, parchment, and mildew roils through me. Right here, a day or so ago, Marat arranged blocky letters, applied ink to parchment, and distributed an article slandering Papa; years ago, to Maman he did the same.

Tears like tiny needles prick my eyes, and I am tired of being the victim in this game. He can suffer. Suffer like I have. Keep on suffering.

I'm just about to pluck up a book on a nearby shelf, perfect for throwing, when a portrait on the wall catches my gaze. It's dark, but the light of the moon allows me to see it partially. I stroll closer, my heart tripping when I find gray eyebrows marking off a peeling face. And when I say peeling, I do not mean the aftermath of a sunburn, but what happens to skin after one has boils or leprosy. The pus! It's disgusting. A turban covers the wretch's head like his scalp is about to fall off completely, and his too-big salt and pepper coat reminds me of how one looks when one doesn't procure a tailor.

Not that I look any better, but I have reasons for what I'm doing.

It's Marat. Has to be.

While I am glad that he looks poorly, I'm amazed that he would pay someone to paint him looking so terribly. Most bourgeois I know who can afford to pay an artist do so with the intent of making them look more fetching—for friends, for posterity. To have an artist paint him as such almost makes me respect him in some small way.

And then I see it. The very weapon he used to destroy my family. Two wooden legs stand so tall they nearly reach the ceiling, and I'm suddenly not so sure whether I'm seeing a printing press or what Marat would have us call the Guillotine.

A platform stretches toward me with matching wooden feet. Between the posts lies the printing mechanism precisely where the blade of the Guillotine would be. Just like the executioner's contraption, Marat's press is tall, impressive, stately. And before I know what's happening, I feel as though I'm stuffed inside the Place de Greve. *Maman is hanging like a bell too broken for ringing*, but now my mind's forging a new, twisted history.

She's bound on the platform on the printing press—no!—the Guillotine? Leathern straps pin her, hold her in place and she's tugging to pull free, but they're placing her head in the wooden brace. The tightness in my chest keeps me from screaming, because the executioner would be pulling the rope and the blade is fallin—

I take a step back.

Marat would have killed Maman by rope, by Killing Machine; he wanted her dead. I do not know why, but he loathes my family.

A long handle protrudes from the front of the contraption, and I know I must try to turn it or take it apart, maybe. So I wrap my palm around the lever, but the metal doesn't budge, only bites into my hand, which is already so caked with blood and sweat that I know I must try something different.

On the platform, a wide flat stone lies, large enough to fit a piece of parchment, and I know this is where Marat branded his paper, sealing Maman's hanging. So, in half a breath, I'm grasping the cool stone and heaving it from the platform to the window and releasing. Shards of glass strike my brow and cheeks, but never before has pain been so liberating.

Trotting back to the printing press, I spot another table whereon lie two fat jars of ink. I grab the jars, flinging their contents about, savoring the sound of liquid black *splish-splish-splashing* the walls, the floors, my teeth.

My heart is a grandfather clock chiming. Ink splashes my arms, my neck. I want to take off my boots so I can slosh through it with barren feet, so I'm just bending over to pull off my boots when a low voice stops me cold.

"What are you doing?"

I drop one of the jars, the clang of shattering glass flickering across the length of the room.

It is dark, but an outline of a tall, strong man snatches my breath away. It could be Marat, but for all I know, it could be a grocer, a tailor. A rather muscular flower lady. Or, it could be a National Guardsman; one who heard my clatter and has run in to investigate.

But until I know who he is, I breathe the cool, even breaths Sister Josephine taught me when I was tempted to snarl something at Mother Superior. *I am but a boat stranded out at sea. A lighthouse, clear and bright and shiny.* What had she said? *Consider your actions, child. Pray.* But does she think that *prayer* will help me? I am tired of sitting around, of waiting.

Besides, the voice was younger than I would expect Marat's to be—far too young for an aged businessman's. Almost appealing.

The man's tense shoulders are awaiting a response, so I gesture to the floor and walls now graced with a fresh coat of paint, unable to stop myself from smiling. "I've taken upon a bit of redecorating."

Adrenaline courses through my veins, and the boat I've become rocks slightly. For the figure's stomping closer like I'm his prey. What will he do? Bind me? Take, take, take from me? My reflexes are quick. I can mark my aim, but no one's invincible. Even our queen, Marie Antoinette, has been locked away in the Tuileries.

The brute is stepping closer, and his form and presence are familiar somehow. He's tall and holds himself with confidence, his shoulders back, his arms strong and wide. His hair, tied at the nape of his neck, reminds me of Saint-Just's. Only Saint-Just's is longer, like mine.

"I have done nothing wrong," I say, my breath barely coming out of me. If only I could make out the man's facial features in the darkened room.

He chuckles, and I've heard that chuckle somewhere before. Perhaps another beggar on the streets? The one who stole my blanket from me? But, no. He's too articulate. A member of the bourgeois or aristocracy.

He glances backward, and I can just make out the bright white cravat wrapped tightly about his throat, but there must be a million men who wear that fashion in this city. A hint of a smile shines through his voice, which has me tensing. "So I take it whoever owns this office asked for you to break his window?"

Relief washes through me like a tumbler of whiskey. He didn't say this is Marat's office, so he's in no way connected to the newspaperman. This begs the question, is he the type to stop a vandal or join in a little merrymaking?

The gentleman takes a step closer as the glass beneath his shoe crunches. Taking a deep breath, he slowly says, "You really should get going."

A frown slides down my cheeks, for I cannot imagine leaving Marat's office so clean. The printing press is still intact. I thought it might be nice to dump his portrait in a latrine. All Marat must do to resume his printing is purchase a new flat stone. Far too easy.

No, this will not do at all. So I lift my chin and command him the way the deserter taught. "Not until you help me."

The man folds his wiry arms but he does not back away, so I point at the printing press like he can see it clearly. "Just help me topple this over and we can leave."

The stranger clomps a step closer, but this time his shoe slips on the inky floor. His arms splay open wide like he might land on his buttocks, but he regains his balance, albeit as clumsily as a doe on too-thin legs. He sucks in a breath. "I'll venture a guess that isn't water."

I wave him forward because who knows what hours the journalist keeps. "Hurry!"

"You really should get out of here."

Oh, the pompous fool. I could scramble apart his brains. Has he no taste for entertainment? Why bother entering the premises at all if he's not up for merrymaking? I should tell him Marat deserves what I am doing. So I face the printing press monstrosity. "Look, I'll strike you a deal. Help me, and I'll help *you* with something."

He grunts like he finds my offer altogether amusing. "You think you can help me?"

It takes all I have not to shove him out of the room without shouting, but against all odds, I find the calm of the boat again. "Everyone needs help from time to time. You might require help securing a lady's affections, for instance. Or assistance with your letter writing."

Laughter bubbles like an infestation in his throat, and he rubs between his eyes like I'm giving him a migraine. I'm *this close* to yanking him by that short spurt of hair of his and tying him to the printing press so Marat has someone to blame. *My scapegoat! How lovely!*

But then the brute's stepping toward me and murmuring, "You have no idea who I am, do you?"

He lumbers another clumsy step forward, and this time the light of the moon bounces off something shining at the back of the room and glints across hooded eyes, and a jowl that's actually smiling.

"*You!*" My voice is guttural, growling. My fingernails burrow into my palms, and I fight the urge to claw out his eyes. His *eyeballs*—

He's a parasite, too weak to live without a host. Too nauseating to be around, to smell. The bourreau is one of the devil's very own, a member of his posse.

So, in my mind, I'm a black cat, leaping, ripping through those round buttons, digging into his chest, and I will *keep on digging*—

I must have moved, because he's gasping, and it shocks me that I've actually gone through with my thoughts—that I'm actually scratching him. He tortured Maman, tortured loads of others, but I am not a killer. I do not want to be like him, so I pull back my arms, inch away.

His voice is strained. "You need to leave this place, Tempeste."

I do not know what to think. He just spoke my name like *mon papa* does—with care. I would almost say with patience, Lucifer help me, but now all I can see is the way *mon papa* hobbled about with his cane, heaving Maman's portrait around town to ask passersby if they had seen a girl who resembles the pale, gaunt woman in the painting. But this boy is *nothing* like Papa. Papa saves lives at the hospital. This boy willingly takes lives.

For pay.

"You must really love your job," I say, jabbing his cravat-wound Adam's apple, "if you spend your free time checking up on the relatives of your conquests."

"Patients," he sputters.

He's daft. He doesn't know what he's saying. "Come again?"

"We call them Patients." He blocks my finger since it appears I've still been jabbing.

Poison coats my teeth. "Oh!" I cackle. "Like you're doctors, right?"

The boy staggers back like he's hurt, and it altogether pleases me to know that I have the power to insult him so easily. I brush off my hands on the sticky ink of my dress, ready to dismiss him so I can get back to my redecorating. "So nice to see you again." I can feel the twinkle in my eye as I add, "Bourreau."

He tramples closer. "Wha—what did you call me?"

His form is so dark and tall—he's half a head taller than me. He's a giant oak tree, branches reaching, stretching. I don't know why, but I find myself shrinking back like he's intimidating. But that is not how Tempeste Guillotine, daughter of Collete de la Croix, responds to threats. Maman, when she couldn't afford medicine, once collected and sold glass she found in the Seine's tributaries. *I* once woke to a rat scurrying across my naval and planted a dagger straight between its eyes, then nailed that rat to the wall to ward off onlookers while I slept. No man in his right mind would consider touching me while I'm asleep.

I wait for the bourreau to offer a half-cocked retort, but all he hits me with is stuttering.

"H-How dare you say that to me?"

So I enunciate the insult slowly. "Bourreau." I bare all my teeth.

He has my wrist bawled up in his hot, thick hand, and I'm trapped. *Trapped!* I'm suffocating. So I'm kicking him in his silk stockings, but he doesn't release me. My pulse slams in my neck. How stupid I am for not running away before he caught me?

I imagine what he means to say. *I'll show you the actions of a bourreau.* The platform is large enough for him to throw my body down and pin me there while he takes and takes. And nobody would ever know.

His firm chest brushes up against mine, and whimpers of fear choke through me. I'm a fetus, *a fetus curling up.* And I'm closing my eyes, holding my breath so that when I black out, I will not remember the time the bourreau, like the man with the sack over his face, *took my kisses, grabbed and squeezed the delicate places on my body. I grabbed a boulder and hauled it to his face. He laughed, saying my anger made him happy.*

As quickly as it started, the bourreau releases me.

I straighten and breathe, letting the cool, cool air wrap me like a cloak.

I'm tethered. Tethered again to sanity.

I should—I should push him away. Scamper through the window and find a hole for hiding. Or, now that we've established that he *will* release me, I should march around him with the air and dignity of the foremost of the wigged members of the Assembly.

But the bourreau's standing before me now, and his height and size are both so large that all I can see is the form of that man who took, *took, took,* and like a spooked rabbit, I'm ducking and sprinting.

The ink is slippery. I skid like an injured bird *injured! fluttering!* and somehow the bourreau's scooping me up and cradling me. His chest is *hot! muscly!* and my breaths are tight. I am a baby boar, kicking.

"What are you doing?" I choke out as he marches toward the chained door. He climbed through the sidelight window rather sneakily. I have to convince him that whatever his plan, he must release me.

My fingernails find his arms, and as I rip through the hair and flesh, he sucks in a shaky breath.

I think he will at last set me down, but now his grip is ironclad. "You're behaving like a deranged animal, mademoiselle."

Deranged. There's that word again. People like to use it for my family. I grapple in the darkness for his finger, but he's pinned it beneath my legs, and for the very first time in my life, I'm finding myself heavy. I must ascertain the location of his other hand, but he's now fidgeting with the lock, clanging the chain like a bell.

Once, while strolling around a pond with Maman, I had

been frightened by a man who was following us. Every time we stopped to feed the ducks, he did as well. When we ran to chase some birds, he did, too. I was small, but even then, Maman cautioned me, *Find yourself cornered by a man like that, grab one of his fingers and bend it backward as far as it will go.*

I am grateful for the wisdom she offered me, so I reach up, batting around for the executioner's paw, until I seize his meaty finger and yank it back as far as it will go.

He's howling in pain.

A coyote stuck in a trap.

I'm smiling prettily.

But still, he holds me like a kitten or a foundling. His thick heart beats like a damned timpani, but seeing as his one hand is trapped below my legs, and the other is still trapped inside my fist, eventually, he lowers me to the ground. "You are nothing but a spoilt little girl."

I release his mangy hand. "And you, *monsieur*, are a mass murderer."

Neither of us reaches for the other, and I am tempted to go for the eyes, kick him in the goods, but that would only mean he would place his grubby paws on me again. And I am tired of this game. I could make one last sprint for the window, but he'd grapple for me in the glass, and I have enough cuts as is.

So I lag.

I could tell *mon papa* that one of Paris' exemplars actually took me captive, or report him to my favorite, the most radical of factions—the Jacobins—but that would mean wasting time talking when all I really want is to destroy Marat's credibility.

Ah!

The image of a weapon flashes into my mind—one with

a long handle and a blade in the shape of a crescent—and all I can think of is what Marat's machine would look like with its assistance. I could destroy the boy's future, but there is not a lot of satisfaction in outright killing. I should align his sympathy with mine. Convince him to retrieve the axe. Get him to work for me.

The light of the moon brushes across my gaze. The moon is Maman smiling down on me. I have destroyed Marat's office, and I've a plan to set him back indefinitely. He won't be able to print lies if his press is smashed to smithereens.

Feeling the victory tugging apart my lips, I say, "You will bring the executioner's axe to me."

8

GABRIEL

SHE SUFFERS FROM HYSTERIA. Worm fever? Blood poisoning. She's not La Magdalena at all, but a bloody siren who's gotten her tentacles round my throat and now I don't know if I can look away. She's destroyed Marat's office with the crumbled printing stone, broken glass, and splashed ink. I hadn't known it was his before, but I recognize Marat from his portrait. Everyone does. The *sans-culottes* will have her head for destroying their favorite leader, who is vying for a seat with the Assembly.

Of course, Père will have my head for taking the carriage to retrieve the axe from our Pillory's locked, hidden case. Add that to my list of transgressions for the week. Not only did I abandon him with his fear of losing our citizenship, but I've stranded him at the Palais de l'Égalité. Normally, I wouldn't dream of taking his carriage, but Tempeste threatened to accuse me of stealing her virtue to any National Guardsman within earshot, and with my family's reputation on the line, I'd be an imbecile not to comply.

I may not be the only person following her, too. More

than once, I thought I saw a trick of the shadows, or a movement around the corner of several buildings. (Not to
mention the piss of a drunkard she made me mop up with
my favorite handkerchief to wring out later at Marat's office
—her fine idea of "embellishment." It is high time I reassess
my feelings.)

Now, though, we have returned with only an hour or so
before the sun rises, and the little sprite must hurry if she
doesn't want anyone else to join our escapade.

"*Merci* for coming with me," she says as if she hadn't just
blackmailed me into smuggling a family heirloom. What
would Henri have done under the circumstances? Cracked a
joke before convincing the girl to grab a mop and broom? If
only he were here to coach me.

Everything remains as it was—window shattered, ink
splattered across walls—though now I smell faintly of urine,
and I've borrowed a torch from a beggar down the street.
Just how many torches would I be holding up if I were dropping lettuce seeds into the ground before putting up my
boots and tightening my violin's strings?

"I'll be right back." She sneers, and all I can do is watch
like a deranged idiot as her hips sway this way and that. The
way Aphrodite would walk, and what a bloody fool I am for
noticing. She's like a sorceress Henri once told me about—
one who bewitches defenseless boys. She lives in a castle,
lures good, faithful men far and wide, only to slit their
throats and tie them up on hooks on the walls, then pet
their faces when she wants to mate.

Mon Dieu, what have I done? Why have I followed her
here? She's not a sorceress—I don't think—but she has cast
a spell on my mind, and I must know her motive for doing
this. Perhaps I can help relieve some of the anger or pain.

When she hoists the blade, I wait for her to ask for my

help—it is rather heavy—and it would be nice to know how her slender arms feel below mine. Help in any way she needs...

She heaves *mon père*'s crescent high, smashing apart the press' legs with such power that I'm a shoddy fool for believing she would want or require any type of help from me.

Splinters and dust surround her in a cloud, littering her hair like potpourri, and the thudding of the blade is enough to make me take a step back. "You are strong." *Very strong.* I try not to make my voice squeak.

Flinging a wad of stringy hair behind her shoulder, Tempeste soberly says, "I like chopping things."

It's surprising that I captured and held her the way I did earlier today. When her entire body went rigid by the printing press, though, the terror in her eyes told me she believed I was capable of doing other, unsavory things. But I would never steal her virtue. The shame of causing a girl to believe me capable of doing that still twists like a cutlass in my gut.

"So what does your père do?" I ask to shift my thoughts away from the way her willowy body trembled in fear just to be near me. She lifts, smashes, lifts, and smashes like she doesn't hear me at all, and the lumber supporting the press is nothing but a pile of splinters now.

She lowers the axe. "He's chosen a few different vocations." She hesitates before lifting and smashing the heap of rubble at her wooden shoes. "He first went into medicine. Perhaps you've heard of him?"

I shrug. Doctors are as plentiful as Patients in this city.

But Tempeste's skulking toward me, her black hair wild with static electricity.

Her breath comes in short bursts, beads of perspiration

dribbling down her hairline, and my chest tightens as one of those beads runs down her slender neck into somewhere a little more discreet.

She pins me with her sultry gaze. "He's spent his entire life treating patients." Her hot breath heats my chin, pulling goosebumps from my arms. "Then, when he saw that our country's policies prevented the poor from receiving the treatment they needed, he made the switch to politics."

Why is she telling me this? I move the torch to my other slippery, sweaty hand.

"But even in politics," she says, swallowing me with her eyes, "his fellow countrymen failed to hear him. He wanted to abolish the death penalty."

We're so close, her dress tickles my stockings, and I all but sink into her like quicksand—when I realize what she just said. *He wanted to abolish the death penalty.* "Your *père* nearly ruined my family!"

She lifts her gaunt eyes to the ceiling and laughs. "Oh, you and I both know how things turned out." She spins away from me, her filthy skirt rippling. "Paris too much relishes killing people."

Don't I know that.

"So, he proposed a machine."

The gears are clicking into place. Because of her *père*, mine almost lost his work. Her *père*. Without him, we wouldn't even have the Killing Machine. And yet, Tempeste loves the contraption. Because it offers the mercy her *mère*— the poor woman I kept missing when I tried to snap her spine—could never obtain.

Fear and guilt crawl like a parasite through my stomach, because Tempeste must never know every detail of what I've done in the past. My history.

Resting *mon père*'s axe against the nook of her shoulder, Tempeste smiles, which all but burns my vision. "*Mon papa* is Joseph-Ignace, proud advocate of our sweet Guillotine."

9

TEMPESTE

GLASS CRUNCHES, and I spin to find a man in a red cravat and a long, olive-toned face lumbering through the broken window.

"Saint-Just!" I say, unable to contain my disbelief.

"Well, aren't you just a doll all inked up like that?" He laughs, and his humor must be contagious because I'm laughing, too. I am not entirely sure why, except I know he's a friend, and when he touched me in the Place de Greve, I didn't pull away. But he's here now, winking at me, and with the ink dousing my frock, what a spectacle he must think me to be.

I open my mouth to ask how he found me here when a rustling of skirts tells me he's not alone, for a girl with porcelain skin in a blue riding habit and high collar is crawling through the window. Charlotte. I expect her to catch her layered skirts on the jagged edges of the glass like I did, but instead she gracefully sidles through the window before settling herself next to Saint-Just.

The fiend.

"Looks like you haven't grown out of chopping things," Charlotte says, snaking her arm through Saint-Just's.

"Some people deserve chopping," I say evenly.

The bourreau stretches out a gangly arm like he means to protect me, only to thwack Saint-Just on the shoulder. "Tempeste was just heading home."

Saint-Just quirks an eyebrow.

So I shoot the bourreau a look that says, *Just because I allowed you to remain with me doesn't make you my willy nilly uncle.*

He drops his arm like I've just plowed him to the ground.

That's right, I can take care of myself, bourreau. I once single-handedly stole a pair of dueling pistols from a pair of guards who refused to share their dinner with a boy, shot out their knapsacks, and pilfered for us the grain.

Now, though, the bourreau's rubbing that spot between his eyes again, like I'm giving him a migraine. Has he any idea what it's like to come within an inch of a light cavalry saber, all because you were defending the innocent and feeding your own belly?

As Saint-Just, ebony hair cascading down his strong shoulders, takes in the disarray of the office, I'm pleased that the torch in the bourreau's hand is enough to showcase my work. Saint-Just's perceptive eyes pause on the walls now splattered with ink and flicker down to the printing press, which is now a neat pile of wood and splinters and pools of sticky ink. He studies the floor, finding the broken ink wells, and I cannot help swelling a little with pride at my fine handy-work. At long last, he trains his blue, steely eyes upon mine, and something akin to a shiver runs down my spine.

"I suppose the newspaperman had it coming." His lips stretch into a smile that's half goading. Has he decided I've indeed *Settled a score, Fulfilled a debt, Made a Difference?* We are cut from the same cloth. *Here* is a man I could rely upon. Had the bourreau asked why I did what I did? Even once, did he lend a sensitive ear? The boy was too busy judging me when *he* was the one who snapped Maman's neck.

I should have trusted my instincts and not bothered with him.

"This newspaperman," I say, wetting my calloused lips. I've wasted far too much time with the bourreau and must cut my losses, and quick. "He destroyed the lives of both my parents."

Saint-Just's chilling eyes widen, but not for long, as it's only half a second before he extends a smooth open palm. "By all means, then."

As simple as that. No *what-do-you-mean-he-destroyed-the-lives-of-both-your-parents*? or *you-are-acting-like-a-spoilt-little-girl*. None at all, for Saint-Just is looking at me like a trained equal, someone he respects, and, oh, for the love of all these long, cold years, what a refreshing change it is.

Saint-Just studies the axe perched upon my shoulder as he tilts his striking head to the side. "I take it you're finished, then?"

I shrug. I could offer a demonstration, but I'm not really one to boast of my accomplishments.

He spreads his full lips into a smile. "*C'est ma fille.*" That's my girl.

Charlotte yanks her slim arm away from Saint-Just's with a scowl. "We came to collect her, not puff her up with flattery."

And *this* is why Charlotte and I are no longer friends. Sometimes, a girl needs something good, something kind. She behaves as if he's pumping me full of a coveted sweetness, of lemon or honey. Now, though, I cannot help thinking of the code Charlotte and I created to alert one another of our presence in the convent when we were forbidden from talking. It was juvenile, certainly, but we used to *cluck* like chickens when we were around a corner or behind a curtain only because it drove the other nuns mad. They would insist we stop our clucking, which motivated us to cluck louder most days. All of them hated it. All, that is, except Sister Josephine, who used to look in all the wrong places—in a chest of drawers, under a stack of papers— pretending she was daft enough to believe there could actually be a loose chicken in a calefactory.

We were limited in our games.

Now, though, Saint-Just is meeting Charlotte's pious gaze with this longing expression like he wishes she understood that I'm a special friend to him in some way. He reaches over to hold her gloved hand, and in the softest of voices, says, "You forget, Charlotte, that I once lived on the street."

He reaches up and runs his thumb along the tip of the blade still perched atop my shoulder when the bourreau stretches out his long arms and launches himself right between us, like a mad, startled gazelle.

He's as thickheaded as half the Assembly.

The lean executioner's rump brushes against the front of my black stained skirt, and he's touching me. I ball my hands into fists; grit my molars, my canine teeth. It takes everything I have not to scramble backward. Slowly, stiffly, like the time a particular brutal *sans-culotte* stuffed me in Medici's cage for days, I take a wide step back.

The bourreau extends a hand toward Saint-Just and says in this slow, even cadence, "I don't believe we've met."

Saint-Just looks down at the young man's hand with a smirk. "It's not every day I have the chance to shake hands with a bourreau."

The bourreau awkwardly clasps Saint-Just's hand, still dangling at his side, like that was an invitation. "Gabriel Sanson," he introduces himself sweetly. "It's not every day I have the chance to wipe piss on a gentleman."

I don't mean to laugh, but a giggle shoots through my lips like a poisoned dart I didn't know I had and everyone—Saint-Just, Charlotte, the bourreau—stares at me like that's the last thing they expected. Even I don't remember the last time I laughed so easily, but they have to agree the bourreau's timing was lovely.

Grabbing the torch from Gabriel's—the bourreau's—hand before Saint-Just thinks poorly of me, I say, "I think it is time for us to leave."

"Oh, so now you're in a hurry?" The bourreau turns his hooded eyes on me like I've hurt his feelings. The boy needs to learn a few alternative facial expressions—two or three, at the very least. If he is truly upset, why is he here at all? It would be so easy to belittle him now.

But the truth is, I'd like to impress Saint-Just, so I tip my head to the side and ever so melodiously reply, "I was only awaiting an invitation."

The bourreau grumbles an assortment of crass words, but he does follow me as we climb through the jagged window. He's getting what he wished for, after all—accompanying me from Marat's office. Of course, I would much prefer leaving with another, more understanding gentleman, but that would mean Charlotte would come, and I haven't yet sorted out what to do about our relationship.

By the time we've settled ourselves in the bourreau's wooden carriage, Charlotte and Saint-Just skirt toward us, his long hair so perfectly combed he could be in the *Journal de la Mode et du Goût,* Paris' best collection of fashion plates. Charlotte's skirt is so devoid of wrinkle that I imagine she won't sit for fear of rumpling the pleats. She wears the humbler mobcap, though—the white one with a blue ribbon tied round the crown—like she understands poverty.

"Before you go." Charlotte reaches her gloved arm out to me, but when I recoil, she drops her hand quickly.

"I mean to offer you an invitation," she says, dropping her gaze.

I take great pleasure knowing that, at times, she feels she must humble herself to talk to me. Makes me feel powerful —like an untitled queen of the plebes.

Still, there's no way in Hades I would entertain any invitation she gave to me, so I look to the bourreau, awaiting the snap of his leathern reins. Though his hands drop to his lap, like he's pausing, as if he's considering what Charlotte said. He scratches the back of his head like a simpleton, like he's deranged. "To what, exactly?"

Charlotte, ever the stoic statue, holds her hands together primly. "I would like to invite you to my Club for Young Ladies, Tempeste."

I bark a laugh, as I thought Charlotte knew me better than to believe I would be interested in such a soiree. "To embroider and panic about which gown I should wear to the next ball?" I laugh so hysterically, I'm holding my stomach, feeling my aged corset's brittle boning. Charlotte can be so witty.

By now, Saint-Just's taking his place next to Charlotte, and they're two starched, model citizens with their spotless, narrow cheeks. He stretches forth his ruffle-sleeved hand, and he has such a manner that I cannot stop myself from watching. "If I may, Tempeste, you really do wish to come."

Who is he to say where I should go, or how I should spend my evenings?

I have a vested interest in politics, true, but I have heard of the nature of these little Clubs for Young Ladies—how they dilly-dally about, discussing which law the Assembly should pass, while the majority of the ladies fail to understand anything about the *true* pillars of our society. I would love to debate the inner meanings of Voltaire, Rousseau, Montesquieu—truly!—but the dimwits would fail to understand me.

Every man is guilty of the good he did not do.

Man is born free and everywhere he is in chains.

Absolute silence leads to unhappiness. It is the image of death.

They would not know these, the hallmarks of our country. Paris is a breeding ground for simpletons, really and truly.

I had expected Saint-Just, of all people, to understand the sacred nature of choice. He made me think so when we first met in the Place de Greve. *Settle a score. Fulfill a debt. Make a difference.* What do the pair of them mean to do? Take my hand, only to deliver me like a shipment of meat?

Slowly, like the deserter taught me, I train a steely eye on the bourreau to prove how much I am relying upon his assistance this evening. Now's his chance. He had better prove his worth again to me. "Shall we be off, then?" My tone is pleasant, but, like Sister Josephine, I'm testing.

The bourreau's dark eyes shift to the side, as if he's contemplating what Charlotte and Saint-Just just said, and then he's staring at the reins in his hands, like he means to snap them so we can leave. But he isn't and he's settling two soulful eyes upon me. "M-maybe you should go with them, Tempeste."

Does he want me to stick a chisel in his neck? How naïve I'd been to believe I could retain safe passage from the ghoul who took Maman from me. I'd pushed aside this very fact. Even now, I can remember sneaking onto his land, past the useless guards who'd fallen asleep, and seeing the liquid crimson pooling over his fingers as he smashed apart Maman's foot. He was trying to extract a confession in private, which was typical at the time. She cried for him to stop. *Cried.* When he set down his mallet, I actually believed he was listening, but he only left the shed to empty his stomach by retching. His conscience knew his actions were guilty.

Stiff as a mummy, I swing a leg over the carriage, unable to believe I've stooped to consorting with him from the beginning. I set him afire with my most venomous gaze. "Thank you for reminding me of why we are bitter enemies."

Gathering up my frayed and ink-covered skirts, I lock eyes with Saint-Just, the friend I had wrongly believed to have obtained, and narrow my eyes to slits to show him how truly mistaken I was. The nuns always tried to convince me how to behave—*look down when your elders speak to you! never run on Sundays!*—but these *things* were never in my nature. I am a roasted chestnut, splitting at the seams.

Now? The three of them can join their own little nunnery.

I spring from the carriage like a jaguar who's gone out hunting. I gulp the city air, dust and smoke roiling through me. A scrap of parchment blows in my path, and I duck to miss a sign jutting out from a storefront. The sun's rising, shining upon a toppled barrel of apples, and just because they're not mine, I pluck one with a surge of victory.

In my mind, I'm taking a bite, savoring the crunching, but there isn't time. Any or all three could be following me. And I do not know my destination, though I know it will be far away.

"Tempeste!" Charlotte's calculated voice trails out to me,

but she can find herself another poppet to bring to these silly Clubs for Young Ladies. I belong in another land— where savage natives hunt and spear and gut and sneak.

Hoof beats *clip-clip-clop*, a frantic echo of my heartbeat. I know they do not believe that I can survive on my own, but I've done it before, and I'll show them. I'll find a new corner. Barter dead men's teeth, sell jewelry.

The bourreau's steering the carriage; I *know* he is, for hoof-beats clop beside me. I have memorized this filthy street, the Rue De Sevres, and in half a block, I'll dart down an alleyway too skinny for his carriage to follow.

I am almost there—the alley's only a few paces away— and while my legs are scrambling faster than they ever have, I tighten my grip round my blade.

At the very last moment, I dart left, knowing they're incapable of following me.

I've made it, just made it into the sand and dank of the abandoned alleyway, when something cold strikes me on the back of my neck. Pain explodes in my skull and shoots down my spine, a sensation I've experienced many times before.

～

*C*andlelight sets a somber-looking Saint-Just aglow before me. The oval shape of his face hangs like a jack-o-lantern in a black room of candles, and clocks are *tick-ticking*. His white blouse tops dark knee-breeches, and his boots melt into the floor, making him more ethereal than a real person ever should be.

"She's awake." His dark blue eyes envelop me, and my head is one colossal lump of pain.

But I can remember the origin of the pain. My hand

automatically rubs the back of my neck, but my tongue's gone heavy.

I'd ask where we are, scramble to sit or stand, but my legs are but a bundle of *chiné* silks—too fluid for standing. My corset *digs* into my ribs like a witch's bony fingertips, and the *fleur-de-lis*-speckled couch I'm waking on is completely foreign.

"Where—am I?"

Head's spinning.

My fingers comb my legs—for blood, for scratches—but it's dark and my legs are as they always are—too thin and clammy.

"Searching for something?" Saint-Just raises a dark brow, and I do and do not want to tell him of my vulnerable state. *Of the gashes in my thighs. Of the white substance dripping down my legs.*

I drop my gaze, heat scalding my cheeks. If he knew what happened to me, he wouldn't be amiable in any way.

"My axe," I say, my throat dry like cotton. The deserter taught me to always be ready.

But the floor is creaking and that damned grandfather clock *tick-ticks, won't stop ticking.* My arms are as heavy as bales of hay, and the back of my neck burns like the red pepper *mon papa* once purchased from a merchant.

It is the same *every* time they take me.

Charlotte and Saint-Just, they—couldn't—be guilty.

Charlotte's curls flounce as she primly takes her place next to Saint-Just. She's all done up in her caraco jacket with its fashionable tight sleeves, her kerchief arranged about her neck like she was born with the thing.

"Did you see who struck me?" My voice screeches like bats. Tell me they are not responsible.

Curtains behind the pair flap, like the whispers of ghosts

from the balcony, and it is like they're telling me to be wary. I do not wish to believe Charlotte and Saint-Just could be responsible, but suddenly I'm gazing upon Charlotte's waist where a girdle of darts loom over me.

"You—*you* were the ones taking me!" The drugs they use —laudanum, has to be—forms cobwebs in my mind, making it hard to think. It was Saint-Just who—who—my heart quivers, fracturing. Spiders flounce in my neck; breathing has escaped. Everything's ragged, dull, strained.

Charlotte nods to the parquet floor like I didn't just ask her something. "You are quite skilled with the blade."

My gaze follows hers to where I find the bourreau's axe propped against the foot of the settee.

The bourreau—he's safe? Undoubtedly.

And I'm launching myself across the floor to retrieve the blade. Because of the poison and darkness, my movements are dulled, slow. Heavy. But the smooth grain of the handle is an embrace. The cool metal of the blade is a kiss from Maman. Always, she's watching me.

Able to breathe again, I mosey back to the couch, settling my gaze on Charlotte. She's always had a talent for speaking without feeling, her face drawn up tight like a quilt ready for tying, but what is her endgame?

"Will you behave?" Charlotte nods at the blade, and I *hate* how she laces all her words with that faux propriety. But I know she has other motives she's hiding.

I settle myself back on the flowered settee. "I'll gladly chop the pair of you, if you would like to watch me." A surge of power like an electrical shock runs through me. "Tell. Me. *Why* you took me."

Charlotte must know that I'm not entirely joking, for at long last she quips, "We wish to recruit you for the Girondins, Tempeste."

The axe in my hands sags, heavy. The Girondins? The group that clamors about for a constitutional monarchy, which is about as appealing as the weevils in the porridge Sister Josephine feeds me. Our country needs to depose of, not work with, the king.

"They're the moderate faction," Charlotte explains, playing with the buttons on her cream gloves nervously.

"I *know* who they are!" Like a cat, I'm springing to my feet. My shoes are too small, they're pinching. And my dress is far too stiff. At least the splattered ink from Marat's office is a small badge of victory. "If I wanted to be a part of a little cult, I'd join the Jacobins, for they're at least willing to execute the king and queen."

Charlotte stares like my words alone have softened the farthest reaches of her brain.

"Cat's got your tongue?" I smirk.

"I can't believe you would want such a thing!"

So I laugh. "But of course, Charlotte." I spin the axe like I'm spinning twine. "They believe in progress. *Oui!*"

Saint-Just gestures out the window—the sun's just rising, sparking smokestacks with orange and pink—and the terror fluttering in my chest reminds me that he might be the one who took things from me. I could slice him across the neck. Watch the blood pool to his boots.

But I am not a killer.

Though, at times, the idea is as glorious as sharp-shooting possums from an abandoned dwelling.

"You are skilled." Saint-Just settles his cryptic eyes on me, and I wish I could see what he would look like with a sack covering his face. Could he be the man who took things from me? "More skilled than we had ever hoped you would be. It is why we kept taking you, testing you, to see your resourcefulness and cunning."

My rage is set to boiling.

"We only regret that others were watching," Charlotte murmurs, toying with the darts in her girdle.

I'm closing my legs, because she cannot fathom what happened to me.

"We saw a man—well, I did, anyway," Saint-Just says, lowering his gaze. "He wore a sack over his face and he was doing unmentionable things. I tried to reach him, but he was too fast and—"

My face comes apart, burns at the seams. "And yet"—the glass in my voice breaks—"you did nothing!"

Saint-Just reaches over, like he means to place his grubby hands on me, and my axe is swinging, an extension of my brain. The widest part of the blade is a fraction of an inch from the ruffle of his sleeve.

He retrieves his hand just in time, and I'm closing the gap, because I am a panther. A viper. They are my prey.

"He got away!" he says again.

"*Never* touch me." Fire crackles apart my corset's embroidery.

Charlotte straightens her starched pleats. "We need someone of your skills to temper the bloodlust of the Jacobins, Tempeste."

I stick my head in my former friend's face. "Did you not hear what happened to me?"

She takes a step away. "For that," she says, nodding her immaculate curls beneath her pious bonnet, "we are sorry."

My mind ripples back to the first time I suspect I was violated. I woke up in an abandoned paper factory without my clothing, legs blood-streaked. It didn't take me long to find my frock hanging on a lantern across the street, nor to convince a passing boy to retrieve it for me. He didn't want to at first, but I promised to teach him how to tie fish hooks with the hair of his own head. Swore to give him a handful of my own, which had grown tougher from rarely washing.

Now, though, Saint-Just's pulling a pipe from his pocket like he's long been bored of me. "We worry that you are too unwieldy."

My ears must have severed apart from my brain. Do they not realize that they are largely responsible for my—eccentricities?

Charlotte grabs me by the shoulders, digging her pointy nails into my robe and shoulder blades. "We realize our methods opened you up to terrible things, but without us, you are nothing but a caged animal incapable of being trained."

I could tell her what I think about her. Of her choice to not seek redemption for her family, but I am not so devoid of conscience to utter such a thing. I think it, though. *Just because the king's army raped and murdered your maman and sisters a decade ago doesn't make you better than me.*

There was a time when Charlotte was once known to laud me with an assortment of praises: *You are so fearless and daring. Show me how to slice this apple? You hold the paring knife so cleverly.* But now I know she was plotting all along to take me—as if honing my skills with such barbarity should ever be okay.

I grip the axe and spring toward her like I really do mean to cut her in half with the blade.

Her porcelain face flinches. "We went too far! I realize that now, Tempeste. We simply needed someone like you to help us stand up to the Jacobins. They're getting far too powerful in this city."

I cannot allow Charlotte and Saint-Just to stand in the way of my quest to discover why Marat's been targeting my family. Am I tempted to spend my energy on finding the wretch who hurt me? *Oui.* But I owe Maman and Papa the diligence of finding Marat. Questioning him will give my fraying mind a semblance of peace. Perhaps a morsel of sanity.

And then the devil knows what I'll do to the man who touched me.

Charlotte, though, and Saint-Just just stand there like a pair of empty-headed puppies, so I spell it out for the lot of them. "Consider me *opposed* to your plan for using my 'skills' for any damned faction in this city." And I spit, just in case they didn't catch my meaning.

Charlotte rolls her eyes while turning for the door, steadying herself on the side of the grandfather clock as she walks way. She thinks she will get through to me, but I am as stubborn as the burs in my underthings.

"I must check in with—" Charlotte catches herself like she mustn't betray any valuable information to me "—our leader."

Saint-Just leans into my starched former friend, clasping her by the hands and brushing his lips against the side of her cheek. Her cheeks redden with pleasure before she lifts her pleated skirts to leave. I have half a mind to tell him I, too, am leaving, but he nods at me. "That's a nasty habit."

He stares at my thumb and I freeze—he's caught me biting the side—something I hadn't even realized I was doing. I thought I had stopped that senseless biting. The skin is so raw and torn, it looks like I've been scratching to escape prison walls all day. Salt bastes my tongue, and my stomach growls. I shove my thumb inside the cool fabric of my robe. "It's a better habit than what Charlotte and you were doing to me."

Saint-Just sighs like he regrets what they've done. "Do you know what I think?" He strolls to the window, his tall leather boots tapping the wooden floor smartly. "You need to set your sights on a worthy goal for conquering."

Did he not just lecture me about pulverizing Marat's printing press?

"Once you have your goal in mind, you simply need to come to me *before* you do anything."

If he thinks I'm going to share with him my deepest, darkest plans, he has another thing coming.

"Do you know what I did when *I* was eighteen?" He turns his head, settling his chilling eyes on me. His lips curl in a small smile, and I could be looking in the mirror at a cleaner, more masculine version of me. "Tempeste, I once burned down a reformatory."

I cannot help it. I'm laughing. "You did not."

"I did." He, too, laughs. I don't know what it is, but he intrigues me. How many people could boast of such a rascally deed?

"Why?" I join him at the window. "Burn it, I mean."

His fingers grip the window base. "My—superior—wanted to control me."

And there you have it. He's a kindred fellow indeed. He knows what it's like to feel trapped, controlled. I can practically *feel* him freeing me from my corset's tight boning.

And yet, he and Charlotte censured me. "I thought you said I was being too unwieldy."

Saint-Just frowns. Walking to a bookshelf lining the wall, he runs his fingers over the spines of the books, those miniature beauties. "Every man has the right to risk his own life to preserve it."

"Rousseau." I can scarcely breathe. It's a quote I thought on when I dared sleep on a bench in lieu of my comfortable bedding. But Jean-Jacques Rousseau goes on to explain, *Has it ever been said that a man who throws himself out the window to escape a fire is guilty of suicide?* I understand Saint-Just's parallel perfectly. I quirk my lips in a smile. "You started that fire to prove a point."

His eyes are like gunfire. "Sometimes one needs to make people pay. In the name of liberty."

"But Charlotte—"

"Charlotte's a little more uptight than me." He watches a storeowner outside set up a ladder to paint a sign jutting out from the top of his building. "While *I* prefer a more proactive spirit, Charlotte needs a little explanation before one does things." He pats me on the shoulder. I tense, because his fingers are touching me, but they are soft, so I do not raise the blade.

"Just tell us what you plan before you terrorize anything," he says.

In him, I've rediscovered an alliance. I know it, surely. But I cannot share everything, so I give him a hint to let him know we're on the same page. "I only need to convince Marat to talk to me."

He grips my shoulder, and like a fiery coal, he's singeing me. But just as fast, he releases his grasp, and I know I'm exasperating him far greater than I had foreseen. His eyes, black and blue with daggers, mirror my own, and I am thankful to have found a mirror of myself in the male species. But he cannot force me how to behave. Neither can Charlotte. They must let me seek my vengeance. It is my salve for suturing back together my two inner halves: Colette de la Croix and Joseph-Ignace Guillotine.

10

GABRIEL

I MOUNT the scaffold for the fifteenth time this week. My hands, so red from blood, have become permanently stained. I've tried scrubbing them with lye and alcohol, so they're also chapped and clammy. My arms ache from holding up heads to appease the crowd, and the sour stench of death coats my clothes—my shoes, my knee breeches, my white cravat that's now long grown pink.

For Père, I must buck up and fulfill my duty, but I would be remiss if I didn't admit that Carvell's offer of land has never been so tempting.

But I couldn't abandon the Master Executioner of Paris when our family's hold on our vocation has never been more bleak.

Our prison cells are so full, I've had to convince the locksmith to loan me more chains. Our food stores have grown so low, I'm only able to offer the Patients mush once per day. Their cries have grown louder, their pleas for us to release them more incessant. Père's begun sticking cotton in his ears when he chops their hair at the Pillory before leaving for the Guillotine.

I should find Tempeste—make sure she's fine, as I'm pretty certain her friends knocked me out while I was driving Père's carriage, for I have no memory of getting home. And I've been too busy purchasing quicklime and shovels to look into what happened.

A goat bleats as I secure a shaky step on the scaffold with today's pudgy Patient who hunches next to me. He hasn't said a word since we left the Pillory. I hope to make this a quick run so I might have a little time to search for Tempeste. Hopefully those friends of hers haven't harmed her in any way.

A skein of yarn whips through the air, smacking me on the shoulder, and I think someone in the crowd might be complaining for me to hurry up when they cry out, "To the Place du Carrousel!"

I glance around to find a row of seated old women, bent over their projects, knitting.

Like a corpse prematurely suffering from rigor mortis, the Patient stiffens next to me, probably because many have wanted to change the locale for executions to the grander square by the king's palace, the Tuileries. No doubt this counterfeiter hopes for a quick death. Dismantling, moving, then reconstructing the scaffold would take all day.

I glance back to *mon père* to ensure that he wants me to proceed, but someone's picking up a large pedestal urn and smashing it at the feet of Père's favorite horse.

The horse, Justice, brays, rearing up on its hind legs, causing the tumbrel to tilt dangerously. Père's large hooded eyes widen as he pulls on the reins. The horse rears up once again, and I'm about to aid in calming him, when the horse's hooves scuffle on the cobblestones and still.

Bien, Justice.

"Are you daft?" Père jumps from the tumbrel while

securing the horse's reins. Patting Justice's mane and running his fingers along the horse's legs to ensure it hasn't been injured, Père murmurs words of comfort to the most faithful horse he's had in years. Only Justice's ears twitch. It doesn't like surprises. No animal does.

The man who smashed the urn sneers up at *mon père* triumphantly. Licking a fat scab on his upper lip, the brute says, "I *said* to the Place du Carrousel, you filthy leech!" He emphasizes his words like insulting *mon père* gives him insurmountable power. I think there's no point in giving him any heed until I spot, between his fingerless gloves, an unlit grenade.

Père's fingers go so white, they match his silken stockings. Panic flounders in his brutish eyes, because there's no telling whether this man has a match at the ready. "My orders," Père speaks slowly, "are to execute in the Place de Greve."

The man twists his mouth as he tightens the grenade in his ripped gloves and seizes the horse's reins. Does he mean to blow up Justice? I grip the Patient's pudgy arm, trying to drag him over the uneven cobblestones in the direction of *mon père*, but the Patient's about as mobile as a boulder. Petrified in some way. The Place du Carrousel is several blocks due west, near the Tuileries, the palace of our king. Why does the *sans-culotte* care at all where this Patient is Guillotined? Does he wish to shame our king further by parading executions outside his window? Flout the Jacobin morbid desire to execute the king?

I've managed to scoot the Patient closer to Père, but the Patient and I spot a discarded dagger on the ground at precisely the same time. We stoop to retrieve it—he might try to get away—when we knock heads and I'm seeing stars amidst the guts of some animal and trash strewn in the street.

The Patient cries out and clutches his head, which is about twice the size of mine. The crowd scurries over the scaffold like ants, seizing boards and ripping apart the edifice which holds our Guillotine.

They'll damage the wood, and the cost of lumber is not cheap. We already had to borrow to erect this edifice. We cannot afford to purchase more wood to construct another.

"Do you not *hear* the people?" the man leers, leaning toward Père with his grenade. A red cap highlights the bright scab tearing open his face. "They want the Place du *Carrousel*, and the *people's wishes* are the wishes of the *Assembly*." His want for food makes his skin stretch dangerously thin over his knuckles and the bones jut out from his cheeks.

A fleet of potatoes pepper Père's black hat and smack his green great coat. He flinches and glances about, feet planted, arms held wide like a fiendish boar ready to defend his family. But anyone who knows Master Sanson knows he never loses himself to emotions. He is a professional by trade.

"*You* should be Guillotined!" a middle-aged woman roars, a crooked finger pointing at *mon père*, and this is getting out of hand. She should be locked up for thinking such a thing. Her filthy, powdered hair grazes the tips of her shoulders, which are cloaked with the tired ribbons of the aristocracy. Maniacal laughter reveals tarred, blackened teeth.

Someone's grabbing Père's horse, Justice, again, tugging his large, almond head to the side. Like it's possessed, Justice opens his wolfish mouth and rears up on his feet. The tumbrel will flip—Père will be killed—so I scramble down the one—three?—stairs of the scaffold and nearly trip over a squirrel that's begun inspecting the guts strewn in the street. But I am too late. Already the tumbrel, like a wooden canon, is tipping over, falling, and I watch in horror as one of the wooden spokes pins Père's chest to the street.

"NOOO!" I cry. This cannot be happening. "*Non, non, non, non.*" I shove a slow, stooped man out of the way, a small child I shouldn't be shoving, and kneel down at *mon père's* side, who's pinned like a creature who deserves to be detained.

Though I've endured the practice of lifting and hoisting newly decapitated bodies, I am not a man of brawn by any means. Sturdy, but nowhere near as strong as Henri. The tumbrel is made of heavy oak—the sturdiest we could buy —and the other assistants are all back at the Pillory. Guarding the other Patients, because the Assembly knows it can treat us however they please. I reach out to secure the spoke and lift before Père stops breathing. The wood digs into my palms and I lift, heave, remembering when part of the gallows fell. I had tried to heave and Henri, seeing my strain, dropped the coils of ropes he'd been holding and aided me. Together, we could lift it, but alone, there is no way.

Père's heavily hooded eyes wince as I grunt. Tears pool in the corners of his eyes, and I have never seen *mon père* cry. This is a reminder, a horrible reminder, of a more sorrowful day. The tumbrel quivers as I try to lift, strain. I recall the afternoon when Père jumped in his tumbrel to purchase supplies, only to roll over a lump in the road. Believing to have rolled over a dead animal, Père jumped from his seat only to discover, face down on the paving stones, his nine-year-old son, Charles. Henri's twin and the eldest brother in the Sanson family.

Père tried to revive him, but the weight had crushed my brother's internal organs on impact. Even now, I remember the trickle of blood that pooled on his back where the tumbrel had pierced his tender frame.

Père had heaved the tumbrel out of the way. Cradling his eldest son in his arms, he rocked him as if to sleep as Henri and I looked on, Charles' head and neck as limp as the horse's reins.

For weeks, Père conducted his duties without any trace of emotion. Sharpened axes and coiled ropes without a word, expecting the same of Henri. I was still too young to help with things, but I remember the silence that folded over our home like the shroud Mère and Père wrapped around my brother's body. The uncomfortable, silent dinners. Père's sharp refusal to speak Charles' name.

In the mornings, Père usually rose to teach Charles to play the violin, as *pères* often did in the Sanson family. But now that his eldest was dead, Henri courageously took up the part, even though he held no interest nor talent. Even though Père shooed him away.

Henri wouldn't take no as an answer, though. He tugged on Père's arm until he rose from bed and scuffled to the sitting room where, before dawn, Henri convinced him to play.

They learned Vivaldi. Schmelzer, Mondonville, Somis. Henri tried cracking jokes, to which Père would scoot back his chair and leave. Henri never gave up, though. Kept knocking on Père's door each and every morning, even though he missed his twin brother more than anyone. Together, they always climbed the huckleberry trees and sneaked pears into their pockets before they'd grown fully ripe. But that's who Henri is—even as a child, he unselfishly helped others despite his own feelings.

When Henri slipped his bow over his sometimes out-of-tune strings, chirping at Père, "To play! to play!" I tentatively pulled up a chair, too, and joined in on my brother's valiant efforts to cheer Père. This is why we all play.

But now Henri is on the front lines. I am here, and the bloody tumbrel is slippery. I have never been the strongest or most musical in the Sanson family, but I have helped—I always try, because I wouldn't be able to live with myself any other way.

Seigneur, aide-moi s'il te plaît. Prayer is all I know to do with bloody scenes. I lift and shove that rackety tumbrel against my blood-stained blouse. My shins, beneath my tight knee-breeches, groan as I grit my teeth.

My gaze imprints on Père's chalky white face. He's closing his eyes. *S'il te plaît, Seigneur, aide-nous.*

Sweat pours down my neck. No one approaches to offer aid but, impossibly, the tumbrel lightens as if made of feathers. My fingers wrap tighter round the wooden grains.

The tumbrel shifts like a rocking horse back into place. The scuffs of shoes clap the cobblestones behind me. And as I kneel and wipe the corners of my eyes, a rush of thick, powerful love washes over me.

Merci, Seigneur, merci!

Père's green greatcoat tightens round his shoulders as he rolls to the moldy paving stones below his knees. I think he might just lay there while I call for a stretcher until his meaty hands grab the rickety side of the tumbrel. Heavy as a bison, he places one knee on the uneven paving stones, then the other before heaving himself up and finding his finely polished shoed feet.

He wheezes; he's a thick-skinned rhinoceros hunching in pain. What must be the recollection of how he killed his son washes over the age spots of his severe face. I wish I could embrace him to let him know it's okay, but his vest and blouse are smeared with his own blood, the color of burgundy.

"Secure the Patient." Père chokes out before nodding in the direction of the multi-windowed Hotel de Ville. My chubby Patient, arms tied behind his back, is scampering past overturned barrels of beer and grain.

Père doesn't say a word as he examines the round gash, so near his heart. I'm amazed he's actually awake. Placing his palm over the wound and closing his eyes as if a vulture hovers over his shoulder, he lifts a heavy arm and claps me on the shoulder, nailing me in place. "I would be dead without you, Henri."

Slowly, I turn to retrieve the prisoner, veering round a broken pile of boards and a bench whereon I wouldn't mind sitting. I snatch up the Patient, who has fallen on the ground as a National Guardsmen holds him with a bayonet in place.

Père may have mucked up my name, but he sees me as Henri, which is a compliment, really. Because he was the son who helped him find his feet during the most trying time for our family.

11

TEMPESTE

FINDING MARAT HAS PROVED as difficult as catching a spider monkey. Somehow the toadstool has secured connections in every damned district in the city. I expected to find him at his office—even watched from the shadows to see the satisfying look on his face when he saw what I did to his *illustrious* machine—but, alas. He never came.

So, I found his apartment. Set a nice little trap—with gunpowder! and horse feces!—but he never showed. So I swallowed my pride and visited *mon papa*—once again.

It was like a rather drab rendition of a Shakespearean play:

Where is Jean-Paul Marat hiding?

You'll lose yourself in this quest, my dearest Tempeste!

It should be against the laws of nature that his voice should be so low *and* so weak. Does he not see that I am already a ruined soul in need of that gilded thread of redemption which only vengeance can bring?

Now darkness enshrouds the Place de Greve like an old cemetery. Abandoned banners flutter from ropes and frayed flags. Flagpoles offset a pile of wood marking the spot where the Killing Machine used to be. Another execution's currently being set up in the stately square of the Place du Carrousel with its conical hedges and geometric gardens, and ha-ha-ha, won't *that* be a pretty sight for our imprisoned king!

Because Marat might be there, I travel the distance to the new killing place, veering around poorly made fences tacked up in a rush and the only grass in Paris that is still green.

I'm just eyeing a sleeping guard's pair of bracers, which would do nicely on my arms that are far too often getting scraped, when a slender figure in a sleek, black robe sidles up to me. The figure's hood is up, so I'm not entirely sure who it is, until she lowers it and the level-headed gaze and slight dimple in her chin tells me it's Charlotte.

Must a girl never earn a reprieve?

Behind her, enshrouded in matching robes, appear to be her friends—the junior members of her Girondin posse—following her lead. They do not approach us, though. Merely hover in the background like my stepmother Élise's gaudy figurines.

It is with great pleasure that I watch as a nearby tree branch lodges itself in Charlotte's hood. She yanks to pull it free, causing it to tear a hole along the seam.

"Our leader," Charlotte says, groaning at her shiny hood's new damage, "has asked that I bring you something."

I can't help but giggle at her misgiving. "Is that so?" I eye the bone-made ivory ring lying on the palm she's holding out me—one which perfectly matches the ring Saint-Just wore the other day. The one she's currently wearing over her gloves—I always detested that fashion choice. Still, an ornate "G" tastefully embellishes the surface of both rings, and I might might find it to be pretty, except for the fact that Charlotte is offering it to me.

"What's the G stand for?" I ask, not too terribly unkindly.

Charlotte's pink lips tighten as she seizes my hand and tries cramming the ring on my finger. I seize the cool, gaudy piece of jewelry and fling it at her stupid feet. Which sends a nice little *cling*—an exact echo to the tambourine some old wretch missing half his fingers is currently playing. The executioners' hammers on the newly built scaffold suddenly cease.

My voice batters the quiet as I say, "What would possess you to believe I'd *ever* ever want a piece of jewelry?"

The robed figures behind her whisper like I've just spoken blasphemy, and Charlotte flinches like I've just painted a mustache on the subject of her favorite painting. She pulls herself up to her fullest height, which is a good three inches taller than me, her skinny shoulders shaking. She spies where I just tossed the ring—in a neat little pile of cow feces—and her voice comes out taut. "It is made of the same material as rosary beads."

An image of Sister Josephine flashes in my mind, but I refuse to allow myself to feel guilty. Just because rosary beads are precious to Sister Josephine does not mean they are precious to me.

Sinking to the ground, Charlotte retrieves the ring with her gloved hand like the damned ring's not actually made of bone, but of diamonds or rubies. The tiniest part of me wishes to know why she cares so much that I accept the ring when a fresh spray of whoops and catcalls curl across the darkened square. I look up, past dirtied bonnets and slouched hats, to lit torches on the scaffold and to our Killing Machine.

It is as dark as the sewers snaking under our repulsive city, so it is hard to see past the commoner-held flags and arms pumping the air like their enthusiasm matters, like it changes things. But I suppose it does. The cry of the people would be the only way to convince the executioners to take their next victim any time other than mid-day.

The blade just fell. I know this, because torches are highlighting a murky fuchsia liquid that is not paint. I step closer, because tri-colored ribbons are dotting *mon papa*'s machine like it's covered in palsy. The fire of nearby torches whips and jerks the flame so that it perfectly enshrouds the wide, diagonal blade.

I suck in a breath. It is beautiful, *oui*, for even in the moonlight, its twin posts remind me of "liberty" and "equality." But I try not to think of the brief blip in time in which the metal *zinged* to the bottom of the Machine. That brief moment Maman would have endured as opposed to gagging. But it's also terrifically horrible in another way. Like a sharp, broken fang—a wolf having munched on rabbit meat.

The bourreau's short hair, tied at the nape of his neck, makes him look a little too cheerful, a little too neat. He bends down and—what is he doing? He's retrieving the head that was just severed by the Killing Machine.

He holds his victim's head high up in the air, like he's a Greek God, like he's Prometheus and Zeus shall grant him the power to spout fire of his own making.

We lock eyes, and if I were a witch, I'd cast a spell in which he's prevented from ever proudly holding up a head that way.

His jaw flexes, and I know he ascertains my exact feelings as cheers, like sprinkles on a confectionary, break out amongst the squared off hollies. The people stir, pant as if they're in heat. They like how the bourreau holds up that head. But of course they do. They are as sensible as grub-shites.

I had forgotten how loudly the people can get when toddlers and wrinkled old women slap together their thumbs, ring fingers, pinkies. When *sans-culottes* seize drums and bells—*banging, clinging*—like the great apocalypse has come this very day.

Two girls about my age are linking arms and dancing. A fiddler, a bit cross-eyed, slashes his bow across his strings like he's playing for the opera.

The people, well. They are giddy at the sight of the bourreau holding up that head, and perhaps he does it because they want him to, but he bulges out his chest like he's happy.

Charlotte murmurs, "It's horrible," before looking away. I bite my tongue, because for once in a great long while, I have to agree.

"You see what that contraption's doing to our country," she says like it's my fault, like I want the crowd to be so bloodthirsty.

I glare at her far-too-fragile face. "Every soul deserves a painless killing." A legless soldier grunts from the effort of scurrying his torso across the square upon palms. "Except for Marat." I add as an afterthought, "And the king." Because he has allowed too many in his country to starve.

Charlotte seizes the locket I'd forgotten she wears round her throat.

"They deserve—"

She opens her rosy lips like she has something else she'd like to indoctrinate me with when Saint-Just, red cravat and great coat fluttering as he walks, bursts through a crowd of dark-suited men, all their backs turned to me. The proper fold of their hands and proud tilt to their heads tells me they might be Jacobins—for they are pleased with the crowd's celebrating.

"So." Saint-Just tucks Charlotte's slim hand into the crook of his tattered jacket's arm. Somberly, he observes Charlotte's second bone-made ring, now garnishing her white glove's palm with the bright stain of cow feces. "She would not receive?"

Charlotte's curls rustle over her collar as she shakes her head gravely.

Saint-Just sighs like I've just cost him a great deal of money. "You are a delectable challenge, Tempeste."

Charlotte swats him on the arm, and I'm smiling.

"I am surprised the executioners went ahead with the killing." I gesture to a group of compatriots, dancing in the patchy twilight round a liberty tree.

"The people's wishes and the Assembly's wishes are one and the same," Saint-Just says, confirming what I meant to say.

Charlotte moans while someone lifts a burning effigy of a priest. "What is happening to our country?"

"The instrument of death," Saint-Just says a bit too brightly.

"You have a curious outlook," I say, studying his long hair, which has become a bit disheveled. The plain buttons hanging by threads have nearly fallen from his jacket's opening.

"A *moderate* outlook," Charlotte corrects as a boy with a soot-stained face tramples over an abandoned kerchief.

I think he's merely passing by when he plants his muddy, too-small shoes before me. He's six—seven years, maybe?—and reeks of sewage, which I know has far too often wafted over me. He holds out a folded, torn note between his fingers, which have never been washed, as far as I can see. For me?

Crouching low to meet his eye level, I ask, taking a chance, "Marat told you to give this to me?" The grub-shite would want to respond to my efforts to rearrange his office eventually, though I mustn't leap before I've secured my landing.

Assent is written all over this too skinny boy's face. He holds out the note until I take it. I pluck up the paper, because it is time to feed.

Unfolding the note with shaking hands, I find the same slanderous scrawl that I've found in his other newspaper writings:

You're about as volatile as your Maman, the note breathes. Marat has spies watching me?

I glance up at the boy, whose bony hand I must have snatched while I was reading. With a flash of guilt, I release his tiny fingers and ask much louder than I mean, "MARAT TOLD YOU TO GIVE THIS TO ME?"

The boy glances behind him, at the robed figures loitering behind Charlotte and Saint-Just, watching me carefully. I must have snatched up the boy's hand again, because he's trying to pull away and I would never hurt a child, but I must know *more* about where Marat wrote this—what is his endgame. But all I get in answer is a splash of saliva as the boy spits a loogie at me.

Smiling at his rascally ways, I wipe the spit with my sleeve. As he trots away, I am filled with the lemon-zest of victory, for I have heard from Marat. And Charlotte and Saint-Just shall not stop me.

12

GABRIEL

I FOLLOWED her here hours ago, but until now, I hadn't worked up the raw nerve to go in. Why doesn't it surprise me that a girl so skilled at swinging a blade would have an affinity for the darkest haunts, nay, the devil's very footstool?

I shouldn't have come, but Père's laid up in bed, and we've talked the Assembly into stalling future executions until he heals properly. Apparently, his ability to take direction from the crowd was "most pleasing." France's spirits have never been higher, so the Assembly has decided to allow us to retain our citizenship—to keep our land, our home, our right to elect representatives from our district to the Assembly.

For the time being.

I still haven't spoken to Carvell after what happened to Père. How could I after he nearly died?

Now, though, I must track Tempeste, for I saw her conversing with Charlotte and Saint-Just in the square, and I am not convinced they mean her well. Saint-Just, well, he seems fishy. Perhaps because I've seen him converse with

Jacobins a bit too cheerfully, as if he really does wish the Girondins were as radical, or as extreme.

As I trail after her into the catacombs, though, there never was a world so macabre, so wrought with diseases and loss such as this. Imagine a stench so foul that it causes even the gravediggers to turn a greenish pallor. A darkness so overwhelming that it's caused many a miner to see things that aren't really there. Their brains becoming puppet-masters.

Behold, the Parisian crypts and tunnels.

I can smell them down the shaft, the decomposing bodies. Like a ripe bowel movement. I try breathing through my mouth, but that only worsens matters. The tunnels are supposed to be a final resting place for the bones of the dead—except that our cemeteries are over-full, spilling into some districts' water supply. So, the Assembly has ordered the removal of as many bodies as possible and displaced down here. But it can be hard to gauge the exact decomposition of a pile of, say, fifteen hundred bodies. Further, the grave diggers are supposed to make candles and soaps from the fats dripping from the eroding figures, but even I would say it would be hard to glean every bodily fluid capable of stinking.

Why, oh why, must the girl come to *this* of all places in the world?

It was the Romans who long ago mined the limestone in the labyrinth below. They didn't begin with the intention of making it a bone-filled ossuary. The Notre Dame? Mined here. The Louvre? That, too. Quarry workers would hammer away, hoisting the massive stones up an endless pit much like the hole I'm scrambling down now, a thick rope clenched between my leg, left behind by the girl I cannot seem to toss from my mind no matter what I try.

About half-way down, the fraying rope slips between my sweaty palms, and I cringe as my shoulder smacks into the cool side of the mining shaft. I will not think of the diseases still brewing on the half-decomposed bodies, no. Cool air licks at my hands as I shimmy down, my fingers embedded with splinters, begging to relax. But I will not allow it, I must climb the entire way.

Down. Farther and farther below.

Glancing about in the pitted darkness and moving away from the hole, I find that there aren't any bones thrown down this particular hole. In fact, the cavern is so small that I have to bend down low, like a troll from one of my boyhood fairy tales. The cave's not very wide, either, but juts diagonally to the side in a slender tunnel much like one I visited long ago. A tunnel I try not to remember but somehow always snakes back into my memory. A memory, just like right now, where I'm pulling off a lantern clipped to my belt, its yellow beam alighting every ghost, crevice, and dancing insect on the wall.

I'd tried *so* hard to reach Henri that day, a year or so after Charles died, only catching glimpses of his blue military great-coat. He had gone with a group of boys to explore the caverns before they became overrun with bones. Believing the older boys to have forked left, when Henri had indeed gone right, I entered a pit so filled with water that I soon found myself swept up, neck-deep, in an impossibly deep pool. When I tried swimming out, my seven-year-old head smacked on the jagged ceiling so hard that I lost consciousness.

Even still, I remember the horror of the lights going out, like the Lord had sent me down to hell.

In the end, Henri found me before I'd completely

drowned, but not before I gained a permanent condition due to the severity of the blow. It would have been bearable for my family if I had been a girl, as females aren't expected to assist with executions, but being a boy, I had to learn to soldier on. It's not like I could complain when Charles didn't survive at all.

It didn't help that for months all I could think about was the taste of the briny water sloshing into my mouth, remembering the sensation of bones snatching at me under the water. Like they could survive if they pushed me under.

Warily stepping through the narrow tunnel to a larger cavern, I bristle at the cool air swimming above my head, telling me the ceiling is much higher now. Holding onto the thin wire of my lantern, I'm just about to let out a slow, even breath, when I spot a large pile of skulls, the stark color of parchment. I shudder even though some aren't as sinister as I tend to remember.

I close my eyes against their black, vacant orifices, but not before seeing the broken crucifixes strewn about like the lime my brother and I scatter on corpses. Why do we work so hard to give the Patients a proper burial only to have them end up in a heap of rubble down here?

A shadow flickers in the corner, and I spin, nearly dropping the lantern. But it's only a rat. A rat and its tail—snaking in and out of one of the skulls' eye sockets. I can handle bodies of the flesh and blood variety, but skeletons?

It takes everything I have not to shriek like a little girl.

Bracing my hand on the cool, wet limestone, I try slowing my pounding pulse, but the moisture is just like the possible diseases simmering on any corpse. I snatch my hand back, wiping it on my knee-breeches, and bite back a curse. Why, in heaven's name, have I come down here at all?

A high cackling echoes through the cavern, and I settle my eyes on a small, willowy figure enshrouded in a black-hooded robe. Tempeste. Black soot mars her face, and I have to ask myself how I can be so obsessed with such a girl. Even now, her cheek-bones cut so sharply, she's but a living corpse, embracing the wild elements with her unpainted cheeks and wind-tousled curls.

Her eyes, set unusually wide apart, shine down on me with contempt, and I have to force myself not to grow small.

"I thought you of all people would be able to handle a few bones," she says.

All I want to do is talk to her—discover what happened outside the Place de Greve between her, Charlotte, and Saint-Just, whom I swear I've seen somewhere before.

She pulls her hood back, two steely black eyes glaring. "Why are you following me?" Her words echo like a murmur in the black tomb.

Not wanting to admit the truth, I point to the mounds of skulls, a few dripping with liquefied flesh. "I wanted to see those."

Tempeste narrows her eyes. "You are the vilest man I know."

I am not the one who chooses to spend my leave in the catacombs.

She sidles closer, my lantern highlighting the satin of her robe, and I can't help wondering how she looks under that robe. Has she the curves I've always desired in a woman? But of course, no. She's a half-starved scarecrow, and the foreignness of that image impossibly makes me desire her more.

Holding one arm a little apart from her body, she hoists a long handle topped off by a crescent blade.

Mon père's axe. I had forgotten I left it with her. I hold out my hand, cursing myself for being so careless with my family's heirloom. But the duties back home have been like a monsoon. "I'll be taking that."

Tempeste casually passes the blade from one hand to the other as if it's hollow. As if she has an exorbitant amount of time. "Come after it, then."

In all my years, I have never met such an unredeemable girl. She's taunting me with *mon père*'s blade. A weapon forged for the express purpose of slaying, at no expense of cost.

I square my shoulders like I must walk another Patient up the scaffold. "Give it back. Now."

This look of anger flits over her dangerous eyes, and I have to hope that she will listen to me. She's not all evil. A little misguided—missing a few screws. She slams the blade into the rocky floor, and the *cling* is a direct prod on my nerves.

Her complete disregard for decorum is so utterly wrong. I reach out to rip the blade from her fist when all I find is the slick rock of the cavern.

To the right, I presume, so I scramble that way. When that direction comes up empty, I shimmy to the left. If my eyes only worked! I know I must look quite the buffoon, swiping this way and that, but *mon père* relies on this weapon. If the Guillotine ever goes awry, we shall need the tool.

But the girl is only laughing, launching her clear voice like a catapult across the bone-filled room. I would almost call her laughter nice—feminine yet full—except I know that I am the target of her scorn.

Feeling about as radiant as horse dung, I watch in defeat as the daughter of the doctor-made-politician sighs.

"What is wrong with you, bourreau?"

Earthiness clings to her body like a kiss from the fertile soil, and all I can wonder is how many times I have endured that insult. Classmates, commoners, noblemen all love to taunt me with that name. I say what I tell all of them. "Don't call me 'bourreau.'"

She's only a finger-width away from me now—or seven, depending on how poorly I'm guessing. Her warm breath puffs directly upon my nose, and *mon Dieu*, even her breath smells like freshly ground cocoa.

I wait for her to say something else, hating myself for hanging on her every word. In one quick move, she locks her stormy eyes on mine while scraping the blade against the rocky ground.

The sound bleeds my ears. I reach out to grab the axe, but instead, grab something round, warm, and soft.

She shoves away my hand so hard that my arm painfully twists backward. Biting back a cry, I watch with wide eyes as she scrambles several feet away from where I lurk.

Her dark eyes, like two black cobras, lash out.

And guilt twists worse than any sword, because I can gather what I just grabbed.

Though I've broken a man's finger-bones one by one, forced a highwayman's head into a trough of water mingled with piss, I pride myself on being a gentleman—if not with Patients, with women, then. And gentlemen do not secure unwanted intimacies from the females they know. Of course, I may reflect on what just happened a bit more happily later on, but as of now, I honestly must tell her it was by accident, because it was. So I lock my eyes with hers.

"I didn't mean it."

She whips the axe around—up, down, to the side—like

she's fearful I'll try it once more. "What in heaven's name is *wrong* with you?"

I consider telling her a lie. *It was there for the taking, and I took it.*

But I'm standing here, looking at her, and all I can think is how maybe, just maybe she is like that Magdalena painting in *mon père*'s house, after all. Amidst all that fire and puff, she's only a girl. A girl who's set her sights on a singular task. Redemption. She wants to avenge her *mère*'s, her *maman*'s, stolen life.

Aside from helping her, I am a traditional soul. One who desires to eventually marry. Tempeste may be wary of such a prospect, but she's the first girl I have actually wanted to consider marrying.

I would smooth her brow. Help her find her happiness. Like Mary Magdalene, she seeks that redemption, and though Tempeste may not have discovered it can best be found in the Lord, perhaps I can help her see a part of it.

Now, though, looking at the way her narrow shoulders are drawn up tight, a tendon pulsing from her neck, I know I have a very, very long way to go.

"My eyes don't work properly," I blurt.

"And?"

"And when I think something is there," I say, pointing to my side, "it's actually over here," I hover my hand in front of my chest.

Tempeste holds the axe in front of her as if scared I will go for the other one now. "You are a sick person, *monsieur*."

I could ask her to hold something out to me just to show her, but the only object she's holding is the axe. It's going to be a little while before I get that back, so I hold out my lantern. "See?" I try handing it over, but at that exact moment the lantern smacks a protrusion on the wall, and even I couldn't have perfectly timed the brashness.

Tempeste just stands there, impossibly quiet now. A bone teeters as a rodent jumps to the bottom of a bone pile, and I watch as it lands on a neat little pile of finger bones.

My stomach churns.

Tempeste eventually says, "You could be lying."

I move the lantern up to my face, or somewhere thereabouts, so that she can read my face. "Do you believe that?"

An emotion contorts her gaze, her brittle cheeks, her rounder nose. I am not too sure what it is, but I know it can't be a sweeping of love sickness. Besides, she's shouting, "You molested me!"

To which I'm tripping over a small pile of bones. "If I wanted to molest you, *mademoiselle*, you would more acutely know."

She cries out. I'm reddening, so I clarify, "Because it would be by your request!"

She huffs as blood rushes to my face. How did we get on the track of discussing the affections I might offer a girl? I know she would never want them from me if she knew everything I know. I understand that better than anyone in the world, and yet, here I am, unable to leave her alone.

"I shall *never* want that from you." She thrusts out the handle of the axe, obviously testing to see if I will grab it, and I'm darting forward, because *mon père* needs it for work. But I end up grasping at nothing but air. She jerks the axe forward, so close that I'm sure she's going to slice apart my stomach. I try snatching it up again, but it's at an odd angle and dark.

She heaves a heavy sigh before pulling it back. "You are embarrassing yourself."

"I'm not the one who throws tantrums in public."

An emotion flitters across her haunted eyes like she's thinking, *you saw that?*

There's this corner of my heart that pleads with me to whisper, *It's okay. I care what happens to you,* but it's not something I can muster. She would pound me to a pulp, then light up a match. She'd smoke away my ashes, and I wouldn't stop her. I deserve it more than she knows.

Even so, another part of me is screaming to do the only thing I came down here to do: show I care.

I want to do it. But I don't. How far can a lowly bourreau fall? And yet, training my eyes on her sharp cheekbones and long, stringy hair, I cannot help drawing closer, trapping her against the cavern's wall.

I shouldn't feel that I've won a victory when she cannot escape me now, but I'm angling my lean frame toward hers, moving one leg so close—and I'm as surprised as anyone— that it actually connects with hers.

She sucks in a breath.

Warmth spreads through our legs, and it's enough to fuel the lantern. Her slender waist relaxes—I can hardly believe it, but it does—and my heart's twisting so wildly, I wouldn't be surprised if she could feel it, too. Maybe there's a part of her that wants what I want. To know what happens if more of us touch. I lean toward her, needing her lips to touch mine, but with my luck, I'd end up kissing one of her eyes, her teeth, her hair, so instead, heart in my throat, I simply reach down for any part of her face, any part of it at all.

Providence must be on my side, for when I reach out, I'm actually finding her cheek, and it's as smooth as satin. This urge tugs through me to swallow my mouth over hers, but if she knew me, she'd never want that and besides, she's already screeching—

"Get off get off get off!"

Her fist hits my stomach, and like a wounded solider, I'm tumbling back. She's already four or ten feet from me now.

The cave is spinning, and not just because she shoved me aside like lettuce. She's a disease, I've caught it, and there's no going back.

I may be a little out of my element, amidst the black and dampness, but I have a good work ethic. Before I lost my vision, it took me minutes to cut an entire quart of wood. I'm good with animals. I loved those dumb, scraggly sheep we had to offer up to the Guillotine to ensure it worked.

But she's charging toward me now, her black hair flying in tendrils like a colony of bats. Shoving me hard on the chest, she cries, "How could you *ever* believe I wanted that?"

My mind flashes to the way she relaxed when I touched her leg. But it's not like I'm about to point that out now, so I keep my jaw shut.

"Do you know what irks me above all else?"

I'm as mute as a leathern basket.

"I came down here to hone my skills, get in a little practicing, but even that, you cannot allow."

I glance at the pile of skulls, a few of them cut cleanly in half, and have to wonder if they fell that way, or if Tempeste did that.

I decide I would rather not know.

Her robe billows like a crow's wings as she prowls. "Why have you been following me?" She prods my shoulder with the topmost tip of *mon père*'s axe.

I consider telling her I saw how she is unlike the others —that she does not feed on the dramatization of a kill. That she, in fact, has a conscience—but I doubt she wants to hear about that, so I mutter, "I wanted to be sure you were *d'accord*."

She swipes the axe impossibly close to my face, narrowing her eyes. "There's something else."

"The Club," I say, referring to the Club for Young Ladies which Charlotte and Saint-Just had wanted her to see. It would have been good for her—reminding her of the refinement with which she must have been raised. It might have been just what she needed to find her feet. But my lantern's spitting, and the two of us will soon be left in the dark. The last thing I want is for us to remain trapped under a mere pile of bones. So, I take a few steps toward the entrance.

"It was a sham." She sniffs. She's oblivious that I yearn for us to leave. Blindly, she flings about the axe. If it had been me, I would have cut off my own foot. "I am like—" she says, raising her voice a few notches "—a caged animal, incapable of being trained."

She must be mimicking another voice. The leader of the Club, perhaps? But then I'm remembering what I last saw that evening—how Charlotte had this carnal look in her eyes just before something struck me on the neck and I fell unconscious. I am not sure how she did it, but Charlotte *was* responsible for my falling asleep that night. Further, she and Saint-Just were obviously singling out Tempeste, so if they were tracking her, perhaps this Club wasn't a typical Club for young girls.

I'm not sure what to think. On the one hand, this sudden recollection makes me not trust Charlotte or Saint-Just at all, but on the other, I do not like the idea of Tempeste being excluded. So I find myself scuffing my boot against the rocky ground. "If I had a Club, I'd let you join."

Inevitably, my cheeks warm, but there isn't time for Tempeste to respond, for there's this far-off sound of rocks or bones crackling. It's coming from the entrance, and just as I look to see what it is, I spot a yellowish beam alighting the tunnel—and not from my lantern. If I were to guess, I would suppose it to be more gravediggers delivering once buried bones. But all at once, Tempeste's shoving me deeper into the cave, and the dark lake I know to be lurking there spurs a wintry chill.

I'm about to protest, insist that we turn back, when Tempeste points deeper into the cave. "Run."

13

TEMPESTE

LIKE A SORE, I am soothed by the cave's cooling balm. I've lured Marat down here and soon I'll know why he's targeting my family.

Fortunately, I've spent a countless number of nights hiding amidst the rocks and rats and skeletons, knowing few people are able to stomach the stench and gloom. Skeletons whisper their secrets; darkness wraps around me like a smooth woolen blanket. The only noise is the dripping moisture of the ceiling and the pitter-patter of rats finding plump wads of flesh.

I've chosen the best smelling off-shoot of the labyrinth, too. Parts of the tunnels are so full of half-decomposed bodies that even I don't risk traveling them. This sector, though, has a scent that's almost sweet as long as you don't get too close to the bodies, and it's the homiest smell in the world—like burnt pumpernickel.

As the bourreau and I dart left, down a low corridor lined with the candles I forged myself, I grab my own lantern on the path, only to have the oaf stumble sideways on a rock on the ground.

Part of me wants to inform him not to bother following. This particular tunnel's just a big loop, anyway. My plan is to circle round, pull up the rope before Marat can follow, and corner him. I'll convince him to spill his secrets. The deserter once trained me on the seemly art of extracting confessions.

"Careful of the stairs," I say as we approach a steep, narrow staircase carved out by an old quarry worker. A whiff of the pumpernickel washes over me, which for some reason changes my mind. "Just jump over them." It's only two or three steps, and the boy—through no fault of his own —is clumsier than anyone should have to endure. He's probably worrying about the likelihood of the ceiling collapsing or the fact that if we get lost down here, it'll be a decade before someone finds us.

I've endured worse.

The boy's form grows rigid like a stale hunk of bread, and I watch in silence as he leaps straight over the stairs.

To his credit, he lands solidly on the lower ground, and I could *almost* be proud, if it weren't for the question shooting from his lips. "Who's following you?"

I could explain all about Charlotte and Saint-Just abducting me, but we've just reached the part of the cavern where the ceiling drops. The walls squeeze so closely together that we must crawl on our stomachs and elbows like hermit crabs, lanterns clanging against the ground.

I peer over my shoulder, and in the narrow tunnel, I find the bourreau flattening his stomach to the uneven ground as we make progress, inch-by-inch. I imagine he's meeting one of my many cave-spiders—perhaps one's traipsing over his forearm. The little critters have a way of darting up one's sleeve before feasting on the tenderest spot of one's flesh, but they simply need to be coddled, plucked. I shrug off one, *two* skittering across my neck, when a low voice booms from behind us in the cavern.

If that's Marat's voice curling toward us through the cave, it's much lower than expected. He never directly spoke with me, though that's about to change. Today, I'll rearrange his bones.

The boy's hands knock into my wooden shoes, but he cannot see, just like *Maman's eyes when the birds' beaks tore into her pupils, snipping away her eyelashes like caterpillars filling their stomachs.* So—since he cannot see, I'll forgive him. For now.

Oxygen's limited, especially with the two of us sucking up air along with our lanterns. I take slow, steady breaths, inhaling puffs of smoke, walking my elbows forward in time to break through to the next phase of the cavern.

The ceiling sails high above me as I break from the tunnel, my lungs immediately flooding with air. Raising my lantern, I find the low, murky pool of browns, reds, greens— like a hidden, liquid rainbow.

Ripples of water pool in the center, and jagged little rocks cut wild, unnatural angles. At the very back of the room, the cavern's walls slope into this asymmetrical arch-way, and I cannot stop myself from tasting the air of mud, sulfur, and water. "Isn't it wonderful?"

All I see is the crown of the bourreau's brown-haired head as he scrambles out of the tunnel, so I smile a *bonjour!* at the shadows dancing on the walls.

If I had known I'd be in the company of a gentleman, I might have worn more than a shift beneath my filthy robe, but I had been rather busy, what with making the candles and obtaining a better rope.

Maybe it's better for him to see the fierce way my skin stretches over my collar bones. I could remind him of how he never so much as lifted a finger to cover Maman when her dress fell at the gallows; but instead I simply throw off my robe.

His gaze catches on my body like I've been doused in a string of pearls. Like I'm mouthwatering—blueberries and watermelon—for he's looking at me like I'm the most delicious of feasts in all the world.

I growl, because goosebumps are tearing from my skin and I do not wish to be desired by him.

I raise both arms to dive into the murky pool that's but a few paces from my feet just as he breathes, "*Tu es belle.*"

If I were Charlotte, I would blush, or clasp my arms round his neck, but I am *not* Charlotte, so I snarl, "I am *not!*" I raise both arms again, axe in-hand, and dive into my secret temple.

It's cold—much colder than I thought. The iciness washes over my shoulders, trickling all the way to my toes, and I have to kick hard to move forward as the axe is as heavy as a millstone. Move away from the monster trapped in my mind—the man with the sack over his head.

I try to peek through the water, but the murkiness tells me to let my eyes lay closed. My one free hand hits something hard, but it's not dense enough to be a rock. It's a bone probably, so I shove the object away with the axe, smiling a little, as even under water, the weapon and I are one.

It isn't until I'm far out in the middle that I break the surface again, the coolness of the cave stinging my eyes and forehead.

Blinking away the pool water, I find the bourreau peering down on me like an overgrown toy soldier. He flexes his jaw, and it makes me feel powerful to see him so nervous.

"I-I'm not going in there."

The weight of the axe threatens to pull me down, so I *kick, kick,* to remain above water. I take in his dark, hooded eyes, his slightly larger lower lip. From this angle, any other girl might find him attractive, but to me, he's nothing but a sad, skinny ogre. With a nice bit of facial hair, I suppose. So I splash him with the water, not wanting him to get any ideas that I desire him. Marat shall arrive any second, so I beckon him toward the dry passage on the other side of the lake. "Jump in!"

He backs away, his boots connecting with another protrusion, and he stumbles backward.

I have to fight the urge to roll my eyes, which is just enough distraction to make me dip down into the water. I'll swim the rest of the way. Soon he'll be joining me on my candlelit path on the farther side. He need only drop that wide great-coat of his, and he'll be ready to join the dark waters of freedom.

As my fingers brush against the brittle, rocky exit, I grab hold of a skinny rock and spring out of the water, feeling his curious eyes surveying me again. I'd bludgeon him in the throat for continuing to stare at me in such a fashion, but I'm not exactly near him, so I settle with folding my arms over my blossoming bosoms.

Shivering, I run my fingers over the pinprick of goose-bumps, his eyes invariably trapped on mine, which makes the cave spin. I'm about to say something foul, something about where he can put those greedy eyes of his, when a yellow light bursts from the low-ceilinged tunnel. Marat. Has to be. I know it's him. The bourreau need's to hurry if he wants me to lollygag.

A giant of a man in a gray-brown jacket and red collar lumbers out of the same tunnel we just crawled through. His woolen trousers button up the side, and disheveled locks fall over his shoulders—not to mention the mouthwatering wooden club he's holding. No, not *not* Marat.

A beastly woman in a linen cap squirms out behind him, harboring a sword so long, I cannot help wondering if it's longer than my axe. The woman's striped woolen skirt, tight-fitting jacket, and apron mark her as one of the *sans-culottes*, and automatically my stomach churns. Why are they here, and where is Marat?

A third man shimmies out, haggard, this one, with a severely pock-marked face, like the unfortunate complexion of so many. They—we!—cannot afford the creams and salves of the rich. We cannot afford soap, much less. Low voices echo behind him in the tunnel, like the skeletons are waking now. But that cannot be them *cannot be them*, so why are the *sans-culottes* following us?

Never would I admit this, especially to the bourreau, but the *sans-culottes* are like dangerous amphibians. I grew up visiting Maman, tiptoeing past their long fingernails and blackened teeth, shuddering at their foul, salty scent. When Maman told me stories about the injustices of the nobility, I'd determined to see past the soot and tar from the city smokestacks that coated their fingernails and cheeks. I wanted to know what they know, to struggle with their struggles, for Maman showed me how silly the rich could be, worrying about the height of their hats. How much powder to put on their hair.

For four long years, I have suffered hunger, pain, and fatigue. I have walked the lonely existence of being spit upon by lords and known what it is to sleep without a blanket on the cobblestones and sticker-filled weeds. I have gotten along with a few *sans-culottes* well enough, but that is in proportion to the thousands who still feel like entities, utterly unknown. Their laughs are loud, open shrieks, like crows spraying the ground. I've bitten down on my fair share of fingers and I can tell you the taste—of vinegar and salt, like laying my tongue on a disease.

I know it's petty, but I often hear this tiny voice saying, *they know nothing of refinement, of decency*, which only makes me hate myself for so thinking.

And, like a fool, I fear what they can do to me, for they are the ones who killed the deserter when he refused to take part in a skirmish over food. They got him six months later —when he was teaching me to fish with my bare hands.

I hate that I hadn't seen the *sans-culottes* coming, but there were so many of them. They were unpredictable. Surprisingly cunning. Which is why I never know whether to turn tail and run or try to talk—though I am about as diplomatic as a Spanish Conquistador.

I had forgotten that Marat, at his beck and call, has the *sans-culottes* army.

The bourreau glances at the group, his hooded eyes stretched wide like a scared porcupine, and he lumbers toward my liquid temple.

In this low, guttural voice, the man with the pock-marked face settles two hungry eyes across the water on me. "Looks like we found her."

The woman with the sword spreads her lips into a curl, and my stomach tightens. My palms ring with heat. Marat has sent them, I suppose.

I take in the man with the red collar, twisting the club in his hand, and the woman stooping down to pluck up a boulder. All I can think about is the way the deserter fell like a rock straight to the bottom of that lake when the *sans-culottes* speared him. I pulled him up easily enough, but the spear had gone straight through his stomach. He was a bleeding tributary, red. Eyes vacant.

I buried him. Decorated his grave with the smoothest of stones, yellowest of dandelions. Sang a song Maman taught.

If I were the heroic type, I might urge the bourreau to scramble faster, but the boy hasn't exactly earned my coddle —with his hungry eyes, he wanted to devour me, and he executed Maman—so I avoid his gaze, pretending not to see his eyes shining out like a fawn's.

I owe him nothing.

I shall wait out the army. Wait for Marat in my favorite waiting place.

I seize the lantern I planted on this side precisely for this moment, which hisses from the water dripping from my shift. It's freezing.

And I turn and trot away, leaving him my candlelit path. He can trail me like one of my pet cave spiders.

SHE JUST LEFT ME THERE. Left me at the mercy of Madam Monster and Monsieur Morning Breath. I would say her wild eyes were stretched wide with panic, but the girl was probably only envisioning what she had hoped would happen all along—for those souls to skewer me alive. An ending that wouldn't be all that wrong.

I take one more look at the man with the club twice the width of my leg and throw myself into the water—the same water where I nearly died when I was a boy—like it's made of nothing but rainbows and licorice. I will not think about the way my head smacked against the ceiling, taking away the sureness of my vision. I will not think about the cholera epidemic, no doubt infecting the water. I will not even think about the bones snatching at my nether-regions. *Non*, no. Instead, I focus on moving my arms and legs, moving in the murky liquid, thinking only on the girl I'm swimming toward. I cannot help it. She is more radiant than I had dared to hope. Her too-small shift revealed several scars. She's practically a warrior for surviving at all. A cut on her neck, another just above the dip of her neck-line. Three slashes on her legs, and those are just the ones I could see with one look.

I once saw a nasturtium in the southeast corner of town. It was a brilliant orange amidst a sea of mud. The thing about nasturtiums is the petals are odd in number, asymmetrical, and easily frayed. They're light, silky, but above all, they're edible. And I'm a bit monstrous for thinking on her like this, but I could bury my face in those too-prickly leaves of hers.

It doesn't take long for me to cross the pool. A handful of the *sans-culottes* are flopping in, too, like sharks eager for a second lunch. The fact that I'm not carrying a weapon means I'm able to beat them by a full ten or twelve seconds.

I lurch out of the water, boots sloshing as I scamper on in the direction Tempeste ran, positive I've terrified her by my enhungered look. But isn't that more of a compliment? To be adored by a worshipful man?

I am lucky, for the ceiling's just high enough that I do not have to stoop, and the walls are wide enough that I don't find myself knocking into them. Plus, she's left me a candle-lit path of burning fats. An enigma, she is. I stumble on an outcropping of rocks, but that's nothing when one considers the fact that, for the first time, Tempeste and I share the same goal—of outrunning the *sans-culottes*.

The tunnel's just opening up to a larger candle-filled pit when my forehead slams into a protruding rock. My temple shrieks in pain, but somehow I manage to remain quiet.

"Are you all right?" Tempeste's willowy figure jumps out.

I yell, so unprepared I was for her apparition.

This wide look of fear splits open her eyes as she steps around me to peer through the darkness. Her sorrowful gaze trips into my vision. She flinches like I've backhanded her, and I shouldn't look at her, practically nude in that shift.

I look down at my water-logged boots, unable to un-see the way her wet shift clings to her slight breasts. "Wh-what do they want?"

Tempeste swiftly turns away, the shift hugging the slight curves of her waist and back. I could swear on the graves of half of my Patients that her skin's prickling just to be under my vision. But my gaze is fastening to her hips as she walks, and my mouth's gone dryer than newly spun cotton.

I force myself to look away. I had better focus, else we'll be overcome by the *sans-culottes*.

"Follow me." Tempeste waves me past a tall mound of bones to a shorter side of the room. It's smaller than the one we were in earlier, but still large enough for the gravediggers to dump their bones. Every wall is piled high with scroll-like femurs and skulls sunken in like a patch of rotten pumpkins.

The *sans-culottes* will be on us at any moment, though, so I trample past the skeletons. I pretend not to notice one of the heads with a patch of graying flesh just awaiting a hungry rodent.

Shoving aside a mound of larger bones, Tempeste, shift still barely eclipsing her like a too-thin bed-sheet, dives into this tiny hole so small that one would need a monocle to notice it.

"Come," she breathes. Wait. She expects me to fit in that?

Rapid footsteps echo into the gallery, and the last thing I want is for them to find me all alone. So I dive in, slamming the crown of my head on the roof of the tunnel. Dark and dampness encase me in a cyclone.

A man and woman are talking, but the blood spinning in my ears from the blow makes it hard to make out what the old *sans-culottes* are saying. Tempeste plants her rather skeletal posterior right in front of me, and I'm not complaining. My view doesn't last long, though, for all too soon she's scuttling, like a spider, back.

Wait—we won't be crawling backward, but up. Fumbling in the darkness and using the light from Tempeste's lantern, I find a narrow hand and foot-hold. Hoisting my body up, I discover that I can hold on with better ease than one might expect. Heaving corpses has a way of strengthening one's muscles, I often forget.

Again, though, just like the other narrow tunnel earlier, I'm finding it hard to breathe and I can't get Tempeste's tantalizing body out of my head. I cough as dust clusters inside my lungs. What I would give to shoot out of these tunnels and breathe in the fresh air of the meadow of that nasturtium.

Holding my breath against a second cough, I twitch, nervous. To be quiet, I need one hand to cover my mouth, and one hand's already holding a rock-outcropping. The other smacks hard into Tempeste's wooden shoe, and above me, she waffles like a pendulum.

I half expect her to snarl something back. I think I might hear a voice coming from the other side, but my throat feels like it's a home for coals, and every inch of my body beads with the hot dew of sweat.

She scrambles backward, one shoe clogging me in the eye. I'm seeing stars again when, in a voice laced with panic, she's crying, "Go back go back go back go back!"

But I've already climbed relatively far, and she's crawling over the top of me, one foot on my shoulder, a knee digging into my back. I fumble for a foothold below, but all I come up with is air. *Sacrebleu!* I sway midair, and the two of us are precariously out of balance. We're at risk for tumbling the entire way down. I dig my fingers into the handholds.

Like a centipede, she crawls directly over me—a foot on my hip, a hand pawing my back—and I don't know whether to grab her and kiss her tiny body or shove her off.

The last thing she grasps is my ankle, which will make me fall at any second. My fingertips are slipping, and I absolutely must place my foot somewhere soon.

At long last, she releases my foot, and just as I'm about to tumble downward, the toe of my boot connects with a ledge. I breathe in a sigh of relief—*bon sang!*—and hate myself for already missing her closeness.

With a scrape to the elbow, I find a second foothold and resume climbing downward. Abruptly, the little outcropping I've just placed the brunt of my weight on crumbles. I whip my arms madly in the air, landing flat on my buttocks.

I could complain that my bum's just been pierced by her sharp metal lantern. Or that my shin's screaming from the lantern's burn, but now Tempeste's crouching next to me, her breath coming out in short gasps. She slaps her skinny, freezing fingers over my mouth.

"Did you see her?" an old woman's voice croaks from the other side of the wall.

"The whore's daughter?" another woman says; younger this one, with a smoother voice.

"Oh, yes." She trudges past the hole in which we're hiding and pauses. Tempeste frantically blows out the fire of the lantern. The old woman hovers like she knows we're here. I try backing away in case she looks in, but Tempeste wraps an iron-clad grip around my arm, then releases like I've scalded her.

I'm as still as a top hat.

Slow, purposeful footsteps echo throughout the gallery. I wish I could decipher precisely what the women are talking about when the old woman croaks, "If only she knew."

"That her mother's responsible for killing so many of our kin?"

The old woman grunts—a sound of affirmation.

The younger woman giggles, which actually comes out so sharp that the hairs on my arm stand on-end. "Pretending she was a prostitute when she was really a noble, no less!"

Tempeste stiffens. So do I. She's grown so still, I cannot help but think that she might be catatonic. Or maybe she's about to hoist the blade, exacting vengeance on all of us. With Tempeste's hot breath warming my cheek, I put together what the ladies just said. They called her maman a noble. I executed the woman as a commoner, a woman of the pre-revolution. A woman who did not have rights.

The ladies shuffle out, so the tunnel must carry on. With any luck, they'll get lost somewhere in the labyrinth. I'm about to ask Tempeste if she knows the route when she shoves me into the cold, hard wall and leaps across the room so fast that I almost miss the gunfire skittering across her eyes.

There's an alcove on the far side of the room, opposite the hole from which she's now scrambling, and Tempeste's leaping into the narrow inlet and disappearing on the other side.

Tentatively, I follow, careful not to kick a rock or trip for fear of causing the old cronies to hear and return. Who knows if there are others about to march past.

After the nook, another angular tunnel twists this way and that, but tall enough that instead of hunching over like a troll, I may fully stand. I dart to the left, then right, following Tempeste's translucent shift and dark hair whipping in tendrils behind her. Part of me follows just to see her better, the slight dip of her waist. Her arms that need to be steadied, perhaps in prayer like La Magdalena.

Another assortment of jig-jags flounder on, until all at once, the room dead ends. I'm ready to fasten my eyes on Tempeste when, to my right, a cluster of ropes hanging from rocks like a human-sized basket snags my attention. I take a step backward in surprise. Of all things, it's a hammock. I'm just about to comment on the brilliance of the contraption in a place where no one could ever feasibly want to lie on the ground when Tempeste heaves herself onto the net, gasping.

But she's not just out of breath.

Perhaps she's hurt; I might have accidentally scraped or scratched her when she scrambled past. As I watch, the black-haired girl I've come to know as invincible knots up two tiny shoulders.

And sobs.

15

TEMPESTE

WHEN MAMAN DIED, I fashioned a song to hold me in its clutches when the wind's fingers reached into my dreams, or in the morning when I sifted through the rubbish in the street. Mostly, though, I would hum the music when I knew Maman's alto would never again meet my own.

How pathetic I was, singing and weeping, like yet another one of Rousseau's melodramatic fools.

Now, the song is a wind-up toy, whirling round and round, and there's no stopping it. No stomping it out. No matter how many times I try to dash it to pieces, drown it in the Seine. Run it over with a wagon's wheels—not just any wheels, but massive ones! with spikes!—my ripshite of a song continues reeling like it's been waiting to mock me all along.

> *the devil's hammers tap the gallows*
> *where Maman will hang tonight*
> *eyes burn*
> *lips chap*
> *throat dry*

perfume clings like a lover to Maman's gown
she tells me not to fight
but she is the teacup
she is the teacup
i will drink from the rest of my life

noose tightens
ground falls
ropes—
—stretch!

the devil's eyes are broken
the devil's eyes are broken
for he fails to break her spine

I'm strapped to that wagon's wheel, and we're rolling; rolling fast. And we're made of steel and diamonds and there's no pulverizing us.

I have learned the truth.

She was no peasant, but a noblewoman.

Her majesty. I spit upon her riches and party gowns. Servants, jewels, courses of food. Hair powdered as high as towers. Gardens, lush. Carriages worth an entire district of homes.

I'm a fallen leaf—a snowflake, already gone. I would say she forged a nest of lies or betrayal or hate, but her arms are only branches gone brittle, snapping at my touch.

All that lingers is my song and it's blurring, changing in a room I share when all I really want is to be alone.

he hovers over me, the devil

with the broken eyes
hot breath
bones trip
candlelight

i drank from the teacup it wasn't a teacup
but a goblet so fine
his fingers wipe the tears
fingers wipe the tears
of shame from my eyes

knees touch
heart trips
ropes—
—stretch!

my sleeping axe wakens
sleeping axe wakens
comes alive

16

GABRIEL

"SHITE!" Burs fill my throat. "Shite shite shite!" *Mon père*'s axe is wedged between my shin and knee and I'm seeing an explosion of blues and greens.

Tempeste paws my shin, my ankle, my thigh. It is nice to have her touching me, truth be told, but the pain is an arsenal of swords. She knows she made a mistake, though, for she's as white as a bed sheet.

"What have I done?" she shrieks, and I was ready for her touches, *mon Dieu,* I was ready for her touches but not these. It's like a barracuda's smooching me.

I had scooted a little closer to allow the girl to rest her head on my shoulder, to hold her close. The ropes of the hammock had groaned, and it was like a canon went off inside her, for that's when she grabbed the axe and swung like I was a soldier groping her in the woods.

Still, the pain's exactly like when I accidentally severed my own pinky when I was sharpening another of Père's blades, and it could be worse. I'm sure, with the proper medical attention, I'll turn out all right.

Tempeste balls up her skirt and presses it into my

wound. I'm whimpering like a puppy, but she's only trying to help, so I nod toward the axe like she didn't nearly sever my leg in half.

"I knew you'd give it back."

Ripping off a piece of her skirt, she shoves the fabric into my leg, setting a cherry-bomb inside my flesh. "Quiet yourself."

True, the *sans-culottes* could hear and find us at any moment, so with a bit of effort, I shut my trap. Besides, there's a pool of blood like warm bath water washing down my leg. It's a little unsettling how trivial I find this detail.

Her touches are like the sprinkle of cinnamon. While she's not exactly delicate, she does have a softness. A touch like Henri's. He once administered one of his own potions he'd concocted from dead men's organs—a longstanding, macabre tradition in the Sanson family—when I accidentally bashed my head on the gallows and ripped open the side of my face. The remedy was this blackish goop, like tar—there's no telling what he put in it. But it helped, which only encouraged him to dabble more in his macabre scientific remedies.

Now, though, I'm sucking in my breath, trying to memorize the swift way Tempeste's dabbing my blood like she cares how I'm feeling.

Tying the makeshift bandage around my knee, she rises from the hammock, her neckline plunging low enough that I may pass out.

"I'll sit over there." She crouches like she's going to sit on the opposite side of the cavern, but I won't have any of that, so I rush to my feet.

"Absolutely not." The stalactites swoop about my head, making me all but collapse.

She wraps her arms around me to keep me upright, and

her embrace is like I'm being housed in an evergreen's branches. I lean in to feel close, but her arm's so skinny, so brittle. Quickly, she releases, so I gruffly wave her back. "*Non.*"

Like a cautious deer, she backs away. I feel her eyes watching me as I find my way to the wall a few paces off. Not unlike my *grandmère* hobbling from the parlor to the dining hall, I lower myself to the rocky ground, wishing that I were staying beside her all the while.

Moisture drips from the ceiling. I'm replaying her rather humane impulse to support me when I nearly collapsed. If only I'd known how to comfort her. Convince her that touching me was good, but instead she's murmuring, "Don't go thinking I care about you, bourreau."

A smile twitches apart my lips. "I would never dream of it."

My leg screams, and her lantern's handle is squeaking. She must be fidgeting with the knob. "I care for someone," she says.

This numskull part of me tenses, like she's going to tell me about a secret beau she has, when she adds, "Have you ever seen a gargoyle and thought, 'why, that's the most distorted creature I've ever seen my entire life,' while at the same time seeing how beautiful it is?"

I scratch my temple, leg a-throb.

"There's an old woman I know—a nun from one of the convents where I used to live. If she and I were stranded on a desert island and there was only one fish to eat, she'd refuse to eat her half while insisting that I eat the whole thing myself!"

If Tempeste's calling the old woman a gargoyle, just how special could this woman truly feel? And yet, Tempeste's actually confiding in me, so I tread lightly. "Have you told her? What she means to you?"

The hammock swings back and forth. "She knows."

I imagine Tempeste's idea of informing her friend. *Nun-gargoyle-woman whom I can barely look in the eye, I swear to never ever take my axe upon you; not on the scalp, not in the throat, not in the stomach. That's how much I love and adore you!*

I envision, too, Tempeste kneeling in the center of a convent, like La Magdalena, surrounded by lit candles. "Sounds promising." I recall the woven blanket wrapped around her, not entirely doing its job.

"She knows I care," Tempeste says, completely unaware of my treacherous thoughts, whilst twisting the lantern's handle. The metal creaks and groans. Her voice goes so low it's nearly soft. "What do you make of what the *sans-culottes* said back there?"

My mind drifts back to the week after I executed the lady-Patient, her *maman*. She wouldn't stop swinging from the rope, and though I hit her again and again to snap her neck, I couldn't make it happen, because a shaman had put a curse on me for daring to execute her in the first place.

Shifting my wounded leg uncomfortably against an outcropping of rock, I offer a falsehood because I do not know what else to say to her now. "Maybe they weren't talking about your maman."

"I have nothing to remember her by," she murmurs, which twists knots in my stomach. She locks her stormy eyes on mine. "You didn't see him."

I'm about to ask who she means, when she kicks the hammock, causing it to swing from side-to-side.

"Marat. He's down here."

I glance at the narrow tunnel leading back to the rest of

the cavern, remembering the surreal sensation of her wooden shoes clubbing my shoulders. How I would sacrifice for her to do that to me again. "That's why you shot back down the wall we were climbing before?"

Condensation drips from the ceiling as she hesitates. "*Oui.*"

The hammock slows, and my stomach settles. If I'd been more watchful, I might have seen Marat or the others tracking Tempeste before I'd moseyed on down here in the first place. I might have demanded an answer of why he feels he must terrify her with these *sans-culottes*. Still, I need to know what she knows. "What did he say?"

Tempeste rolls to her back as a puff of air rises from her lips. "He said nothing."

I puff my own cloud of air on my now-freezing hands, seeing she's obviously offering a falsehood. Marat told her something, but the only way I'll convince her to tell me is to show her I care.

I glance about, my eyes traipsing up the ceiling to a patch of angry strokes of reds and browns—paintings of skeletons, I think. She's painted another rendition of the Dans Macabre, the dance of death. And it makes sense for a girl so bent on pushing away the comforts of home to paint it. A pile of bones looks the same whether you're a lowly merchant or a person of means.

"*C'est bien.*" It's nice.

"Nice" isn't exactly the most fitting word, but the bold smattering of colors proves she has talent. Still, Tempeste says nothing, so I babble onward. "You and your *maman* were close?"

Tempeste cuts me a glare that could slice apart the limestone. "I'm not talking about her with you, bourreau."

"Just so you know, I've wiped the floor with people who have called me that name."

"Go for it, then." Tempeste stares blankly at the ceiling.

I press my parched lips together, for what am I supposed to say now? *Sorry that I killed your* maman? *Sorry my family, out of every bloody family in the entire country, was chosen for killing? Sorry I'm not more like Henri, who always knows how to crack jokes?* She already knows the gist of this, so I stare up at the painting again, taking in the outline of the smallest skeleton clutching something sharp like a weapon. She's smiling at a taller skeleton, both holding hands, and I know I have to be looking at Tempeste and her *maman*.

"When I painted it," Tempeste says, "I always felt like I should have drawn her in something grander."

My heart hiccups as my smile falters. "You believe what those old cronies said?"

"You didn't hear Marat on the other side of the tunnel." She hugs the lantern tighter. "He said, 'Eighty-nine ghosts to haunt you, *cochonette*.'"

He called her a *little pig*? The unholy bastard. But I must convince her that this bit about eighty-nine ghosts cannot be right. The cold and darkness of the tunnels are getting to her. Ghosts never will be real. She needs air, to walk around. So in an attempt to have her follow me, I rise to my feet.

From the pain, I nearly collapse to the ground.

The mural spins above me like a chandelier all lit up, and for the briefest of moments, she watches me instead of the mural. Her knuckles, so taut around *mon père*'s axe, seem to tremble as I secure her in my vision. Her chest heaves like she, too, is feeling the impossible heat of the moment. But instead of accepting or broaching the topic, she looks away, voice streaming out in a rush.

"She used to say that number. When she was asleep."

My lack of air tells me I need to take a breath. Maman. Her *maman*. She doesn't need heated looks, but comfort.

She lost her *mère* when she was so young, which explains why she uses the child's name for her. In some ways, she is so young.

If I could but figure out what to do. Secure for her a doctor that can help her resort the troubles of her past? Her *père* is a doctor, though, so she already has one. Henri would know what to do—how to cheer her from this revenge ailment—but Henri is so far away, and all I have is myself.

"She would never explain." She avoids eye contact.

I stare at the puff of air floating away from her breath, not entirely sure how to offer comfort. I'd amble closer. Hold her in my arms in that hammock. But her aversion to touch is very clear, and her obsession with revenge is worse than I thought.

"We walked past Les Innocents once, when I was a little girl, and when we saw a throng of bodies piled so high that they were spilling out of the gate, Maman started muttering that number over and over before running away so fast that she forgot to take me with her."

A pit rises in my stomach, for I know the cemetery, Les Innocents, well. It's not the sort of place one would want to stroll through on Sunday evenings. It's where Death opens his shutters to dump out his realm's chamber pots. The smell is worse than spoiled eggs and milk and boiled cabbage. It's worse than corpses, sitting out in the sun all day, because the graves are already full.

"Why do you kill people?"

My eyes snap across the stone wall to meet hers. She's rolled to her side to face me now, and I cannot help traipsing my gaze over the near-translucence of her wet shift. Her curves, slight, but still there. Her shoulders and bosoms rising and falling with every breath. Her legs shining with a radiance I'd give anything to touch.

I gulp for air, only to choke on dust. "The Assembly kills people. I simply do as they order, as a servant to the crown, or now, as a servant to the people."

"The revolution doesn't mean much to you."

I run my hand over the moist wall of the cavern, seeing the bare skin of her legs from the corner of my eye. I listen to the low, far away footsteps echoing through the catacombs, sure they're not drawing near. "I like the idea of people gaining more freedoms from what they've had."

"But if you had your choice, you'd go back to the way things were with the monarchy."

I flush worse than before. She understands that my family did, in fact, better thrive with our larger earnings from the monarchy. But there's more—the revulsion that shined in her eyes when I lifted heads high into the sky. The romp and celebration of the people bothered her. But it's like she doesn't know this type of celebration should be had for no Patients. If she likes the revolution, then that means she likes the idea of murdering the king, and I would never have that.

"The truth is," I say, wishing we could, I don't know, for every execution, have a brief moment of silence. "I am scared for our country."

She curls her lips, which are blood-red. "Scared for yourself, you mean."

If she only knew the truth of what she's saying—when one goes too far to defend something. How *mon père* holds our family's future in his grasp by a string, so I tell her what I now know, throat chalky. "We know no boundaries."

She raises an expressive eyebrow.

"We do not look to the Lord for answers regarding our country."

She scoffs. "You think the *Lord* cares about what happens to the likes of you and me?"

I think how, in the Place du Carrousel, Père was nearly crushed to death because of the hatred of that man. But the Lord helped me lift the tumbrel when I was too weak. I did not drown in the catacombs that day, either, but a skeleton propped my head above the water until, hours later, Henri found me. That skeleton should have sunk to the bottom the minute it started holding my body, but it didn't. It saved me. The Lord answers our prayers. He cares about us. "*Oui.*"

Her gaze burns holes into me again, and for the first time, I cannot hold her eye contact. It's like she's seeing my inner soul, my worst, dark secrets, and I clutch my leg. I do not even know if I hold her interest.

"Why do you stay—in your vocation, I mean?"

Her question catches me off-guard. Has she seen me chatting with Carvell? Perhaps she can see that I truly despise our living. "*Mon père* requires my aid. As his youngest, I'm essentially all he has." I do not bring up my dead older brother. "With Henri gone."

"Who's Henri?"

My voice falls to the pockmarked walls. How to describe a brother who's given my family so much happiness? A boy who probably has his unit up in stitches? "He is the brightest star of the Sanson family. He is the reason why I know we are still good." I do not tell her of the laughs and jokes. How Henri has the type of spirit that can lift even the soberest of days. How once, when I complained of digging holes for our Patients all day, he stole my shovel after tickling me so long, tears came.

Père is alone, and he needs me. I may well and good

have dreams, but how can I be so selfish that I ruin the very livelihood of our extended family? I do not much see my uncles or cousins, but they rely on our reputation. If I abandon post, I sacrifice the very Sanson name. Not to mention Mère and Grandmère, whom I rarely see. But they rely on me, nonetheless.

"She had a past, you know," Tempeste says, and I scramble to redirect my thoughts to what she means. "I would ask her about her life, but she would never tell me about it."

I could point out that my past is riddled with an assortment of unsavory memories—about the sheep and corpses we had to decapitate to ensure the success of the Machine. How, when the original curved blade did not properly sever head from spine, the king, of all people, suggested we use an oblique blade. But I doubt she would care, so I add, "They have records at the Palais de Justice. Maybe you could find records of your *maman*'s birth there."

Her eyes snap to mine. It's the look I'd like to see in one of my Patient's eyes before setting him or her free. *The Assembly has pardoned all your wrongdoings.* Or, *bringing you here was a mistake.* There's gratitude there. Appreciation. And a smile's tugging on her lips when, all at once, she sours her expression with a foul smile.

"What?"

Her eyes are full of fireworks. "I have no use for young men who wish to be with me."

I've never believed that words could bludgeon. But here, now, they are a studded club to my chest. I detest that, with her raven looks and siren-like touches, she has power such as this. One would think with what I've done in the past that my care and conscience would be snuffed out. But she can never know what it's like to be me, all that I've done, so I scoff. "You think—I want—don't be silly—" It's well past time for me to return to *mon père* and forget this dalliance anyway.

I could tell her of my plans. Of my utmost fancy. *I'd like to move to a grassy knoll, raise goats, and make my own milk and cheese.* Of the stretch of land, probably already sold by now, that Carvell offered.

She would call me a goon, which isn't much of a stretch, because I do not have the money.

Even so, I find myself squaring my shoulders, praying that she will see in me even a sliver of promise. "I am a little different from what you might think."

To which Tempeste leaps from the hammock, and I can't decide whether she might give me a chance or if she's going to take out my other leg now, when she nods toward the entrance. "The old cronies should have passed."

I kick at a pebble because there's nothing else to say. "And the other eighty of them?" I miss the pebble.

"Do *you* hear anyone?"

I shrug, wondering if she might like another tactic. Is she the type of girl who would be wooed by love poems? Or flowers?

Tempeste lifts her lantern so as to see farther in the tunnel, and the action unwittingly steals my breath. I must get out.

"I'll only be a moment." Her thumb runs down the wooden handle of the blade, and she's petting the damn thing like it's her pretty beau from another township.

I shall pace—I'll stymie my feelings—but there's my stupid leg, and besides, her wiry frame bounces back like a fevered toddler in all of three heartbeats.

"There are still some of them coming through," she says, tone sour, but even still, she looks and smells like cocoa beans. I want to hold them, smell them, work with them to see what they might offer.

Tempeste stalks past me straight for the hammock, and I can nearly make out her spidery ribs beneath her dress. The enticing dip of her belly button, which in no world should be enticing at all.

"We should light some candles before my flame goes out." She cuts a sideways glance at me.

I drop my gaze so she won't catch me staring and turn to see what she means. I end up half scooting, half crawling to the corner next to where I sat before as my leg screams. The corner dips down about half a foot, and already she's reaching and lifting a rock to reveal a handful of tall, skinny candles, a thick, worn book, and some other objects. It is hard to tell.

Curious about which book she would be hiding, I reach in, but she blocks my hand with her wrist's bones.

"I'm relying on you." Her words are a lead-filled crate. Wisps of her hair tickle my neck. She seems to realize our proximity, though, for she sucks in a breath.

"I only have two candles." Her voice is strained, and I have to wonder if she, too, feels the heat. "When it's time, I'll light them both, but since you don't have a weapon, one of the candles will be your weapon." She takes a shaky breath. "The other will be for light, naturally. I'll use my axe, but do not forget for a moment that you are lighting the way for us, Gabriel."

She just called me by my Christian name. A lump forms in my cravat-bound throat.

Her hair brushes the length of my cheek, and the edge of my pinky just may be touching the edge of her pinky. I really don't know, and I do not try to look because I don't want her to move. *Dieu, aide-moi.*

She must feel what I'm feeling. The heat between us is as warm as the suds of a hot spring. Everything is still and radiant and, for once, neither one of us is talking. She's staring at my throat. Maybe it's because she's too shy to look all the way up, but then she's raising her eyes and in the smallest voice, she says, "*Merci*. For helping me."

I'm taken aback. I never believed she would thank me for anything. I want to move closer, take her hand, but I also do not want to move because, for the first time, she's looking at me like she *wants* to see me.

An ocean of longing, of touching, tears through me. What if I were to scoot a mere inch closer to graze her waist? Shift our conversation from survival? To what the future might bring?

And then the shock of all shocks happens.

"How is your leg?" she asks me. She places her fingers on the fringe of my breeches, not an inch from where she set the blade.

I do not know what comes over me, but to be touched even by the threads is more than I had ever hoped, and my hands twitch at the fringe of her thin shift, hungry.

She's so close that I can feel her breath on my neck. Warm perspiration tickles me. I could take her hand, feel the tiny bones of her fingers, but I do not deserve it. I want to deserve it, but if she knew me, *really* knew me, she'd shove my fingers away.

My voice sounds surprisingly normal when I ask, "Do you have any idea what they believe your maman di—?"

"No." Her cheeks darken as her eyes swim over me. She's leaning in and toward me. It's like the fireworks the nobility once used are silently shooting celebratory spurts of gold and green.

"You really are not cruel," she murmurs, squeezing the edge of my knee-breeches.

I want to grab her hand. Cover her lips with my own.

I fall into her eyes, which are two deep endless pools. "I try not to be." I have a clogged throat. But if she really knew me, there's no way she'd have this, so I break her gaze. She raises her hand, absently, to bite the edge of her thumb.

"Do you think Marat would be open to chatting with u —" I begin.

"He wants me dead. Hands down. That's it."

"*Je suis désolé*. I'm sorry," I say. "For your *maman*, I mean." I run my fingers through my unkempt hair, wondering what the devil is the matter with me. I should have grabbed her by the waist. I should have seized the moment. But when she knows what I've done, she'll crucify me. "If it helps, I was going to break both her feet, but I only did one."

As soon as the words are out of my mouth, I realize the gravity of my mistake. Is there a way to make her forget, to take back the words I didn't mean to say in the first place?

Silence wraps around us like an impossibly warm cocoon. I expect her to slap me, kick me in the face. But instead, the ropes of the hammock groan as Tempeste wordlessly crawls atop it. I think maybe she's just stalling before climbing back down to bash my skull in, but instead, delicately, ever so delicately, she settles down her lantern, and in the quietest of voices she says, "I'm going to sleep now."

She was close. As close as my bleeding shin and knee. And instead of grabbing her by the threads of her shift and pulling her closer, I let my damned guilt get in the way.

Now, my only option is to settle lower on the dewy rock and listen to the moisture drip from the ceiling.

And obsess over what Marat might have told Tempeste.

17

TEMPESTE

THE SOUND of a chicken clucking awakens me. At first I think I'm back in the woods training with the deserter, but it isn't until I open my eyes to see the bourreau grasping two lit candles that I remember the *sans-culottes*. We are their chosen prey.

Plus, that's no chicken. That's the signal we used in the convent—that's Charlotte's tepid voice.

She had better not hinder my chances of getting to Marat. I need answers more than I'd like to sink my teeth into a squirrel's tangy meat. So I spring from my hammock —a gift from the deserter upon his death—and storm past the boy just as I'm hit with an armor-splitting reality.

He touched the fringe of my dress.

And I *liked* it.

Coals sparked like lava inside my throat and other places I'd like not to name.

Coals which never ever before were intended for lighting. Coals which always scalded, burning me.

It's like the bourreau of all people saw the warmth I needed; I never would have believed I wanted it.

Was it an anomaly? An aberration? But I did want him to touch me. To see how his hands would feel on my arms, to hold me around my ribs. Is this what love is, then? When a boy's eyes, like the long tongue of moths sucking away nectar, lure you in?

I do not know how to think on it. I'm supposed to hate him. But he is kind, gentler than I ever imagined. When I thought he would grab me on the hammock and pin me down, he simply offered me a shoulder to sob upon.

Too bad I rewarded him with the swing of my axe. I really should have Papa look at the wound when we get return.

Not entirely able to come to terms with these newfound emotions, I simply point to the tunnel with the tip of my blade. I mustn't forget about my goal here. To find Marat.

Thinking on the clucking—Charlotte's clucking—I explain. "That signal is for us." I force aside the invisible magnetic pull I feel toward him and swallow the dank, cool air, allowing my voice to be filled with a murky indifference.

I half expect him to spout off a slew of noxious questions, but he simply plants his clumsy feet like a baby giraffe. I mean to move out immediately, but the river of blood leaking from his tourniquet proves his wound is far worse than I had originally supposed. I could tie another— the deserter taught me well enough—but that would leave me with relatively no clothing for myself.

We haven't time, besides. Like my father's favorite manservant, Charlotte's awaiting us. So I trample over boulders and smash apart finger bones, promising myself that I'll patch him up soon enough.

Behind me, the bourreau lights the spidery ground, but not so bright that our enemy would be alerted to our presence, so I take in a steadying breath, drawing strength from the cool handle of the axe. Just a few more twists of the tunnel, a giant step up to the alcove, and then we shall meet Charlotte. And she can explain why she's following us.

As I peek around a wall covered in fungus, my stomach tightens. A woman, *not* Charlotte, holds a butcher's knife, her broad back to us. Though an apron wraps around her middle section, I pause, for she boasts the beefy arms of a fish-wife.

The fish-wife.

Merde. I had rather preferred to not see her again.

The bourreau's hot breath—no, the candle's hot flames! —singes the back of my dress, and I whip around as he scrambles back.

Guilt flashes in his eyes as the candle drops from his hands. *Plunk!* My blood screams in torment. *You—you distracted me, and look what happens.*

The woman's gaze shoots to me like an arrow finding its target, and in her burly voice, she says, "Thought you could escape as easily as that?"

I think of the starving women's rage in the market— the women who do not have enough money to feed their children. I could sink my blade into her aproned gut easily enough. But as of yet, I have never killed another person, and I would prefer to stay like that. So, like nothing more than a spooked gerbil, I duck, hair flying round me as I roll past. The grainy ground crunches beneath me akin to crunching glass as a handful of *sans-culottes* march toward me like they're taking a chattel from a nobleman. I am *not* the enemy! Shovels, rakes, sickles, scythes—despite only being four in number, they possess every type of farming weapon, and I must admit I quite prefer seeing bayonets.

A new woman with the same dark hair as mine clutches

a sickle twice my height. She might be the twin of the beefy-armed fish-wife.

"You shall pay for what your mother has done!" the woman cries with bloodshot eyes, like she hasn't slept or eaten a proper meal in months. "For my sister, for my nephews." The scythe trembles in her fists as she lifts it to the sky, and I must applaud her sense of vengeance.

But, I am her target, which splits what I mean to do like a gooey cantaloupe in half. I could cut her down, I could do it easily enough, but here is yet another *sans-culotte* testifying that Maman did something unpardonable. How could I hurt her before knowing what happened?

So I duck away and survey a small group hunched at the back. A girl in a red cap and long narrow face winks at me. My heart wrenches, for that's Charlotte. And she's not alone, for next to her slouches Saint-Just, smoking his pipe, donning a crumpled-up hat. Perhaps he shall witness greatness from me yet.

Still, I do not know whether to snarl or bark a laugh, because he and Charlotte took me so many times with the intention of forging me into a weapon. Saint-Just told me to set my sights on a mission—do I forget what they did like toppled refreshments?

Noiselessly, Charlotte stoops down to retrieve a dagger from a boot so worn that her stockings peek through. I expect her to follow my lead—try to talk some sense into the *sans-culottes*—but all at once, she's spinning on this woman little more than a child and clocking her on the head with the butt of her dagger.

So she *is* capable of acting without mulling things over for months.

Two women in white bonnets and smudged faces turn

on my former friend, who merely boosts a slender shoulder. "She wanted to make mutton stew out of my friend."

My stomach twists as Charlotte's gentle eyes lock with mine, and I do not know whether to thank her or shoo her away to a boat on the docks.

The beefy armed fish-wife has found me again. When she raises her knife, her bodice stretches so wide that the front splits. And what's revealed is something I never wanted to see: between her bosoms, a thick wad of black hair.

I suck in a breath. *Merde!* Sometimes, life gives you a raw deal all around. I flip the axe around and smack her on the head. Better for her to drop quickly before she realizes I saw that.

The bourreau swings his candlesticks round and round —like there's actually someone close enough to harm him. He's not unlike a circus performer, juggling torches. A day ago, I might have laughed at him, but now I understand he's doing his best regardless of his weakness. And just as I'm about to tell him to take a step forward to light up the posterior of a woman about to implant Saint-Just's crumpled hat with a scythe, a man with a shovel and a black bicorn hat snickers, "Just look at him!" The scythe carrying woman, just like everyone else, is distracted.

Burning hot tallow drips like melted water onto the bourreau's hands, and the fact that he hasn't yet dropped the candlesticks is a wonder in and of itself. He's scampering toward the man, swiping his candlesticks up and down again, but he's still a good foot away from him and the tallow must be hot, and I hate my instant worry for him. Could I forgive him for executing Maman? Am I capable of that?

At long last, the bourreau's hand flinches, and he drops a candlestick.

Plink! Roll.... Which draws a quiver of laughs. But the bourreau marches toward the man with the other candlestick. The man laughs and points like one of those dumb wind-up monkeys *mon papa* once bought me. And I'm throwing myself into a spin, setting the axe into the stupid man's shoulder, because those monkeys were irksome, and I threw mine out the carriage window first chance I had.

The bourreau's and my eyes lock like a key turning pins in a chest. And my mouth twitches, which proves I'm going soft in the head. I'm nearing the depravity of a love-addled milksop—and I *refuse* to be a love-addled milksop. So I roll my eyes like he's rice pudding, altogether bland.

Charlotte, Saint-Just, the bourreau, and I all fight together against the remaining *sans-culottes*. I would say we're like soldiers in a battalion, but we're more like ninjas on a hidden island—invisible, synchronized, working with finesse. We spin and fight and at one point, Saint-Just's firing a pistol precisely into a particularly fearsome *sans-culotte*'s chest before complimenting the bourreau on a blow he landed, and it's the closest thing to friendship I've ever had.

All at once, much too soon, the cave grows silent. I didn't kill anyone—only wounded, but bodies squirm like heaps of potatoes wrought with maggots. The smashed apart skulls littering the ground twinges a fair amount of guilt in my chest—did Saint-Just need to shoot that *sans-culotte* in the chest like that?—but he, we *all* were defending ourselves. I haven't gained any wounds, and we'll be finding Marat soon, so I swallow the guilt of Saint-Just's murder, and stretch forth a dirty hand. "I don't think I've ever experienced a greater contentment."

The bourreau ducks his mouth into his arm, stifling a

laugh. I catch sight of a new scratch, which runs the length of his cheekbone. He all but collapses into a nearby wall, so I run over to support him.

My pulse slams in my throat, and I hate the worry tearing open my mind, but I murmur, "Don't die."

He cracks open a smile, fingers grazing my hand, my wrist, and a surge of embers are floundering through my skin. I stare up at his dark, pain-wrought eyes as he murmurs, "Sansons aren't so easy to kill off."

I assess the blood spilling from his leg. His face, far too white.

Charlotte shoves a slew of broken bones out of her path. "I cannot believe you're fond of this place, Tempeste."

"Now, now, Charlotte." Saint-Just pulls his pipe from his teeth. "Aren't you glad we found her when we did?"

I smile, because my fellow egalitarian is seeing me in my element. But they needn't have rescued me. The bourreau and I were more than capable of rescuing ourselves.

"Besides." Saint-Just fixes his chilling gaze on Charlotte like he's reproving her. "I believe there is something else you wanted to tell your friend?"

This is it. Where Charlotte apologizes for taking me, and they tell me they were wrong to censure my actions in destroying Marat's printing press. But when I try to read my former friend, deciphering her China-doll face is about as easy as reading an encrypted ledger. Her porcelain eyes are affixed without emotion, and her chin juts out much like—well—much like mine does.

Just when I think the statue will not crumble, her bottom lip quivers.

"I am so, so sorry about everything that's happened. How we took you without asking. For Sister Josephine."

A tremor of emotion rolls through me, which I'm

tempted to squash out. My softness for the bourreau is messing with my head. But if Charlotte were truly sorry, she would know that our fair Sister has not found a remedy for her wounds yet. Sister Josephine hurts *every time* her habit moves, every step she takes around the convent. And Charlotte needn't be so controlling. *Like a caged animal incapable of being trained.* If only Saint-Just could convince her to amend *her* ways. Find balance in her perspective.

I curl my fingers around my weapon, because this is the Tempeste I've always been. "She suffers daily for what you did."

Charlotte, red-capped, dirty-aproned Charlotte, wilts like one of the damned lilies *mon papa* showed me. I was foolish enough to like them. Why has he always felt the need to cheer me up, to protect me? *Why* did he think to place me in a plastic case and feed me half-truths when the truth has always been the *only* way? Did he know how I would fissure once I discovered Maman's noble birth?

He should have been honest.

The bourreau and Charlotte want me to forgive them. And I could be wrong—*I am probably wrong*—but I wonder if maybe I could. Because Marat's the one I'm angriest at, anyway. He's the one who sent Maman to an early grave. These two are helping me. The way Saint-Just is.

Still, there's no way I'll ever join the Girondins, the hypocritical faction that professes to be so morally minded when they condoned repeatedly taking me, paving the way for the man with the sack over his face to defile me before anyone could stop him. They say they meant to "train" me, but isn't that crossing the line—even if Saint-Just understands more of what I am?

The cave's walls moan; it's the sound of thunder, but that's not it. We have conquered a roomful of *sans-culottes*, true, but scores of them could still be anywhere in the cavern. And Marat, like a barnacle on clothing, must be dealt with.

So I point back toward the lake, the one the bourreau behaved as if he was too scared to swim across. We should swim back toward the entrance, find Marat, and force him to explain what Maman did to those *sans-culottes*. And if the bourreau's too weak, I can help him swim.

"I have something for you." Saint-Just digs slender fingers into his trousers' pocket. I think he means me—he *is* trying to recruit me as a Girondin—but instead, he extends a confident hand to Gabriel. The bourreau, that is.

Gabriel stares at the folded paper in the dark, a question mark tearing apart his chiseled forehead. "What is this?" He painfully leans against the cavern wall for support, blinking toward the rumble of the approaching *sans-culottes*, looking as pale as a ghost. I should tell him to hang on, rewrap his tourniquet. But there isn't time.

"Just open it," Saint-Just says as Gabriel tries to retrieve the note, but snatches at the wall before Saint-Just plants it in his palm.

"Indulge me," Saint-Just says with a wry smile, but the torch in Gabriel's hand swirls and spits—it's losing its firelight. Why are they lollygagging like this?

As Saint-Just straightens his torn waist-coat, his silver buttons glinting in the fading torchlight, he winces as if he's endured a wound somewhere—perhaps he got jabbed in the stomach.

"Are you all right?" I'm becoming far too conscientious.

He bats my concern away with his pipe, which I most appreciate. "You are a marvelous fighter, Tempeste."

I'm about to ply him with compliments, because his aim with that pistol, though cold, was particularly grand. But an earsplitting shriek soars across the cave—like cats screeching as hawks pick apart their bodies—and I'm covering my ears. So is everyone else. Saint-Just's taken Charlotte in the crook of his arm, and the bourreau hunches like he doesn't know if he has the power to read this note Saint-Just gave him. Except those aren't cats but *bats*, waking. I would know, for I once naively woke some whilst trying out a six-barreled musket. Lovely gem.

Now the black winged creatures are flying toward us— miniature vampyres, *flapping! hungry!*—and I know what the frightened creatures mean to say:

Marat's army? They coming. They feast on us.

18

GABRIEL

MY ARMS and leg sting in pain as I hunch in a hidden corner with the others, hoping the *sans-culottes* will run past us. I mean to read the note Saint-Just gave me, but why did Père send this along with him? How did he know that Saint-Just knows me or would see me at all?

I am a fool for stealing the time to look at it, but I can decipher the words from the torches of the *sans-culottes* barreling past. And I must know if Père is well. Has Henri been injured? Why has he written?

So I hover round the corner from where marches a trail of *sans-culottes*, Tempeste but a foot away, showing me her back. And I linger, always linger at the slight lines of her frame before crackling open the paper. My fingers shake from nerves and blood loss.

My dearest son,

I have spoken with Carvell. He has divulged unto me your desire to leave our vocation and purchase his land to farm.

You have broken my heart. I had thought I could rely on you the way I could Henri, but I suppose I was wrong. If I had known you were set on leaving so quickly, I could have made necessary precautions, but now you have left without a word. I can only suppose you've been planning this all along.

Your decision has put our family in untold jeopardy. The inspector says the Assembly is deciding whether or not they'll send us to the Conciergerie for you abandoning your post. Is this what you wanted, son? For us all to be locked up? Return home, son. I implore you—

A barefaced *sans-culotte* prowls into our nook. I had hoped we were sufficiently cloaked, but he's as real and bald as a baby's buttocks. When he flashes his gold teeth, my mind is still reeling. Father knows. We're to be locked up in the Conciergerie, but I haven't even actually left. Not yet.

More men doting black wigs, swords, and pikes snarl, prowling into the nape of our enclosure, like wolves closing in on supper. Tempeste may be throwing herself between me and them, but she cannot withstand thirty or forty, which may be the approximate number trickling in.

When the slaps of wooden shoes echo throughout the cavern like applause before a beheading, I know we're surrounded. Red embers fly from torches, the foul smell of body odor wafts off the bald *sans-cullote*. I'll never have the chance to see *mon père* again.

A girl as slight as a rail jabs her spear at Tempeste. But it's not an ordinary spear—it's topped with a half-decomposed skull, writhing with larvae. Just one more reason why the catacombs is my favorite place in the world.

Tempeste nods at the half-decomposed skull. "He looks a little like you, pigeon."

The girl glowers, accentuating the multiple cuts and scars covering her face. Tempeste's response wasn't exactly the best way to pad the girl's violence, but I offer Tempeste a faint smile of encouragement.

Tempeste blushes like she doesn't know what to with that, and the starving girl's curling back her lips. She reveals blackened gums just as two old biddies hobble through the arched entry. When every head turns to face the women in quiet, in reverence, I know they are the leaders of this little band.

The oldest of the pair stretches out an aged, gnarled hand toward Tempeste. Her hair, as white as snow before a killing, reminds me of our country's obsession with spilling blood. "Time to answer for your mother's sins, *infante*."

Charlotte pulls a dart and miniature bow from her boot, but I doubt even this secret weapon will convince the *sans-culottes* to stop killing. Saint-Just checks his pistol's chamber, but he'll run out of ammunition quickly enough.

A man in a blouse so low that I can see the lint in his naval shimmies past a pile of arm bones. Tempeste raises her mouth to the dew-covered ceiling, gesticulating toward her own navel.

"What has *happened* to Parisian fashion?"

With thirty or so *sans-culottes*, we are surrounded, so it's time for me to speak. Save us all, if I can. I'll speak for *mon père*, for the fact that he believes I've deserted my family. Speak for Henri before he's dishonorably discharged from the army. I'll remind the *sans-culottes* how true republics do not murder suspects on sight, but bring them before a tribunal. I'll promise them the coveted front row seats in the

Place du Carrousel, at the grand head of the Tuileries. Anything to protect Tempeste from this horrible band.

But one old man's already swiping at Tempeste's wooden shoes, and she kicks him while he yelps like a spaniel. A man's turning an obviously stolen gold-plated pistol in so many hazardous directions, he might shoot Tempeste.

Non. The only way to stymie this group's fever for blood-lust is by reminding them of something else they love. The thing that saved my family once.

They do not know that they love it. Most don't, to tell the truth. I didn't learn it until I'd been playing those duets with Henri and Père for years. It's something Tempeste could benefit from.

Listening to the hum of our violins, we wordlessly mourned the loss of our brother. Henri, never a natural, would hum along, too, and Père would jab him with the bow, only to make Henri giggle. Henri wished to improve his skill with the gun—he was never as good of a shot as the men in our family—so Père let him enlist. "This is why I have two sons," Father said, unable to speak of Charles. "Gabriel will help me at home."

And I was only happy to do so. Was desperate to make up for my eye-related deficiencies. And then, when the Assembly began breathing down our necks and Père asked me to learn to empathize with the desires of the *sans-culottes* so that we might anticipate their responses at the executions, I had the most surprising of revelations:

They love music as much as anyone else.

Most consider notes to be a collection of trinkets, a waste, because it's not something you can hold in your hand or steal or barter for grain. Mère once said our family is never more whole than when we are playing our instruments. After a long day of clubbing men's toes, we can easily forget our misdeeds by diving into refrains and notes.

The working class, too, sings and dances and shouts every time they feel their liberty expanding. I do not blame them.

They sang when they destroyed the Bastille. Sang when they booted the King and Queen from Versailles, their palace in the country. The group carries instruments. This people, the working class of Paris, has discovered what the bourgeois, the aristocrats, the clergy, my family all know— good music fills us when we need filling up.

I could wait a moment or two for when Tempeste insults the brood (whether purposely or by accident, it's bound to happen). She smiles at me, hinting at the fact that she's about to dive for the saber already stained with blood, but I give her a swift shake of the head.

She snarls a rebuke, as if saying, *I can do this,* but she will get herself killed, so I clomp toward the old woman with the white hair. Because even the *sans-culottes* honor the elderly. Reaching out, I swipe for her hand, and it only takes me twice before I'm gripping her brittle fingers like I'm holding the hand of Marie Antoinette. With my most respectful tone, with the honor and respect I reserve for Père, I say, "It is an honor, Madame."

Tempeste grunts, but she must see that I do this for her. To atone for all that I've done.

"You seek vengeance?" I ask the old *sans-culotte*, knowing that she does. When she nods her wispy hair, I say, "But the girl is not what you would expect."

I know what the old woman is thinking: *She is the daughter of a noblewoman, so let us get on with it.* But I cock my head to the side and offer her a tight-lipped smile like I am holding a coveted secret. When she narrows her eyes to snake-like slits, I exaggeratedly grin and bob my head up and down like one of the mimes who perform for children. I know it's humorous, because Père and I always laugh when Henri does it. My exchange is so utterly unexpected that the old woman barks a laugh.

"You're a long way from home, bourreau." She takes in my bloodied knee breeches.

I detest that insult *every time* someone offers it. But I am on the way to gaining the old biddy's favor, so I pretend that I do not hear it. "She is a composer." I nod toward Tempeste like she's an anomaly. "And she composed a song for you."

Bored, the old woman raises her veiny hand like she means to tell the *sans-culottes* to "get on with it," so I jump to an explanation.

"All of you." I hold my arm out like a sop giving speeches. "She wrote it for everyone in the working class."

Now, for all I know, Tempeste is as tone-deaf as a cat on its deathbed. Even now, she's staring at me like I've just sprouted horns from my head. But I must convince them that Tempeste's their compatriot, so I spread both of my arms toward her like she's the Savior they never knew they had.

The bald *sans-culotte* sporting the golden teeth folds his massive arms like he's waiting for the perfect moment to tear my arms from their sockets. "Let's hear it, then." If I knew better, I'd tuck tail and run. And yet, if ever I learned a singular skill in all these years working for *mon père*, it is how to put on a show like they'd never expect.

I do not know why, but I know how to grimace and scowl and laugh right when the people need it. I prod a Patient forward *precisely* when the peoples' pulses slow and they need to feel excitement. Once, when I hadn't garnered their attention, I tripped on a rosebush on my way to the scaffold, and they laughed. They became attentive without even realizing it.

So I spread my arms to each and every sap in the candle-filled gallery. "It is about the short jacket you wear," I explain with ease and confidence. Slowly, like I'm pointing at the pope's regalia and insignia, I gesture toward the torn jacket the bald *sans-culotte* wears. "You know, the *carmagnole*. The symbol of your rising power."

To tell the truth, this is the most worrisome part. Either the bald *sans-culotte* will agree with my assertion—that his people are gaining greater freedoms from what they've had—or else he will grab my Adam's apple and take a munch.

My wound, try as I might to forget it, pounds like a war drum, but I smooth my brow like my heart's not pounding in my chest. Like I can feel my toes and hands.

As mild as the breeze which washes over the sloping hills west of the city, I say, "Won't you sing for us, Tempeste?"

The ethereal girl looks like she might battle axe my face, though with her barren shoulders and complexity of expression, she is La Magdalena again. In that portrait, Mary Magdalene is repentant, yes, but also torn. She remembers her transgressions and is tempted by them. But she also feels what I feel. There is something strong and right between us.

A blush fills her cheeks, which she never before had, and light's shining in her eyes as she extends a dirtied hand.

Her fingers brush my hand, and it's enough—just enough for me to sing and whoop—even if it means I die in the process.

Murmurs trickle like land mines throughout the cavern. Charlotte and Saint-Just duck so closely to one another that it's impossible to know what they're planning, but Charlotte apologized to Tempeste earlier, so I believe she'll help me protect her friend.

Rubbing my hands together, I pray I can soften the blows they intend to offer. *Dieu, aide-moi!* Smiling so that my dimple arises from my cheek, I blubber, "I shall sing the song, for the mademoiselle taught me it!"

Raising my mouth to the dew-filled ceiling, I close my eyes, pretending that I am also singing for *mon père* and Henri, because the National Guard could be dragging them off to the Conciergerie at any moment. Tenor notes fall from my lips, and I'm as startled as anyone that I do not squeak nor strike a false note. It's a tune I've hummed many times to myself when Père asked me to find a way to understand the poorest in our city, and it wasn't long before I composed a song—never once dreaming I'd be performing it in front of them.

It's akin to many of their other tunes. The *sans-culottes* love the spirited, the sturdy, and somehow the music comes from my mouth like inside me there's the low notes of a trombone. I hope they're truly listening, because it's my only plan to shield Tempeste.

The white-haired woman, though, doesn't tap her foot nor smile her wrinkled lips. The bald *sans-culotte* grimaces, so I know I must sing like a bugle garnering courage for an army.

The low pounding of a drum taps a rhythm that matches my singing, and *oh la vache!* I cannot lay my eyes on the drummer—with the assortment of figures in mismatched clothing, I cannot even tell from which direction he's playing—but the old woman's eyes dart about because tears are pricking them. And she's blinking them away like she's nervous. But that's what happens when music hits you unaware and you have suffered in the past. I must not let her forget. Not forget! I must get her to look at me the same way my *grandmère* does when I'm playing my violin.

The Lord must hear my prayers, for no one has decapitated me yet, and so, with the gusto of a French horn, I sing about the King and Queen and how, together, they destroyed the lives of the peasants. And I'm stretching out a finger, showing the *sans-culottes* that it is for them I sing today.

I tear off my greatcoat, because it is not the jacket I should be wearing, and the bald *sans-culotte* is tearing off his coat—the *carmagnole* to which I had before been pointing—and without a word, he's holding it out to me.

I take it, amazed that my little tune is working. I drape the short jacket over my shoulders like it's made of taffeta, and I raise the key of the tune up a notch to help them feel their expanding liberty.

I sing like they could sing this round one of their newly planted liberty trees. I belt out the music to remind them that they shouldn't be the ones forced to pay all the taxes when the aristocrats pay nothing. And they must be thinking the same thing, for even now they're linking arms and skipping.

Their reaction is better than I had hoped. And I'm singing better than I've ever sung. The words tumble from my lips, and to my utter astonishment, I find that some of the *sans-culottes*, on the chorus, are joining in:

> *Dansons la Carmagnole*
> *Vive le son,*
> *Vive le son.*
> *Dansons la Carmagnole*
> *Vive le son du canon.*

I sway my arms this way and that. Tempeste bites the side of her thumb like she doesn't know how to handle it. Then slowly, ever so slowly, she lowers her thumb, and I could swear that she's staring fondly at me. She *can* forgive me for executing her mother, but I don't know if she ever truly should.

Her eyes are round like she's startled that my voice doesn't sound like a dying ostrich, and her mouth opens like my Christian name is on her lips again.

A handful of men in black wigs and bejeweled robes stomp between us, and a woman with an oversized cockade pinned to her blouse wraps her possessive arms about me. While she smells of urine and sweat, I shoot her a smile like she smells of nothing but roses. Because that's what I must do to protect Tempeste.

When the girl with the skull-topped pike bounds up to me, we link arms, which forces her to drop her weapon with a clink. We skip in a circle, and the entire cave is bursting with the music I composed to help me empathize with them.

Tambourines cling, clubs pound, and the walls shake with so much rhythm that the cavern could bury us alive, but nobody seems to care. Not a one of us.

A pair of mademoiselles with blouses so low that I can see their dumplings clutch at my shoulders, my arms. I'm just about to paw them off on another dance partner, when the older one cups my buttocks, and I let out a little whelp.

But it works—I was supposed to sing a high note, anyway. And another's slapping my stomach, my wound. Like bear claws digging into cuts.

I heave as stars swim in my vision. The cave, full of darkness and candles and lanterns, spins like a top. If I stop, though, so will everyone else, and I must keep singing to protect Tempeste.

I am just slowing my spinning when the room slows and I'm face-to-face with Tempeste. It's like the room's devoid of oxygen.

Dark circles rim her eyes, and I itch to sooth the edges.

Breath traps between us. The others keep singing, dancing their jaunt. She's a blown tree, a black willow. Hair ripples like fraying flags.

A fever crawls up my neck. Because, though I've whipped souls, snapped the bones in their arms when they didn't properly fit in the wheel, it all pales in comparison. For we are going to kiss.

The soothing smell of earth and yeast cling to her smooth skin. Her fingers grip my fingers. She wants to touch. But I think about the fact that a Patient once ripped open his own wounds, preferring to bleed to death rather than face what I had in store for him.

I buckle, swoon as Tempeste grips me by the back of my shirt. She says my name, eyes wide with worry or regret. Many others are saying my name, too, as the brassy notes of a trumpet blasts. Women grope each and every square inch of my body, and Charlotte and Saint-Just swirl around me like a lollipop.

But she's touching me, a foreign softness in her eyes and face.

I close my eyes. I cannot keep them open.

More hands paw my body. She cradles my head, like she's really and truly sad.

It shall all be worth it if they believe this wasn't my song, but Tempeste's.

19

TEMPESTE

THE CLUMSY LITTLE oaf faced off the *sans-culottes* like he was a tribal chief. I thought *I* was spectacular, singular even for shirking *mon papa*'s luxuries, but the bourreau? The filthy mongrel bourreau? He put his life on the line after knowing me but a few days.

And then he sang.

My, how he sang.

It's nonsensical how one display of aptitude can alter the emotions of even the most sensical of beings.

And now he has fallen and that ugly emotion I refuse to feel has sparked to life all because those girls wrapped themselves like leeches around his rather fetching body. What the devil is happening to me?

I know about music, tidbits Maman taught me. But when the bourreau said that I composed a song for the *sans-culottes*, I thought I might use *mon papa*'s tweezers to pick apart his cerebral cortex. But then he ended up being damned entertaining, and I had no bloody idea that he could perform that way. I want to hear him sing another song, watch him dance a few more refrains. But I'm going soft in the head. Someone had better fetch a doctor, *mon papa*, because I obviously need a draft of opium to ease me off to dreamland.

We march through the tunnel—he, Charlotte, Saint-Just, the *sans-culottes*, and me—and I'm glad he's falling in and out of consciousness, because I'd be tempted to draw close to him again. I'd reach up and run my fingers over that cravat, because it's rather fetching on him.

A pair of *sans-culottes* drag him like a sack of potatoes toward the surface, and I remember my mission. To interrogate Marat. Even though Maman was a noble, I still have the right to question him. He stole Maman. I mustn't forget that.

And as for the bourreau, the filthy, stinking, unabashedly handsome bourreau whom I can't get out of my head?

I may just insist that he take me to supper after we're finished with all of this.

As we reach the mouth of the cave and I seize my waiting rope, I hug my robe a little tighter, grateful that I once again collected it. The satin soothes the coolness of my skin, and I secretly pay a *sans-culotte* to fetch my father to tend to the bourreau's leg.

When we reach the surface, a hay-filled cart nearly topples me. I throw a dried-up cow patty, because it's hard to excuse old habits as Charlotte, three inches of mud on her skirts, trots up to me.

Her hair, normally carefully curled, lays limply, and the ribbon around her dress frays. She leans close, the heat of her breath warming my arm. "They may try to recruit you for the Jacobins, Tempeste."

I take in my former friend's red cap before dropping my gaze to the darts she pulled from her boot. *Why* is it that she's lurking about? I told her I wasn't interested in working for the Girondins. I'm not her sister, her friend; I'm not even her political ally, so she should let me, as the headstones say, "*repose en paix*"!

"You have so much talent." Charlotte ducks below the branches of a chestnut. "And yet you are unwilling to help our country." She extends her blackened glove out to me, that white-boned ring in her palm.

I fight the urge to shove her in a latrine. "Leave it alone, Charlotte."

"Please take it."

I glance at her with side-eyes. She's so calm, so serene, like a bloody harp.

Charlotte stuffs the ring on my finger, the cool, chilling bone absorbing my skin before I can think how to deny it.

The bourreau's ruined me—next thing I know, I'll be visiting hospitals with *mon papa* and relieving the pus from growths and warts and *merde, merde!*

Staring down at the ivory ring on my middle finger, I do not know if I can accept it. As Charlotte mentioned earlier on the night when Gabriel held up the freshly cut head, it is made of rosary beads. Sister Josephine must know about it, for I still remember the day Sister Josephine received her first set. Mother Superior could no longer horde them in the cupboard where she kept them. Sister Josephine had just come out to show me where I was having a bit of too much amusement pruning a copse of hollies with a pair of shears from the convent. When Sister Josephine called out my name, I whipped around and snapped that brand new pair like the itty-bitty hair of an infant.

Beads littered the stony ground, like bulky, oversized snowflakes, and I remember the guilt that crawled through my gut. Instead of plying me with punishments, or insisting I scoop up every last one of those beads, Sister Josephine simply bent down and started searching them out. I joined in, but she never chastened me. Later that night, she invited me to join her in her office, where, together, we listened to Charlotte read passages from the Bible while we restrung the beads. I'd found a sturdier cord made of horse hair, and Sister Josephine smiled that gummy smile for bringing it.

We strung and listened and even laughed when Charlotte inserted quotes with American accents. We walked a little sprier in the morning, knowing we had found a stronger, higher level to our friendship.

"What will you do," Charlotte asks, whilst I twist the "G" so it's perfectly aligned with the top of my knuckle, "when you've obtained all the answers regarding your *maman*?"

Like a chandelier, my memory comes crashing down on the cobblestones, for I loathe every time she talks piously like that. My chosen path and questions are never elevated enough for her contentment. Has she no regard for my queries? The things I must know, what I would like to ascertain?

I clutch the chilling ring on my finger, tempted to fling it off, because I'm not "balanced" enough to be wearing it. She has other friends with little robes that ripple over their little bodies like silver staircases.

I am a decagon when she thinks I'm square-shaped. I shall never fit in her order the way she wants. Girondins, bleh! Why must every word that gives me the heebie-jeebies, like God and Girondins, start with a "G?"

I nearly fling the ring to an abandoned broken candle sconce. But her hurt-filled eyes remind me all over again of those ridiculous accents she would assign the king when he threw Daniel in the lion's den:

"Thy Gawd whom thou servest continually, heh will de-leh-ver thee!"

We'd gone through the convent, mimicking her accent the rest of the week. It was ludicrous, imbecilic really—so I don't entirely want to, but I keep the ring. Stuff it into my pocket until I know what to do with it.

Like I've just delivered her fondest hope, Charlotte releases a breath. Why does she care so much about it? She doesn't dare to talk, though, and I *know* Charlotte has these grand illusions of what I am—like Sister Josephine does. Is that what they want? For me to aid the moderate, level-headed Girondins like a *maman* to their tribe?

But the Jacobins have all the power, and I thought that's what I always wanted.

Charlotte should lead the Girondins. She's compassionate, level-headed. She's *far* more suited for it than me. I do not wish to hurt Charlotte, which is all but shocking, but she doesn't seem to know how to take "no" for an answer, so I don't say anything. Not one word at all. That is, until I spy the locket she's always worn beneath her kerchief, which holds rubble from her family's home in the country.

"How can you not wish to avenge your *maman*'s and sister's killings?"

Charlotte's eyes wilt like she thinks I'm finally seeing what she's always seen in me. "Revenge is hardly a worthy cause, Tempeste." Her pretty face softens, like we're the friends we used to be.

And I care how she feels, but I should have known she'd believe I'm on a level of which I'm not ready. She was always the one who refused dessert when the convent offered it. She never slept in, even when Mother Superior was away.

She's *always* been better than me.

Even if Maman was a noble, even if she did terrible things, there's an explanation for her actions—and Marat will pay.

As the heady scent of horse droppings swells over the alleyway, the black wigged *sans-culotte* dragging the bourreau stops to raise a cup of ale to his lips.

He's awake.

I should like to talk with him, but, like I've drunk far too much syrup, I do not know what I would say.

I take in his maroon greatcoat, the long tails, how a button on his vest has nearly been pulled from the string. I never noticed it before, but it fits him perfectly. From jumping in the lake, just at the end, his hair curls, and his boots slosh with water. And dear, God, *no! Lucifer,* help me, because I'm finding nearly every aspect of him appealing.

As we parade past butchers' shops, my shoes splashing in dead animals' bodies, I try not to think about that moment just before he passed out. How, despite the room being clogged with *sans-culottes,* it was like we were quite alone, and every single nerve in my body screamed for his lips to be on mine.

But how can I want that when I have been soiled in the past? When the man with the sack covering his face took everything that I had?

We stride past the Place du Carrousel, and I watch how the bourreau's eyes tighten at the massive line of victims to be felled by the blade.

A boy, far too young to be assisting Master Sanson, marches a man up the scaffold, performing the job Gabriel typically does. The boy, trying to keep the criminals in place with chains, cries out as one twists out of a loop that was tied too loosely, and Gabriel reaches, trying to help his *père.* But the *sans-culottes* pin him down with pikes and bayonets, dragging him past the row of boards hastily constructed to block off the Killing Machine.

I have ruined his plans.

Perhaps even his *père*'s trust—that he'll fulfill his duties, because I cut him with an axe. He is not there to aid his family.

His family.

A pit rises in my throat, simmers in my stomach, and other places, because we are not so very different, him and me.

When I spot a pot of dead cut lilies, I allow my thoughts to skirt away from the bourreau because it's all so very frightening. I'm reminded all over again of the time Papa and I used to smell them at the Palais de l'Égalité. I was so delighted how their sweet scent eclipsed the foul stench of smoke and cow dung in our city.

But we're on the Rue Denise, far away from any parasols or tinned candies. Slaughterhouses are as plentiful as the maggot-filled cabbages the *sans-culottes* and I must eat, and the burning scent of melting tallow is as strong as any decomposing body. The church bells toll like a jest, one Sister Josephine actually believes, that the Lord cares about what happens in this city.

We've reached a bottleneck in the road. A woman in a broad-rimmed hat stands atop an overturned carriage, holding a paper and reading. She's spouting off lies like a herd of heifers, and her lies are from Marat's paper, probably.

A hand nudges my wrist, and I tense, blade lifting when Gabriel's hooded eyes, torn open with grief, nestle into mine.

"Another kiss of the blade?" he says.

My cheeks warm, searing. He's mourning the loss of his ability to aid his *père*, and he's bothering with me. I close my eyes, remembering again the strength of his fingers beneath mine, and I do not know if I can be this bird, free-falling, brave enough to try its own wings. But he smells of liquor and ash—from all those torches in the catacombs—and I'm reminded all over again of how deeply I cut him.

He should not be watching, hoping to touch me. His eyes, swollen with fear and longing shouldn't be laced with desire—like every bell is going off in his body.

I feel the tolls, too. Like someone's lit a match in my bloodstream. And I shouldn't be wanting to reach for him like this, desiring to cup his face.

I want to ask, *Are you okay?* But that's an insidious question, because I'm the one who cut him in the first place, and this terrifying thought hits me.

I have absolutely no problem forgiving him for what he did. For killing Maman. It was his job, a task he *had* to do for his family.

He angles his soot covered blouse toward me and butter-flies—*moths! black!*—tear through the neck of my shift all the way to the mucked shoes I'd managed to pull again over my feet. Reaching up, he brushes away the cobwebs in my hair, and it horrifies me that I actually *want* him to touch me. What happened to indifferent, goal-minded Tempeste?

His hand drops to his side, grazing his bloodied leg. I would try to make sense of what he's thinking, why his filthy brow is creasing, but he's a book too difficult to read.

He staggers over a broken bale of hale. "You m-mean to avenge your family?"

I grab the bourreau's strong, albeit lean, arm to help him right his footing, though the *sans-culottes*, like gnats, are in the way. I do not let go, though, and his arm is thick and sturdy. I study his pale cheeks. Search for his dimple, which is currently missing.

He asks if I still desire vengeance? "It's all I have."

An uncertain emotion flits over his eyes, like he's corresponded with many brands of people and still has no clue how to correspond with me. I do not blame him for his hesitancy, because, in the past, I would normally pluck off each and every one of his fingernails just for looking at me. Even so, I glance down at his wound and murmur, *"Je suis désolée pour tous vos soucis."* I am sorry for your pain.

I let the words linger. Perhaps he doesn't remember when he said the exact same words to me, but then this other, softer, emotion flits over his eyes, like maybe he remembers me spitting upon him in the Place de Greve. He cracks a smile.

"You should feel sorry for nothing," he says

I search his eyes. His exhausted eyes. Does he mean that, truly? I am amazed by his quickness to forgive me for hurting him. I hold onto grudges like squirrels horde acorns. It's a little liberating knowing that I can forgive him for executing Maman. The idea—it's dizzying.

Wishing I had the resources to wrap up his wound properly, I gesture at his knee with the sharp end of my blade, but I shouldn't be doing that, because the poor wretch is flinching.

"Sorry." I heave the iron axe behind my shoulder and march past a mirage of broken barrels held together with twine.

His eyes twinge with sadness, and he shakes his head like even now, when I'm trying to be kind, it's not working.

His lips have gone blue; he's lost so much blood. At any moment, he'll lose consciousness again.

"Tempeste—" He grips me by the arm, holds my robe, and I actually want him to hold me in place. I look up into his dark, hooded eyes, a little bewildered that I truly desire to know what he means to say. I've never been fond of romantic words or gallant offerings, but—he makes me want to be a better person. Steady. I *want* to listen, so I bend closer to his filthy blouse and crimson leg. I will not miss a thing.

A decrepit hand wraps its brittle fingers around my shoulder, squeezing, and I know it's the leader of this *sans-culottes* posse. I fight the urge to swing at the mangy thing—the bourreau had something important to say!—when the old white-haired *sans-culotte* croaks.

"Come, *infante.*"

I do not wish to listen. I detest interruptions of all kinds, and yet Marat from any rooftop could be waiting to sharpshoot me. I've allowed myself to get soft, to let my guard down. I may have forgiven the bourreau, but I must not forget what I've come so far to learn today.

So I leave him, with his tender words and broken eyes, and skulk beside the old woman. Peer at the whitewashed homes strung with lines of clothing, wondering if this strange happiness sparking in my chest is here to stay.

When the old, bent woman raps at a door with green peeling paint, my pulse springs, for I'm a carrot, waiting for Marat. Dangling. I should have prepared a few notes. I should have taken a hostage—though I am the hostage today.

As the warehouse door cracks open, its hinges squeaking, I'm hit with the heady scent of paper. I know we've found where Marat should be hiding. It's a bit unfair that he's probably found another printing press already, but I needn't focus on his assets, only my plan: answers. And if necessary, *pain.*

I expect the white-haired woman to lead me inside, but instead, her stony eyes crawl past me. Looking past a throng of children chasing a couple of geese and around the pot of dying lilies, she settles on the now filthy Charlotte and Saint-Just, whose clothes are as torn and dirtied as mine.

"*You*," the old woman spits on the sand covered street, "are nothing but thorns in our liberty. Leave!"

Ah, so she knows what their rings mean—that they are spying for the Girondins, with their "sensible" plans for our country. Saint-Just, in that torn silver buttoned coat of his, should explain he's not really so blasé, but he keeps his full lips closed. Like he has a secret he does not wish to say. Shouldn't he be trying to convince me to go with them? Try to escape? It wouldn't be hard as I still have my axe and I am not in chains. But I want to be here, for Marat is my trajectory. He is the score I must settle. Saint-Just understands my journey.

A pair of *sans-culottes* jab Charlotte and Saint-Just in the backs with pointed pikes, and there's no way for me to stop them now—until Charlotte dives low and throws herself like a beggar at my feet.

With tears stinging her eyes, she cries, "Do not compromise your morals, Tempeste!" The red cap on her hair is so loose, it nearly falls to the street. It's a marvel Charlotte, always so prim and proper, is allowing herself to be seen in such a ridiculous way.

Still, I remember the way she used to help me understand a few Latin phrases during our transcribing. Always gentle, ever patient. Never full of names.

I look at her dirty, hopeful gaze and cannot help thinking that while we used to be friends, we've grown apart. She hasn't lost what I have. Well. She hasn't the spirit and *need* for justice, like me.

"I am sorry, Charlotte," I whisper, throat chalky, and I could swear that Saint-Just's murmuring something to one of the *sans-culottes*, but perhaps he's convincing the ogre to ease up on his pike poking. Let him and Charlotte depart in peace.

Charlotte sobs as I turn away, but I have not come this far to let her high-minded principles get in the way.

So I pound the door of the warehouse with the sharp peeling paint, because it is long past time to act. Marat's inside, and he'll reveal his exact connection to my family.

The white-haired *sans-culotte* woman coos near my ear, "Can I get you anything, *mon ami*?"

At first, I think she's talking to me, but then realize her wrinkled eyes are settled on the bourreau, and my chest twists like—jealousy. And my, my, if his tune hasn't secured a new admirer rather quickly?

The bourreau shakes his dark head, causing his hair ribbon to flutter to the street. And this itty-bitty part of me squirms to pluck it up, smell it before handing it back. Won't someone please bludgeon me? It's only a ribbon and it's black—the color most citizens wear when they hold a light for the monarchy. And yet, he saved my life, stopped the *sans-culottes* from trying to kill me, so I bend down, snatch it up, and hold it in my palm. Cover it with my fingers for safe-keeping.

Without another word, the old woman's nudging the door open, and inside, we're walking.

One of the black-wigged *sans-culottes* prods me with his bayonet, pierces the flesh on my back, so I show him my canine teeth.

He backs up a little, and I've still got it, all right, so I'm downright cheery.

It is time. The very moment for which I've been training. Even now, I can hear the deserter's patient instructions. *Find your mark, and do not look away.* I think of the times I've shot an arrow at a target, lowered a machete. The weeks he trained me with a rifle, improving my aim. If he were alive, I think his quiet soul would nod me forward from the corner, giving me the very courage I need.

When we pass a misplaced statue of Christ draped with a red cap and blue, red, and white cockade, I want to laugh at the absurdity, but my stomach twists because I know the image would bother Sister Josephine. And the bourreau's pausing at the little spectacle like it hurts him, too. But he and I know this is only one instance of how the *sans-culottes* flaunt their abhorrence for the clergy. Their disrespect is almost tantalizing—all disregard for authority is applaudable, really—but it bothers the bourreau, and it would bother Sister Josephine, so I bite my tongue. *Maybe* they're onto something.

When the bourreau sways a little to the right like he might career into a nude painting, I grab him by the collar and straighten him, because the goal now is to get to Marat in one piece. I carry the brunt of the oaf's weight, and it reminds me of when Charlotte tried propping me up after I lashed my own body in imitation of Sister Josephine's wounds, but I do not dwell on that old memory. I hold onto Gabriel's belt, his trousers, his blouse, the utter warmth and smoothness of his clothing. The heat of a lantern trickles from his waistband to my sleeves, and I'm reminded of how he saw me in nothing but my shift for the better part of two days.

Fortunately, I have my cloak now. Plus, I've hidden a dagger—or three—in a few compartments up and down my sleeves. Any terror I might be feeling from facing Marat is like a specter leaving me.

The bourreau's shoulder presses into my cheek. I could be wrong, but I think his body's gone into shock, for now he's trembling. I would throw a blanket on him. I have none, so I give him what support I can. "I had no idea you could sing that way; you should be on the stage."

He grumbles something obscene.

I have to laugh, because if he only knew how earnest I'm being. I have to tease him now, just to distract him from going into shock. "You should put on a little show before every beheading."

He growls. "Do not mock me."

I grin. I pay the bourreau a compliment, and he still believes I wish to pull off his fingernails while he's asleep.

We round the corner in the long hallway with a newfound spring in my step. I expect to traverse more, smash apart a few urns or fountains, when the sight of a man with rags wrapped around his head stops me cold.

Marat. From his painting, I could recognize him anywhere. I'll cut him in sausage links.

I take in the patch-work of *sans-culottes* patrolling the room, survey the boxes of gunpowder, which, with the proper fuse, would explode.

I weave past rakes and scythes, and I'm just tiptoeing past an abandoned money pouch—almost wishing I could raid its contents—when something shiny catches my eye.

A harpoon. The spear-like weapon for whaling, and it's so new it looks fresh from the blacksmith.

Automatically, I hold out a hand to the scrawny *sans-culotte* clutching it. "For me?"

He shakes his lopsided head, shooting spittle at me. I reach for the weapon, just to tease him, but he jerks the weapon high, tensing.

Laughing, I bat it away. "Only bluffing."

Chest alight, I watch as the white-haired woman treads toward Marat, who's hunched over a desk of quills and parchment with candles and brandy. He's wrapping a new string of rags about his scalp, sores festering. The cleansing scent of vinegar hits me, and the bourreau's tripping over a wooden crate.

I help him up, because we are friends now, he and I.

Brushing my fingers over his hand just once, a rush of warmth passes through me. I square my shoulders, readying myself for justice for my family.

The white-haired woman whispers in Marat's ear while he fastens the end of the rag behind it. And when he lays his hand on hers, a look of understanding passes between them. Ah, she's his wife, probably.

I expect the old woman to linger, but when Marat passes her a stack of papers, she staggers away, probably to print more lies. I would light them with a torch, rip them up and stuff them in the sewers, but I must not get distracted, especially when the old goat hasn't even bothered to look at me. No, he's studying the bourreau, the peaceful bourreau like he finds him interesting.

The bourreau squeezes my arm like he's trying to reassure me, which sends happy grasshoppers hopping inside of me.

Marat says, with the flair of a court jester, "I hear, mademoiselle, that you've been looking for me!"

My mind flashes to the day I found his apartment— empty. Of the sewers I searched before settling on the catacombs for our little soiree. But I underestimated his gift for planning. *Eighty-nine sans-culottes* had been a strong hand, indeed.

Marat peels with laughter at what must be the look on my face, so I tighten my fingers around my blade. Why doesn't he order his soldiers to capture me, or confiscate the axe, at the very least? The black-wigged *sans-culotte* still prods me with his bayonet, true enough, but I could take care of him with one fell swoop. Might be pretty.

"I must tell my wife," Marat wheezes, "to find better hiding places for our machine!"

Why is he not more hostile about seeing me? And why does he not order his guards to get on with the decapitating?

Marat waggles his caterpillar eyebrows. "Would you like to hear a most delectable tale about your precious *maman*, dearie?"

I take in the gargoyle's overlarge lapels, having to wonder if this is truly the Marat I've always been hunting. Perhaps, even now, he's a ruse. I'm dreaming. The toadstool is nothing but a gnome—a leprechaun sent to distract me. There's supposed to be a drum, a war cry, a battle of wits and stories. He's supposed to throw me in the dungeon and feed me nothing but rum that tastes like piss. Watch on in horror as I strangle his guards to death before breaking apart my shackles with nothing but my canine teeth.

But now the bourreau squeezes my arm like at any moment he'll soon be toppling, and Marat must sense the bourreau's urgency, for the little man's raising his fingers, trilling the air like he's playing an invisible instrument.

I have to smirk, because I'm not the only one with a few idiosyncrasies.

"Antoine," he says, "attend to the bourreau's wounds, please."

One of his *sans-culottes* in a floppy bicorn hat, striped trousers, and greatcoat with far too short sleeves shakily lays down his musket and marches to Marat's desk of oddities. Picking up a flask and rags, the soldier marches toward the bourreau, avoiding my gaze. It is nice to know that I've instilled a little fear in somebody.

But Marat spreads his chapped lips into a smile so

hideous that like hives, he has me itching. "We wouldn't want an *executioner* to die on us, now, would we?"

The bourreau's grip has gone so limp that at any moment, he'll be losing consciousness. I won't have him insulting my friend, the one I have not entirely vague hopes will kiss me someday, so I nod, albeit hesitantly. "One wrong move," I sneer, "and I'll vivisect the both of your spleens."

The *sans-culotte* drops the alcohol to his feet with a loud *clank*.

When Marat's turban slips over his forehead, he pats it back in place. "Did you know that I was your *maman's* personal physician? A bit of a hypochondriac, she was. Always requesting work for this and that." He trills his fingers again. "It bears little wonder that I fell for her beauty, heh-heh-heh!"

My stomach parries. Maman once told me that she couldn't help falling for Papa because he was so well-groomed, clean. Marat, on the other hand, makes *me* look unsullied.

"She was the daughter of a highly-respected marquis. He owned some of the most coveted land in all of the country. But there was a water shortage," the fool explains. "Her *père* grew ill, so much of the duties fell to her. The tenants were drinking from a river wrought with contaminants, so I asked her to allow them to drink from another creek."

His eyes light up like an unrelated thought just occurred to him, and he snatches up a quill to jot down something. He doesn't set down his quill until I've spouted gray hair and even more crow's feet.

"Where was I?" His green eyes flicker before brightening. "Oh, yes, yes. Lovely!" He licks his crusty lips. "Your delightful *maman* told her men to guard that other unconta-minated creek water instead of sharing!"

The goon leans forward, laughing. He's so reprehensible that I cannot help prowling toward him just to put the creature out of his misery. I'm careful to keep the bourreau fastened in the corner of my eye—just to make sure he's fine. He must survive long enough for *mon papa* to look at his wound so he can return home and recover with his family.

The nervous *sans-culotte* is still trying to pull off the bourreau's boot, so I offer the bourreau a weak smile. *Hold on for me.*

But now Marat's waggling his eyebrows like miniature limbs reside inside. "Anyone who tried drinking the water would be shot—and not just the offenders, but their families! Seems she had much to prove to her *père* that she could keep a handle on things." He giggles shrilly. "It only took a few days for her tenants to die out from disease. Eighty-nine men, women, children, and babies!"

Eighty-nine. The exact number of *sans-culottes* he sent after me. I cannot look at him; he's lying. The *sans-culotte* tending Gabriel is ripping off his stocking. The wound's so deep, I can see the bone. White as a baby's bum. My stomach roils.

Marat licks his lips like there's not enough saliva in the world to sooth their aching. "It wasn't until she saw the bodies—how I piled them up like husks of corn—that your *maman* felt the scourge of what she'd done to all those families."

I'm but an arm's width away from the fiend.

"Of course," Marat says, trilling his fingers again, "I made sure to leave the little ones closest to her door so she could see their chubby legs. It wasn't long before she ran away and whored out herself rather mightily."

Tears burn so hot my eyeballs bleed; I'll snip apart each

and every one of the old man's veins. Smother him to death with that turban he's wearing. I *full well* remember Maman furiously powdering her neck, her chest, her cheeks at her brothel where I wasn't supposed to be. When I begged her to join me at *mon papa*'s house—to stop his marriage to Élise —she refused, claiming the only luxury she deserved was the too-dark rouge she wore on her cheeks and lips.

Marat's tongue has stopped wagging, and the nervous *sans-culotte* has finished patching up the bourreau, so it appears it is time to end the newspaperman, at last, finally. I didn't truly intend on killing him, but after such a pack of lies, he *deserves* to die. He ruined my family.

I tighten my fingers around the smooth handle of the blade, my breath so caught in my throat that it's hard to speak. "And so," I croak. "You sent her to the gallows—in the name of all those families."

The old man waves his skinny fingers like a swath of chicken bones at me. "No, no. Nonsense, dearie! I wouldn't dream of stirring up those old memories." Sticking his finger in the cup of salve, he rubs a little on the wound festering on his cheek, and it occurs to me that maybe—just maybe—this is precisely the medicine Sister Josephine needs. I'll swipe it once I finish with my killing. Run it to the Madelonnettes Convent.

But then the little gnome murmurs, "I didn't want to bother her. Your *maman* was already suffering so beautifully."

My goal is trapped in my brain. I'll—I'll rearrange his arteries.

The foul old man saunters so close to me that I can smell his breath—soured, stale coffee. And—wait—wait. Now he's looking at me like, for the first time in our discussion, he can see me quite clearly. And I know if there's any bit of truth in this old man's heart, it will now unveil itself.

So I tense, gripping my axe, ready.

He licks his lips like there never was a bit of news more mouthwatering. "If you wish to know *why* I denounced your *maman*, dearie, just ask your bourreau, for he's the strapping young brute who persuaded me!"

20

GABRIEL

THE JITTERY EYES of a fox have taken over Tempeste. She's looking from me to Marat to me again, and I know she doesn't believe him yet because her axe isn't swinging.

Is it true? Do I deserve to be dropped from the highest tower, drowned in the farthest depths of the Seine's tributaries? I never wanted her to know the truth. Never wanted her to find out this way. I wanted to tell her, but there was no way.

Oui. I am the scoundrel who begged him to write that story.

I had nearly fooled myself into believing I wasn't guilty. Focused on my obsession with her, pretending it never happened. I wasn't the fool who went to great lengths to impress his *père*, to safeguard the jobs of his entire family. I wasn't so black of soul that I was willing to execute a woman just to make the *sans-culottes* like me.

I shift my pounding leg, and already I can see the fuse of questions simmering in Tempeste's gaze. In my mind, my words are already coming out fluidly. *I am so, so sorry, Tempeste. Let me explain.* But to admit it out loud to her right now would be akin to dousing myself with lime and digging my own grave.

Marat's giggling that damned high chirping of his, and if I had my favorite club, I'd strike him across the face. He must be so proud, so pleased with himself, for he has ruined me.

Why does he not start from the beginning? How we received notice on a Tuesday? That the Assembly was "forlorn" to say that they "no longer required" the services of our family. We were too much of "a drain" on their resources when they were desperate to embrace a "higher" form of liberty. Just like they're probably telling Père today.

Was Marat there to see the pallor of Père's face? How he suffered a stroke and nearly died, so unsure was he about how he would feed our family? *No one will hire me,* he murmured from his favorite settee. *And you? Henri? We have all been branded as killers. No one will pay killers a salary.*

So I nursed him back to health, wondering how we would ever find a way to make ourselves indispensable to the Assembly.

Marat skulks toward Tempeste like they're bloody allies, and I haven't come this far in our relationship for him to knock me down the ladder. "You can leave," I say.

I know my words are useless, though. Tempeste, independent, ferocious girl that I've come to know, will be riveted to every word he says. She will never forgive me.

I will never forgive me. Everything I've done has been for my family, and even still, they're bound for the Conciergerie. Not today, for I just saw them in the square, but maybe tonight.

Marat giggles as the *sans-culotte* who patched me up scampers away. "It's time you join the Jacobin cause, dearie." He flitters his fingers in the air like a damned circus performer or something. "Take the life of the one who's truly responsible for destroying your family."

Tempeste's not exactly skilled at veiling her feelings, but the way her shoulders are angled away from Marat and the sheer and utter shock in her eyes makes me think she doesn't believe what he's saying.

I've only a fraction of the time I need to explain things properly, but I extend a heavy arm anyway. "You do not know everything."

Her eyes are miniature bonfires blazing.

I should tell her how, after reading the Assembly's letter, I wanted nothing more than to cut our losses as executioners and leave, but that wouldn't put bread on the table for Mère and Grandmère, my nieces and nephews, all who relied on our services for food.

It also meant abandoning my uncles and cousins who served in the other parts of the country. And once Père recovered from his stroke, he wanted to think on our options, but he was called away to assist in a faraway beheading. For the first time, when I heard him outside the Pillory, yelling in frustration, I wanted to help. Oh, how I wanted to help. Go in his stead, but I would never be of any use when it came to the precision required of a sword's beheading. And Henri had already left for the army.

My lips are moving before I can think through what I have to say. My cravat's wound so tightly around my gullet I might stumble over everything. "I was wrong when—when I thought I needed to do *anything* to safeguard my family."

Tempeste turns away from me, as if to see what someone else has to say. Charlotte, maybe? But Charlotte is gone. So is Saint-Just. It makes me wish they were here, because they might convince her to show me some mercy.

I do not deserve any semblance of mercy.

But I will tell her what happened, try to explain. How, when Père left, he grabbed me by the collar and pled, *Think what we can do! You may have injured your vision, son, but you may yet prove your worth to this family.* He didn't mean to cut me down, but I felt the censure. It was time to show my worth. I could, even yet, be an asset instead of a liability.

But Tempeste's staring at me with this disbelief—*non*, with complete and utter loathing. She still hasn't moved, though, which makes me wonder if she's still deciding if this is all some big mistake. She's waiting for me to say that Marat is lying. That I'm the newspaperman's scapegoat. That we are sharing a joke for some larger strategy. But now that she's heard the truth, I could never outright lie. Omitting the truth is as far as my conscience would let me take things.

She looks at the wooden floor, axe swinging like the ticking hand of a pocket watch, and even my pulse is ticking.

She drifts toward me like a spirit—quiet, soundless. I should be afraid. I know it's a death wish, but I reach out to move a stringy wad of hair out of her face. As long as I'm alive, I shall always move her stringy hair out of the way. But I miss—of course, I'm missing. I succeed only in nudging her nose with the side of my thumb, which is like the dainty tip of a bird's beak.

Her shoulders draw up tight, her body refusing to bear up the pain, and a lump forms in my throat because the tightness in her brow tells me she *doesn't* want to believe. She just stands there while I linger, propping myself up against the wall. I doubt there will be another moment like this in a decade. So, knowing the foolishness of what I'm doing, I cup the smooth side of her face.

There's a brass-knuckled slap to my cheek.

I knew it would happen, but my vision goes blurry.

I'm reminded of when I accidentally molested her down in the cave. And when I touched the fringe of her dress, how she let me. But I forbid myself from pulling back, because I deserve every ounce of pain.

It's the only way I can atone for the choices I made.

All those years ago, I voluntarily met up with the news-paperman after Père and I met him when we went out for drinks. I took note when the newspaperman told us about the lady-turned-whore who deserved to die more than anybody. But he'd chosen to let her rot in the streets. And later, needing a Patient worthy of dying and not having anyone on hand, I was determined to prove once again to the Assembly that the Sansons are the ones capable of giving the show the common people seek.

Everyone knows the common people, the largest popu-lation in Paris, love bloodlust above everything. Without them, the Assembly would crumble like the Bastille did when the common people got angry.

Stooping down to pluck up a small-sized boulder, Tempeste says, "To think that I fought for you. That I had *almost forgiven you. You!* Who destroyed my family."

If she only knew the weight of the coin I paid Marat to write that story.

With bloodshot eyes, Tempeste screams, "On the name of Maman, noble woman and whore, I will kill you while you are asleep!"

Marat pulls a pistol from a drawer in his desk, and I do not know whether he means to use it on her or me.

"While we would all relish such a dramatic, tension-filled killing," he cries, "will you not even now do the deed?" He cocks the weapon, holding it out for Tempeste, and I should have known his plan is to sacrifice me. For the Jacobins, he would want the powerful Tempeste. But the girl

I've come to know would never accept a weapon from him—would much more relish using Père's axe for the deed.

And she *should* do it, for I broke apart her *maman*'s foot, not because I needed to extract a confession, but because it would force the lady-Patient to hobble her way to the scaffold, which always builds up tension nicely. I chopped her braid, not because I feared it would get in the way of the rope, but because it's easier for the people to scream out for vengeance when they do not find the Patient to be pretty. And I allowed her *maman*'s dress to fall down to her waist, because the crowd revels in all things shocking.

The people were ecstatic with the show I've always been capable of giving.

Tempeste, though, is as still as if her spirit's left her body. She's a ghost, and when she joins me after I die, she'll spend the whole of the afterlife haunting me. And because I had ultimately been successful in convincing the Assembly to retain our services for the city, I got what I wanted: job security for my family. For the time being.

I am not the only one who is willing to do whatever it takes for their family, though, and it wouldn't be fair not to allow her the same luxury. So I lay my hand on her arm, fully aware of the cobra I'm prodding. "Do it." The room, the soldiers, the desk, the quill and ink, are all spinning. "Just do it before you change your mind, Tempeste."

21

TEMPESTE

I AM THE WIND. I am the rain. I'm the Bay of Biscay flying over meadows and cattle and sheep and dumping the whole of the contents over this ripshite of a city.

I'm snatching up the filthy bourreau by the back of his leg—my fingers, from his blood, stick—pressing my palm into his wound because I'll crumble him into itty-bitty rocks, mash him into itty-bitty cracks and seams.

His whimpers, his bloody whimpers are angels, baby cherubim singing.

His whimpers tear through me.

I wanted to kiss him. Wanted to know how love, with him, would be.

His pain—his choking pain—is a symphony of strings. A dissonant chord that breaks apart the depths of my heart like shattered rubies.

Sparks of anger and betrayal and compunction tear through me, and *at last* I understand why Maman chose my name.

Like a storm cloud, I'm squeezing out the sun's rays. Curling the darkness like wisps of fog settling each morning. The earth, with one small breath, shall soon be bits of glass, and with one swift kick of my shoe, I'll be toppling mountains, smashing apart valleys.

I can *smell* the bourreau's screams, *taste* the whimpers from his disgusting mouth, because that's what you can do when you become a natural disaster. Senses intermingle like soil and moss and peat.

I stare down on those dark, dark eyes, mortified that I actually allowed him to get to me. I actually believed he was not a ghoul. A kind, gifted singer. I let him *touch* me. Smiled like he mattered to me.

I am inside the very cyclone I made. I'll stretch those hoods of his eyes so far that the skin snaps like bits of pie crust I've stolen from the bakery. Mash those eye sockets like eggs, smear the yolk so that they bleed.

The rake never should have targeted my family. I don't even have anything to remember her by. Not a pendant, not a quill nor shard of clothing. He stole everything. My heart —*no*, the burrs I've carefully constructed around it are weeping.

My fist throbs. I'm still holding his ankle. And my hand has fallen asleep. Because the butter knife's not mine anymore—*his! always!*—I throw the pissy axe to the ground, hoping it bends indefinitely.

I miss my shoe by only a margin of an inch, and the *sans-culottes* stir like bright, miss-matching larvae. But I do not care.

Do not care.

The bourreau, the generous, *disgusting* bourreau, lied to me.

Marat huffs as another valve to my fractured heart seizes, so I pulverize him with my gaze.

"Do you not wish to join the Jacobin faction, dearie?"

My chest flutters like a parasol, broken but expanding. Join the one faction I admire? An absurdity.

Not an absurdity.

Killing the bourreau—killing the bourreau?—shall not exactly be easy.

Just a moment ago, I breathed in the ale on his breath, held onto the lean muscles of his body. Snatched his black silk ribbon, so I release it now, fluttering, the cobwebs of my ill-constructed heart sinking to my filthy, shoed feet.

This is how Maman felt when she learned that Papa would marry Élise. Must be.

I shall *scream*.

It is pleasant, rather pleasant, to know that once I end the bourreau, I shall fit into the Jacobin club nicely. *Oui!* Perhaps they'll have me assassinate Dukes and Lords, since my soul *my fractured soul* shall be unredeemable already.

I shall cut apart each and every one of the bourreau's ribs and make candelabras for my hammock for proper lighting.

Stick his eyeballs on pikes before I mash them, because it shall be nice to stare at them a little while longer to understand how I fell for his lies in the first place.

Gunpowder, fuse already lit, courses through me.

But this itty-bitty voice is saying, *Do not compromise your morals, Tempeste.* Charlotte's? Cold, cold, condescending. At first, I believe these are words of the past, but the timbre of her voice is bouncing off the windows. The room's high beams.

And *sans-culottes*, nothing more than distractible children, are turning to see.

So I blink. *Blink-blink.* Because there's Charlotte, red-capped, out of breath, mud-streaked. Her marble face, etched with pain and alarm, makes me feel smug to know that I have the power to evoke such worry. And like she's our next great Catholic Saint, she's extending her dainty ringed fingers toward me.

I stuff my hand in my pocket and fling the ring to the bloody flooring. Compassion? It has no precedence in me.

Charlotte cries out, "No!" But I have no time for decency. Still clad in her *sans-culotte* apron and work boots, she's exactly the antithesis of what I remember her to be. Pious? —always. But I cannot help remembering a time when Charlotte told me of the gowns in her wardrobe, lined up, starched and shining. How she spoke in reverence of a muslin gown so soft and white, she almost believed that snowflakes made up the stitching. She owned a gold-striped sash, an exact replica of our queen's. Her red satin gown, the robe a la Turques, with so many embroidered flowers, and tassels and fur so ornate that a duchess once asked her where she purchased the thing.

I do not know why I remember, for luxury of dress is— *and should be!*—waning. But Charlotte, *my Charlotte*, knows fashion. She even cried a little when she donated her wardrobe to the poor. I loved her for that, because even though I couldn't care two stitches about the clothes I wear, it was her idea to donate them. *Not* Sister Josephine's.

About her more recent apparel, I have thought snide, snide things. But she has not worn anything the good and proper would not wear as of late. She merely dresses too fancy for my taste. No tassels nor fur this time. For her beloved France, she is changing.

"If you will not listen to me," Charlotte says, and I have never heard her voice shake so fiercely, "perhaps you will listen to Sister Josephine."

I think she might be soft in the head, because Sister Josephine would never leave the Madelonnettes Convent, and besides, the only person behind Charlotte is Saint-Just, in his crumpled-up hat and pipe sticking out between his teeth.

But then there's this soft *tap-tap-tapping* of wood and a spray of white hair peeking out from a veil.

And my breath is strangling me.

My one true ally is here in the flesh, along with a gaggle of other robed figures with curls coming out of their hoods, exactly like the ones I saw in the executioner's square the other day. It doesn't take long for her to observe the axe in my hand. I am leaning over the bourreau, *the beautiful insidious* bourreau, watching the blood pool on the ground below his leg.

A carriage sits upon my chest. Three.

A windmill, its blades *slap-slap-slapping* me.

When I lived at the convent, how many times did Sister Josephine implore me to release my hate?

She doused me with cold water and gave me a bucket for pulling weeds. "Accidentally" caused me to trip, so that I knelt when I prayed.

Now, though, Sister Josephine is clutching her rosary beads. "My lamb." Her gentle eyes, taking in my trembling hands, are battle clubs smashing me.

I look away, because she's not supposed to see. I'm supposed to kill the bourreau, light off fireworks, drink champagne. And then? When I see her next, forget to mention my other, unsavory activities.

Charlotte's bending down to whisper something to Sister Josephine. The other girls tiptoe around the guards like they, too, deserve to know my secrets. But none of them are supposed to be friends. Their allegiance? I'll smash it like a grape.

Charlotte bends down and retrieves the ring at her feet.

Straightening her apron as if arranging a pile of lace, she says, "You do not have to go through with it, Tempeste."

The robed figures draw closer just like beetles—*no!*—my conscience is choking me. But the *sans-culottes* are blocking them off. Knives and pitch forks block their masterful principles and holy ways. Besides, I do not wish them to be near.

I tighten my fingers around the handle of the blade.

The *sans-culotte* with the harpoon is pointing me out to a whale-of-a-man who's just joined the scene, and even now it's like they're awaiting this final performance. Where I kill the bourreau and Marat has something else shocking to write about my family.

Sister Josephine's eyes are lances, piercing my very being. Kindness shouldn't be so sharp. Cutting. I shouldn't care what she thinks, but she's the one person who believes I am somehow redeemable. Actually believes.

So I stare down at the target at my feet, the devil I nearly fell for, the one with the broken eyes. They're soft, brown, understanding. Like he doesn't blame me. But what must it be like for him to look at me today? Surely, he must see a girl who's deranged. Truly he cannot harbor feelings for a girl as unstable as me.

He comforted me on the hammock, dangled his life in front of the *sans-culottes* to save me. Touched the fringe of my shift—*I wanted him to touch other things!*

Marat snickers like he's enjoying each and every choice I make. "If you will not kill the bourreau, child, then you must dispense of the clergy!" He gestures to my one true friend, like I would ever kill Sister Josephine.

My arm quivers. The blade of the axe falls dangerously close to my knee.

Charlotte's eyes, too, are as wide as the wooden shoes crammed on my feet. Marat, clever Marat wraps his shriveled hand around Sister Josephine's waist. *What is he doing? I'm the brunt of some joke. This is a test. The Jacobins do not truly wish to harm the clergy.*

But Marat's licking his flaking lips like they're an unending supply of salted meat. "To join the Jacobin faction, to prove your talents for justice and proactivity. You must choose one, dearie."

Sans-culottes file into the room like there's an endless supply of reserves. Tens of thousands of them inhabit this city. Saint-Just—a strangely quiet Saint-Just—should be offering some tidbit of advice—*imploring me to act! settle a score, fulfill a debt, make a difference, oui. Sometimes one needs to make people pay. For liberty.* But all he does is stand there in his crumpled hat, mute as a turnip, as *sans-culottes* perch behind boxes of ammunition like they're waiting for something.

Even now, as I try to catch Sister Josephine's eye, I cannot help remembering the most ludicrous advice she ever offered me—when Mother Superior ordered those lashings, and she told me what Jesus would say. I've repressed it, always. But the words rush toward me like a tidal wave, and there's nowhere to go but straight.

Turn, turn, turn, she said. *The other cheek.*

Her words are strong, green vines strangling me. Not strangling. *Holding.* They are not only Sister Josephine's words. I heard them before. It is why I work so hard to repress their teaching. For, just before Maman left, just before:

noose tightens
ground falls
ropes stretch!
She murmured, "*Turn the other cheek.*"

I pretended not to hear it—just like I always do—with

Papa, Charlotte, the nuns—anyone—who tries to reason with me.

I have broken noses and stolen enough food to feed both the Prussian and French armies. I've spent countless nights dreaming of hunting down Maman's killer and severing his fingers one-by-one just to hear him shriek.

But murder? *Sometimes one needs to make people pay.*

No. No.

Like I've just scalded my hand, I drop the axe to my feet.

22

GABRIEL

SHORTLY AFTER HITTING my head in the catacombs, I visited a cathedral—the Notre Dame. The purple and red stained glass windows glistened like peppermint candies, and chandeliers dropped from the ceiling like giant snowflakes, glowing.

While the choir boys sang, their voices like airy flutes, I felt this indescribable warmth wash over me. Comfortable. Sweet. Candles flickered orange and yellow; the Corinthian columns simultaneously lifted and grounded me.

When a thin crucifix snagged my attention, though, I buckled. How could our Lord, our great, powerful Redeemer, allow himself to be nailed to those awful beams?

I pulled on *mon père*'s coat, which even back then smelled of blood and quicklime. "He died for our sins, Père? Every one?"

Père watched an old woman blow her nose into a handkerchief, and I imagined him thinking of rolling over his oldest boy. Someone coughed. A priest strode toward a confessional, and it wasn't until Père found his own meaty fingers clasped together in prayer that he managed, "*Oui.*"

I believed everything Père said, especially after picking himself up and continuing on with his thankless job after losing Charles, so one can imagine the awe I felt once I realized that God could die for every last one of mankind's terrible deeds.

The choir boys' voices rose toward forte, and the guilt of what I'd done, hurting my own eyesight, churned like rancid cream. Dust and mildew tugged through my nose, and I realized with horror that at any moment I would be crying —for guilt, for shame for letting down my family—and I panicked at the thought of Père seeing me cry, so I took a bold step sideways, only to bash my knee on a nearby wooden seat.

A woman wearing a hat twice my size turned to glower at me, and Père snarled, "Mind your own worries." He gripped me by the shoulder and led me from the cathedral, and I didn't lift my head from the checkered flooring the entire way.

It wasn't until our carriage jostled over a bridge of wooden beams that Père asked, "Why were you asking about our Lord's mercy?" His hooded eyes ebbed with worry. It didn't occur to me back then that he might be worried about his own soul with all that executing.

I clutched my throbbing knee. "Because I have done a terrible thing."

Père seemed to take in every emotion warring inside of me—the remorse for going down to the catacombs, the embarrassment that I hadn't been able to swim well enough to prevent my eye injury. The fact that I would never be a full-fledged assistant to him.

He could have given me any number of sermons that day. About obligations. Duty. Choice. But instead of lathering me up with platitudes that would have bounced right off the Artois buckles of my shoes, Père quietly reached over and laid his meaty palm over the bruise on my knee.

I decided if God was anything like *mon père*, I rather liked him that day.

Our Lord and Savior has suffered for our transgressions; every last one of our dastardly deeds. So from that moment on, I determined to try a little harder. Love, serve, teach. It's why I took Tempeste's *maman*. To atone for letting down my family.

But by doing so, I hurt another family, and it's doubtful that Tempeste will ever forgive me. Just because she didn't slice me apart with that axe doesn't mean she's ready to run to the hills and mate chickens with me.

I should find a way to leave Paris—follow my dreams. And yet, how can I? She's stuck on my soul like tar, like licorice candy. I should drop this silly attempt at wooing her, and yet I cannot help indulging the feebleminded hope that she *will* forgive me.

Perhaps this is why I fell for her in the first place— because this hidden part of myself knew all along that I could never be happy until I helped her find her happiness.

And if she finds her happiness with someone else?

I may require a healthy dosage of therapy.

Now, though, a low, lyrical voice is laughing, and it must be important because everything's gone quiet in the factory. Too quiet. Like the time I inadvertently groped an elderly nun not unlike Sister Josephine.

"Such a pity," the man's saying, and it isn't until I peek through my lashes to find his red cravat and tall riding boots stepping over me that I know it's Saint-Just. His arms—his very being—seem to come alive with electricity. It's like he's suddenly more than a man. He's more of a force, a beast.

"Your talents were so promising," he says, and I must

have lost more blood than I thought, because it sounds like he's censuring Tempeste.

He laughs this loud, open shriek, and a chill tears through me. I've heard this laugh before. Years ago. On the east side of France. And I *knew* I recognized him when I first met him in Marat's office with Tempeste.

It was in the fall. Henri's unit was low on supplies, so I drove out a tumbrel full of blankets, ammunition, crates. The Assembly hadn't lessened my family's salary yet, so we had plenty.

Henri was so cheered by my arrival that he invited me to meet their fastest rising officer—a man with long, dark hair, and the sort of indescribable charisma that commanded a stage. He was holding his hand over a blazing fire—not for a fraction of a second, but for five long seconds, garnering whoops and cheers from all the soldiers. Some of the men were shouting for him to hold his hand longer. Others were burning their own hands just to feel what he was feeling. I must admit I was astounded by his behavior—even found him oddly brave —until I saw the curve of his back, the way he lifted his face to the sky, shrieking with the *same* exact laugh he's laughing now. *Pain!* he cried. *Freedom can only be harnessed through pain.*

I am loathe to admit that I did not recognize Saint-Just sooner, but there were many dark haired men surrounding that fire. And the Saint-Just Tempeste introduced me to didn't seem all that evil until today.

Gunfire shakes the room, and he's laughing this terrible laugh—like his voice alone will soon topple the building— and with the way his men were worshiping him, I wouldn't say it's outside the realm of possibility.

"Paris is an explosion of color," he muses. "Itty-bitty

faeries lighting up the sky with their pained laughter and screams."

I may not be the only one suffering from brain softening, except Charlotte and Tempeste, too, are looking to one another like they have no clue what he means.

He parts the window's curtain. I'm on the floor, so the angle's all wrong. It's hard to see outside, but deep through the latticed, murky window panes, it looks like a red-capped *sans-culotte* is setting a torch to a priest's floppy robe.

Wait. This cannot be what I'm seeing.

Orange flames lick the black habit. This is the first time I've seen a *sans-culotte* actually physically lift a finger against the clergy besides burning effigies. Marat has urged them to do so for what feels like a decade—they've enacted the charade—but now I must force myself not to jump to my clumsy feet.

The girls, in their tattered clothes and blackened faces, spin around to help, but Saint-Just's bringing his fingers to his lips and whistling. Something like thirty men in the factory point their muskets at them and Charlotte and the others, ready. It seems Charlotte has more friends in her Club for Young Ladies than I had supposed. In their chilling robes, they appear to be exactly the type of group I could see Tempeste joining.

Charlotte's gentle voice pitches like she, too, did not see his betrayal coming. "What is going on, Louis?" Her whole being shakes.

Saint-Just, the apparition, laughs. Like he's merely won a game of cards. Like he relishes our misery. "Man has the right to deal with his oppressors by devouring their palpitating hearts."

Marat giggles, and I know Marat wrote that. I remember the issue, because Père talked about it with Henri after he begrudgingly introduced me to Marat when we went for drinks.

I should close my eyes. Snap them tightly shut, for it won't be long before Saint-Just or Marat catch me and pledge to hurt the girls. See for themselves that my family's locked up in the pointed, Gothic towers of the Conciergerie. I'm about as defenseless as a turnip, anyway.

"We haven't *room* for everyone," Saint-Just explains, and Charlotte sways like she's about to faint. She reaches for those poisoned darts of hers in her girdle, but they are not there. "We simply need to dispose of the clergy. You've seen how they spend exorbitant amounts of money on architecture and decor when people are starving."

I am loathe to say he has a point, but threatening and killing people is not the moral way.

Charlotte's reaching for those darts in her girdle again, but Saint-Just casually points to a spot far on the other side of the room. "Sorry, *mon cherie*. Your darts are out of harm's way."

Charlotte flinches like she's just been clubbed in the face. Tears prick her typically veiled gaze. A few of her robed friends reach for their own darts, but a bare-chested *sans-culotte* cocks a rifle, causing them all to freeze.

I'm just bending my knees, pain tearing like needles through me, when a minor explosion shakes the building. My nose tickles from tar or smoke. Is something burning?

Someone shrieks from the other side of the window. And I do not know what it is until I spot the raw glint of a machete.

An aged man wails through the window glass. I'll never grow used to that sound. Saint-Just presses his fingers to the lattice panes. Charlotte's robed friends, too, are shrieking. Some outstretch their hands, wincing in pain. One, a bit pudgier than the others, reaches for the broken tip of a bayonet, but the barrel-chested *sans-culotte* kicks her with his boot so hard, her cheek splits open and blood splatters from her face.

"Tempeste wished to find Marat," Saint-Just says, "and we hoped a little reunion would inspire her to join us in our efforts today. Remember what I said, doll?" He rearranges the ruffles of his sleeves. "I realize I may have marred your trust, what with my Girondin spying, but I stand by what I said before. Sometimes one needs to make people pay."

Tempeste wrenches a musket away from a man as large as a mammoth, and it doesn't take long for him to backhand her across the face. Robed figures grab, scratch, claw, but Tempeste flies into a wall like a poppet. I'll slaughter a thousand men just to—

A deep gash tears open the cheek of La Magdalena's seraphic face and Saint-Just? I go for the knees.

23

TEMPESTE

A SCORE of *sans-culottes* are pinning me to the wall, and the bourreau's just launched himself half across the room, nearly through a window. His hooded eyes are trained near Saint-Just, so he must have been aiming for him, but he missed by a furlong.

The bourreau flexes his jaw in frustration. "Tell your men not to touch Tempeste."

Words have never held more beauty, though even the devil can hold bouquets.

My neck stings from that *sans-culotte* throwing me into the wall, and splinters dig into my palms from where I braced my landing. He's a big oaf, the *sans-culotte* who threw me like a javelin.

I would turn about, demand he try again, only with me ready for him, but we are well past a few good scratches and pops. We're well past chicken-fighting. Perhaps I should remind Marat and Saint-Just that the Assembly will not approve of this senseless murdering.

Or will they? Just like the benign intent of our sweet Guillotine, the road toward freedom is slippery.

Saint-Just was supposed to be a friend, but he's nothing more than a bramble, a thistle in need of burning. Counterfeit. He's counterfeit. My eyes sting. His expressive face smears with a smile, and like a wolf, he's all teeth. "Someone adjust that bandage, please?"

He points to the bourreau. He must not want to harm him for fear of the Assembly. The Assembly likes tools, and the bourreau is a tool for securing liberty.

A tool who was given the wrong job. A tool who *hurt* Maman. My family.

The same *sans-culotte*—Antoine—who helped the bourreau earlier steps forward, and I'm just about to point out the probable recourse from the Assembly for targeting the clergy when Saint-Just murmurs, "Have you ever run up a hill and enjoyed the burn in your legs so much that you wanted to ratchet up the pain?"

His eyes glint through Charlotte's robed friends, past the *sans-culottes* as he locks eyes with Sister Josephine, and I do not know why he cares what happens to her or all the clergy. Someone's crying—crying outside the window—*pain*—like they're being skinned alive. And I feel those shrieks, because twenty paring knives are digging into my arteries. I *know, I know, I know*—

> *two dark slits*
> *burlap sack, covering his face*
> *knees pinning my hair*
> *cannot tear away*

The bourreau should tie me to a wheel, take a club to my bones, because I've felt nothing since that day. *I've felt everything.* The deserter taught me to always face my enemy, but how could I when he covered his face?

When he stuffed his falsehoods inside of me.

Charlotte's trying to pull away from Sister Josephine—Sister Josephine's brittle fingers squeeze Charlotte's trimmed sleeves—and I know Charlotte is as desperate to grab those poisoned darts as me. Sister Josephine's holding her like a baby bird, her skinny arms the cage.

Someone spits tobacco. A wooden rake scrapes. A church spire through the window stabs the sky when Saint-Just says, "I never believed in your Girondin philosophies." He cocks an eyebrow as Charlotte reaches the spittoon wherein he placed her darts. A *sans-culotte* shoves her in the back so that she falls to her knees. "You were simply the source the Jacobins needed to gather intelligence," Saint-Just purrs. "*Darling.* Though I am quite pleased that you fetched the nun. You are useful in so many ways."

Charlotte's calm rips from her face. Like someone's slipped a torture serum inside her brain. Her eyebrows cinch, shake.

Sister Josephine hobbles toward Charlotte, reaching out like she means to smooth her worries when, through the window, black habits flutter up like crows flying for safety. A *sans-culotte* pounds a priest's face with a club so many times, I think of a crude bale of hay.

And I'm rocking. *Burlap sack covering—*

Somehow, some unearthly way, I feel the bourreau's tender brown eyes upon my face, and I'm crimson, broken sheets, because I do not want him to see these secrets inside of me. But my lips betray everything. My eyes join the conspiracy. Settling Saint-Just in the crosshairs, I say, "I *know* what you did to me."

Saint-Just pulls his pipe from his teeth. "You quite pleasured me."

my body isn't mine
scuttles away
hot hot coals groping me
i'm dropping to the ground
curling
because
perhaps he won't want to take advantage of me
        this way

Something sails through the air—one of Charlotte's poisoned darts?—but the object is too wide, and a paving stone breaks in pieces round my feet. The bourreau shouts like he's at last found a smidgeon of victory.

One of the robed figures is slamming into a wall. A freckled one, as her hood falls from her face. She looks to be but twelve, and how is it our children must sign up to fight our battles in this country?

Saint-Just curses—*merde, shite, shite, shite!*—while a burly *sans-culotte* clubs the bourreau in the face. I flinch because blood pours from his eyes. Hurting him makes *me* bleed.

Shouting sprinkles through the air, the musty warehouse air infused with the scent of paper printing. Sister Josephine's holding out her aged hands, pleading with Saint-Just like he's worthy of saving, and Charlotte's tugging on his greatcoat like he'll magically change the way he behaves.

Fat hands grope for my ankles. Seize my shivering skin, shackling me. And like a beaten cobra, I *slink* to the dirty floor like the deserter did when he sank into the lake.

Saint-Just cackles, a warlord securing his victory. He's a dark, vast shadow, ever looming over the fallen bourreau, girls, and wooden crates. "Let us be off to the Guillotine!"

~

*D*rums *tap-tap-tapping.*

Saint-Just leads us past shuttered windows. Whitewashed buildings. Piles of broken wheels and doors and crates.

Books burn—ash, fluttering. Even sacred writing is being burned, as the Jacobins have no use for God's word in their imperial reign.

When I stumble over a disrobed clergy sprawled, dead, his white buttocks showing themselves to me, Saint-Just explains, "We have been planning this for weeks."

Amidst the stuffing being torn from a settee, Sister Josephine removes her veil and gently covers the dead monk's impropriety. His skinny arms and pale skin peak through like the stark wrappings of a mummy, and I cannot believe this is the Jacobins' plan for our country. To kill, and I had wanted the same thing.

"Don't worry, doll," Saint-Just says, checking the chamber of his pistol as a rogue chicken darts out of a cafe. "This is merely a precursor to greater things."

Stone-made cherubim lie broken in pieces at my feet. A grotesque which had once guarded a cathedral is currently being smashed by the hammer of a boy not much higher than my waist. Rock dissolves, crumbles, and I know he is not old enough to properly discern what he is doing.

Saint-Just steers us past a vineyard of bloated grapes, their pointed branches scratching through my robe to my knees. He trolls us over a bridge, beams rattling. A fisherman sobs over a corpse; his twisted fish net abandoned, empty. Paris was dangerous before, but only in the last few hours has it become a great hunt for game. Saint-Just is right. The attack against the clergy must have required a great deal of planning. And is this the Jacobins' plan all along? To tighten their belt against anyone who doesn't believe as they? I always thought, on a map, it looked like the buckle of a belt, the Île de Cité.

I have been driven by the need to hurt others, obsessed over finding answers for my family. There was a day a year or so ago when I went around,ncutting the angry word *Greed* into the doors of any apartment that took more wine or grain than they needed. The deserter and I once broke into a marquis' garden and made off with a statue of some fancy aristocrat—used the rubble to sink a newly ported boat and stole all the fish meant for a rich man's family.

I've fought *so long* against the rich, the entitled, but what happens if one goes too far? Is there any hope of redeeming the soul they were supposed to be?

The percussionist is *tap-tap-tapping,* and we're mounting the scaffold—Charlotte, Sister Josephine, and me. I suppose this is how it all ends, where I'm killed for considering unmentionable things. I *thought* I had some grand purpose in life, but without knowing I was doing it, I'd become one of Saint-Just's blind, demonic sheep.

My friends and I, wrapped up in shackles clang our newest tambourines. Seems Saint-Just and his friends are only too happy to add a few nameless captives along with our party. Charlotte and her girls do not walk fast enough, so a *sans-culotte* prods them with pointed spikes. A girl with half an arm missing sobs into another girl who has a bandage wrapped around her face. Ropes strangle their wrists. Sear red. Is this why Charlotte wanted me to join the Girondins? To stand up against the Jacobins and help innocent girls like these?

Sister Josephine prays so loudly and with such devotion,

I think God might reach down from those thick early morning clouds, which have grown pink, sopping up all the blood spilled by our Killing Machine. Sister Josephine's voice is raw; scraping. I would sooth her vocal chords with the herbs of an apothecary.

The bourreau, the dirty, filthy bourreau—we left him behind. He is safe.

I hope. I think.

Men in striped trousers fight over a pig down below for a bit of meat. A poultry farmer's shoving a chicken in a cage, and I count one—two—seven blue, red, and white flags fluttering, rumpling in the stagnant heat.

A gray haze settles over the square like the breath and mist of deity. Saint-Just grabs a bowler hat from one of his men, and he throws it to a girl holding a dolly.

He lifts his arms wide, and his filthy face is as two-faced as the *livre*.

"Whose head's rolling today?" calls out a man with missing teeth.

Saint-Just holds up a finger, his long greatcoat flapping. "You shall see."

Sweat tickles my chest, beads on my brow. The scaffold spins like a carousel, and my head throbs. I could sleep for a week. So this is what it's like to die. Where one's senses contort what's really happening.

White-bonneted women pull up seats, settling in for their early morning knitting. Taking pleasure from his growing audience, Saint-Just rises on the balls of his feet. "Won't you all meet the *good* nun, Sister Josephine!"

Jewels smack the wooden posts of the Guillotine. As rose petals drizzle through the air, I spot jade and sapphire—my one true ally's rosary beads.

When Saint-Just bends down to whisper, his breath is hot, scalding. "You're not the only one she tried rescuing."

I recoil.

He's referring to the girl who drowned her own baby; the man who ripped apart his best friend's stomach with a scythe. But how does he know these things?

I try to catch Sister Josephine's eye, but she's looking at Charlotte and the other girls, strewn down the scaffold stairs like spilled wells of ink. Pain splits apart my splintered friend's face, like all she wants to do is help them find the solid ground. Fight for *real* liberty.

Saint-Just turns to the crowd like they should care about what happened to him in the past—his history. "She watches everything!" He gestures to Sister Josephine, arms bursting with energy. "When I burned down my reformatory, she actually believed *prayer* would change me."

I have heard that guidance myself—to pray daily—but he's lifting his once comely face to the sky, which contorts and flashes with lightning. His blue eyes glint like the bourreau's sharp, crescent blade, and he's laughing. Ah, so she's the one he meant when he said someone was trying to control him.

One of the robed girls leaps within inches of Sister Josephine's wooden shoes, but a *sans-culotte* snaps her twiggy arms. Twigs as if from a sapling, and she cries in pain.

Sister Josephine flinches.

Others, down below—my estranged brothers and sisters of this country—laugh and clap like pain is peace. I had thought *mon papa* was malicious for not admitting the truth to the Assembly, that Maman was our family, but perhaps I had been wrong to judge him so sharply. The truth, well. It can be pounded and pounded and molded into an ugly shape. The toothless smiles surrounding the scaffold make me feel like we're all on a stage. Is that what they want? Life has gotten so difficult that they feel we must all weep?

Seizing Sister Josephine's brittle shoulder, Saint-Just lowers himself so that they're face-to-face. Her lips quiver—and so do his, but because of laughter, while she is crying. Opposing reflections, in a way.

"*Now* do you believe me?" he asks, like he means to be gentle, but all eyes are riveted to him on the stage.

Sister Josephine's gaze crackles—the face she makes when she's about to quip about the "delicious" weevils in our grain. "I always believe."

Revulsion contorts the radical Jacobin's face. His blue, blue eyes are so foul, they are dagger-like shards of ice. This is *not* what he means. "In *God.*" He backhands Sister Josephine so that his Girondin ring slices open her tissue-thin face.

She staggers, nearly trips over the Guillotine's wooden feet, but she rights her footing and bravely perks her lips in a bittersweet smile. "*Oui.*"

Saint-Just shoves her down hard on the horizontal platform—the sound of a butcher slopping down a slab of meat—and hovers over her like he's dreamt, for many years, of this day. His hands ball into fists, and he breathes shallowly. "You disgust me."

I'll throttle his odious face, scatter his bones in the vilest part of the catacombs where I don't even dare to venture, but chains clang like the crash symbols percussionists use in this city. Feet scramble on the steps as robed figures flee their captors to save their Sister Josephine, but, like flies, they're swatted down. Flattened. Discarded from the stairs completely.

One robed figure falls from the scaffold—an upside

down spider, legs quivering as she shrieks. My ankle twists —my shoe slips and I'm swatting at a *sans-culotte* who's settled his fat rump upon me. Spears pin my shoulder and a scarf stuffs my mouth, my canine teeth.

Saint-Just grasps the rope, swinging like he's pulling a scarf round a liberty tree, and he must stop, because Sister Josephine's head is below the blade of the Guillotine.

Two years ago, I was eyeing a pair of shears. I didn't want to bother with the lice and tangles that had embedded themselves in my hair. Without a word, Sister Josephine sat me down and plucked a comb through every single gnarl. Took hours, and I only complained.

Before that, a thick cloud of darkness blanketed my mind and the streets. That white goop drizzled down my legs. I needn't worry Papa. The deserter had died in that lake, so I wandered back to the Madelonnettes Convent from which I'd run away.

I could see the questions in her eyes, but instead of insisting on answers, she took me to a quiet room far on the opposite side from everybody. When I threatened to tear out her eyes for touching me, she brought me a bowl of soup and silently, with her calm gray eyes, watched me eat.

The man with the sack over his face had taken all that I had, and all I really wanted was to press my knees together. *Keep pressing.* Sister Josephine urged me to talk, but from that moment on, the man with the sack caused my mind to rattle about like a stone in a cage.

She drew me up a heated bath, pretended that type of luxury was for girls like me. Waited as long as she could to tell Mother Superior that I had returned to share their meat.

Now? Sister Josephine's grown impossibly still, her white hair whipping in the air frantically. Her head is bent. Praying. She's accepted what will happen, but shouldn't she be putting up a fight like Charlotte told us about, like Joshua's army?

Someone in the audience is clapping. Children punt a ball, which bounces off a headless statue that looks like it's been Guillotined. The people—they've grown weary, though a trio of National Guardsmen are fast approaching. They shout, pointing at Saint-Just's unsanctioned use of the Guillotine.

A bony woman's shaking a fist, a dog barks—*won't stop barking*—and spotting the blue uniforms of the National Guardsmen, Saint-Just opens his hand with the rope. "Good-bye, Mother! Say a prayer for me!"

What is he saying?

Wooden posts groan. As footsteps clatter up the staircase of the scaffold, robed girls weep.

Metal slides on metal, and there's a *humph* as the blade sinks through the neck-bone of my fair Sister Josephine.

Sans-culottes frantically remove my chains as National Guardsmen surround and shackle Saint-Just—*shouting*—for wrongful use of the Guillotine. *Stand down, citizen*, someone brays. Another Girondin leader. *You have no authority.*

The heavy clouds release, and rain spits as I limp toward my one true ally. Curses pepper me from the crowd, but they're of no consequence. They're little bits of mashed up larvae.

The platform grips my shoe. My other stockinged foot sticks to dried blood from another killing. Wind tousles midnight hair against my chin and prickly teeth. Sister Josephine is a collection of bones and skin stuffed inside a too-coarse bag of clothing.

Her fingers are warm but inflexible like twigs from a young tree.

Arms scoop me up in a ball. The tall, lithe figure and the

wood and metal cane laying atop me tells me it's Papa, limping and carrying me away from the ghastly Killing Machine.

I am too numb to make out his words, but they are there, impossibly low, comforting. He holds me to his chest, his silken cravat my only balm as I weep. He marches down the wooden stairs as I cover my eyes, mentally burying my one true ally.

there was a time
i dreamt of the person i might have been
the person i wanted to be

where i studied moths
pinned patterns
peered through
a monocle for studying

purchased cabbages for the poor
handed them to little ones
who were hungry

assisted Papa
with surgery!
helped rotten girls
almost as rotten as me

there was a time
i dreamt of the person i might have been
the person i wanted to be
but only

when
i was near
sister josephine

24

GABRIEL

SOMETHING PRODS MY BOOT. In the back of my mind, I think it might be Carvell come to offer his land one final time, but instead the gangly *sans-culotte*—Antoine—who patched me up earlier stands over me. Same drooping hat, same striped pants, same coat with too short sleeves.

"You dead?" He prods me with his bayonet a third time.

I try to open my mouth, but I feel so sluggish, like I've had a fever for days. I raise a hand before letting it slap to the wooden floor in a heap. *Mon Dieu,* I am so weak. My leg's as heavy as a bale of hay. My head is like one of Père's assistants pounded spikes into my brains. Regardless, the poor sop needn't point that musket at me.

Throat sticking like I haven't had a drink in weeks, I mutter, "Don't you have somewhere to be?"

The boy sets the tip of his bayonet to the wooden floor. "Not when you're bleeding."

I glance around, lost as to his meaning. The room is torn to bits. Gunpowder lies like a layer of dust over abandoned papers and broken crates. A hole the size of a *palais* tears open one wall. It's a miracle I'm still alive, not to mention in one piece.

The young, freckled *sans-culotte* rests his chin on the butt of the gun, staring at me.

I'm not sure how I've gained his attention, so I ask, "Saint-Just tell you to look after me?"

He, Antoine, shakes his head, hat flopping. "I wanted to be sure you were okay."

Now, the days' events have been somewhat of a whirlwind, but wanting to be sure that a bourreau is fine is a rare event, indeed.

I consider asking him if he has an eye on my job—that's why he's helping me—when he finally shrugs like the secret's not worth holding onto, anyway.

"You helped *mon père*," he says.

I have been accused of doing many things. Of tying a rope too loose or tying it too tightly. People have screamed that my Patients asphyxiated too early. Once, I didn't wait long enough for the Assembly to order the torture of an inmate. Another time, when I cut someone's hair too short, their loved ones said I was guilty of "butchering."

Needless to say, "helping people" is not exactly my forte. He must have me mixed up with someone else. Perhaps Henri. So I grunt and try to sit up, which only has my leg screaming like a legion of needles are digging into me.

It's embarrassing to have him witnessing my pain, so I mutter, "Maybe *you* hit your head."

Antoine bends down and grabs me by the back of my shirt. "There's a doctor not too far from here."

I would fight, but consciousness is a slippery beast.

～

*B*irds twitter, purple gourdon flowers comb Père's fence, and I am limping. Please, don't let Père already be taken to the Conciergerie.

The Good Samaritan, Antoine, eases my arm off of his shoulder as I grab hold of *mon père*'s metal gate. "You're sure you don't want me to help you the rest of the way?"

I take the axe from his other gangly hand, nearly missing the handoff but I catch it, just in time. "I'd rather explain things to Père my own way." If I am not too late.

"You'll visit the doctor again in the morning?"

I nod this time. Maybe not the doctor where he took me, as Père would have a conniption if he saw the rats and the condition of the instruments the doctor used, but my family's physician, probably.

The boy sighs like he would have to content himself with how little he's been able to help me, so I lay my hand on his shoulder. End up grabbing a clavicle like a chicken bone instead.

"If it were not for you, I would be dead."

He shrugs, smiling a little at my mistake.

I take in his nose's smattering of freckles, the way he slouches while he stands, and the complete and utter sameness he has with all the other *sans-culottes*—and yet he's not as bloodthirsty as the rest of them.

I let my hand fall back to my bloodied leg and begin to open the fence to search for Père without alerting Antoine to my worries. I stop in my tracks one final time. "Who was your *père*?" He says I helped him, but the only way I spend my time is by buying quicklime, holding up heads, and driving the tumbrel for my family.

The boy scratches the back of his head beneath his floppy hat and says, "You held his letter."

At first I think of Henri's letters, but then I see an old Patient who cackled at my jokes which weren't even amusing. *Hold it to my cheek, won't you?* the old man begged.

Antoine explains. "You gave *mon père* the one thing he wanted. I didn't get it to him until he was *en route* to his execution, so he didn't have time to read what I wrote before he died that day."

I hadn't realized his *père* hadn't been able to read it. If only I could turn back the hands of time and insist all the executioners stop so he could have the time to read.

I look to the stony ground, wishing I were better than he believes. I could ask what he wrote to his *père*. If they were close like *mon père* and me. But I do not deserve these details, nor do I have the time. The National Guardsmen could, even now, be on their way. So I murmur what I always say. "*Je suis désolé pour tous vos soucis,*" while trying not to think of the fact that Tempeste echoed those same words back to me.

The young man takes up his musket, readying himself to leave. "Better for him to die at *your* hands than that Jacobin, Saint-Just's, yesterday."

His boots clomp the earth as he turns, and my own heart is clomping. If only I had woken sooner and helped Tempeste and the others instead of lying unconscious in that factory. If only I had told Carvell not to come to my home and let on to Père about what I had been dreaming. But I am being selfish in my concerns; my family, as yet, is alive. And, according to Antoine, Saint-Just's plan all along was to murder Sister Josephine—something about past vendettas and her being too controlling. If that was Tempeste's good friend whom she spoke so fondly about in the caves, I am truly sorry.

At least the Assembly has locked him up—according to

Antoine, anyway. As of yet, no one uses our Machine without the proper authority. And while it pleases me that Saint-Just is behind bars, there was a time when matricide was punishable by death, and not of the quick and painless variety. I have an ancestor who once dragged a boy by horses and cut him into pieces—four to be precise—after slicing up his intestines like spaghetti.

Sometimes I miss the old days.

I pause, unsure whether or not I should take the time to replace the axe before *mon père* sees. A trivial detail, but, for him, it would be one less worry. It's been nicked and damaged in so many places, it may not even be in good enough condition to use. Blood stains the handle, and, though over a century old, it's the first stain, because we always clean our weapons following a beheading.

I'm just nudging open the gate, hoping against all hope that Père hasn't been dragged off already, when a low voice cries, "Son?" There's a thud like he's just dropped a pile of wood to the earth, and he's cursing. No doubt he just dropped a healthy-sized log on his toe.

Boots slap the earth, and before I know what's happening, he's rounding the corner and engulfing me in arms so powerful, he's smashing my rib cage. His eyes are so anxious; he hasn't looked at me like that—ever.

I, too, am stifling a sob. "You are here." I smell his greatcoat, which smells of blood and quicklime, as always. "You are here." I hold onto his shoulders, willing myself not to cry. "I hadn't—I didn't mean—"

Père's hooded eyes are watering. "Everything be okay."

Still, he doesn't release me, his massive arms like the boulders of Stonehenge securing me in place. I didn't inherit his size, nor his throaty voice, but I did inherit the

Sanson circles beneath the eyes. Everyone has them. Even Henri.

When I was a boy, I asked Père if Sansons were cursed, because all my ancestors bore these. Père laughed in his throaty way. *Oh, no, my boy. We bear those marks because we bless this city. Some people would enjoy killing, but we? We lessen their pain.*

Of course, I believed Père to be a madman, for he often told me to club Patients' fingers harder, make them scream louder, to give the show the *sans-culottes* sought. But that day, Père took me to the stocks in the marketplace and pointed at the widest hole where the head belonged. *We are trapped in our vocation,* he explained, *and every few years, we must prove we are worthy. But once we've retained our commission, we ease up any way that we can.* He patted the wooden top of the stocks, proudly. *I built these myself, and if you were to measure, you'd find that the holes for the head and hands are bigger and closer together than the others in our country.*

At the time, I couldn't understand why he was so proud of widening a few holes. We asphyxiate people to death. Torture them for money.

But now, after this little ordeal with Saint-Just, I cannot help thinking that maybe, just maybe Père is right. He did instill in me a conscience where I feel horrible for killing. I have made mistakes, but I do not feed on death the way Saint-Just does. The way Marat seemed to enjoy the massacre of those priests.

At last, Père squeezes my shoulders one final time before settling those dark circles on me. *Have you changed your mind?* His gripping eyes plead, but how can I explain that I never meant to leave in the first place? That I wanted to, but now there is no earthly way.

He looks so hurt, so aged. I try glancing away—to our

half-fallen down shed, Henri's laboratory where he stores the concoctions he mixes from dead men's organs. *Ça me saoule.* But even now, Père's mature eyes plead, *Talk to me.* Just like the one and only time Henri and I came to blows, or when I accidentally dropped the bag of quicklime we use to ease the smelling of bodies and speed decay.

I want to tell Père why I left—that I was only planning to be gone for a few hours at most. Of my adventures with Tempeste. But he wouldn't understand, and I shouldn't have abandoned him in the first place.

So, gruffly, I raise the axe, pointing out my thievery. "Sorry I took it without asking."

His meaty jowl frowns as he takes in the blood stains. But then his gaze falls lower to the wrapping round my leg. Again, his worn, aged eyes plead, *Talk to me.*

A crow pecks at a pile of sludge on the ground, and a wind chime tolls through the stinking breeze. I cannot speak. It is all so very complicated, and none of it would instill his confidence, which I have striven my entire life to obtain.

It isn't until he's settled me before a fire and placed a glass of brandy in my hand that I find a bit of comfort for the first time in weeks. My toes smolder from the fire, and I almost believe I never left in the first place. But then the fire's tendrils are like her wild hair, and I can see her large, doomed eyes. The way she bites the side of her thumb when she's considering something. The too-high set of her chin— so annoyingly imperial and almighty.

Père stokes the fire, golden embers glistening. Ash floats like ruined feathers to the ground, and he replaces the poker, his dark green greatcoat fluttering slightly as he moves. "Was Carvell's land not to your liking?"

The brandy in my mouth sours as I shift painfully in my seat. "I did not go to Carvell."

Père leans against the mantle like he at long last has me in a cage. "He told me of the cabbages you wanted to plant. The chickens you planned to raise."

I adjust my knee, because cabbages and chickens are the least of what I had planned in the beginning. I'd wanted to purchase cattle, too, but knew it would be a very long while before I had the proper funding. I would start small. With pear and apple trees. But Père would not wish to hear any of this. He would want to hear of how I've had this great epiphany. *Never mind, I cannot believe I ever wanted to leave!*

Père's wide face falls in shadows. He stares into the fire as his throaty voice lilts. "Has it been so very awful working with me?"

It wasn't about working with him. *Non*, not a single day. I would express that, but then he would try to be more cheerful just to comfort me. He would offer to pay me more, and, with the debts we've racked up, I could never accept that kind of charity.

I toy with the neckline of my blouse, thinking of the basket full of heads, of the sheep heads, newly severed, too. Of the blood I wrung out of my cravat after giving it a thorough washing before creaking up the stairs, unsure of how to look Mère in the eye when she asked about my day.

She hardly leaves upstairs. Shuts herself off with her old texts and tea. I cannot blame her, for I can barely handle what we do in this family.

I tug on my cravat, because it's nearly black now, which only reminds me of those catacombs enshrouding Tempeste. Is she mourning the loss of Sister Josephine with her own père? Will she fare okay?

"I *know* our job is dastardly," Pere says. "Sometimes I have to drag myself out of bed just to perform my duties." His otherwise stately voice hitches up a few notches, though, when he adds, "But when Carvell came knocking at my door, I didn't know what to say. Gabriel? *My* Gabriel?" His voice croaks, and he waves his hand in the air the way he taught me to perform on the stage. "He wouldn't openly betray his family. That's what I thought." He lowers his voice, nodding to an opened letter sprawled out on the writing desk behind me. "Until I read your last correspondence with Henri."

He folds his arms, massive biceps bulging.

If I admit the truth, that I've yearned to leave my entire life, he'll throw me out. Say he wishes I had died instead of Charles that day. But I couldn't tell him how much I've desired this when he's being so forgiving. He could have thrown me out the minute I showed my face. I've heard of sons being disinherited by their *pères* for doing less.

"What about the Conciergerie?" I fidget with my bandage, not entirely wanting to know what he has to say.

Père collapses his powerful body in the wing-backed chair beside me. It's like being seated beside a bear who will always have the jump on me. He stares while I reach for my glass, which has me setting the glass down—which is blasted slippery.

"Now that you're here," he sighs, "we needn't fear such things." But he draws silent, like there are things he does not want to say.

I reach for my violin, because I must do something with my hands, but my fingers slip over the strings. Maybe he's wishing Henri were here, who's always possessed the gift for making us cheery. I know I wish that, anyway.

I'm just clutching my instrument's neck when Père lays a meaty hand on my forearm. "I have long known that you do not possess the stomach for killing." His massive chest heaves, and I think he's about to censure me. Instead he says, "Perhaps it is time for you to leave."

He doesn't want me? I know I'm being infantile to think such a thing, but it would probably be best for me to go if that's how he feels, anyway.

But the love and concern pouring from his large hooded eyes isn't a show. I *know* Père loves me, so I misunderstand his meaning. His suggestion is exactly what I've been wanting, for years, for him to say. But it is wrong. Ill-timed. I could never abandon him when he could be locked up in the Conciergerie.

"I've gotten by without you." He shrugs his monstrous shoulders as if he doesn't possess a single care. "The last couple of days."

Perhaps he's tired of me. I've overvalued my aid. "But the Conciergerie..."

"You needn't worry about the Conciergerie," a cheerful voice, a bit like mine, launches from the doorway.

As if we're in a play, Père and I look up to find a military-coated figure hunching in the stark center of the doorway. Chest puffed out, his jaw flexes as he purses his lips in a perpetual tease.

My breath catches in my throat.

Henri.

25

TEMPESTE

CHEESE WAFTS THROUGH THE AIR. Rain spits as I stare at the door where I often met Sister Josephine. The porch is wet *cold* and all I can think about is the way her eyes shined with disappointment when she saw me holding the axe over the bourreau. The handsome bourreau. Memories can be crippling.

My throat's as raw as my feet. My ears ring like I've been sitting too close to shooting. I do not remember the last time I was able to sleep.

Charlotte, re-clad in her tight-fitting caraco jacket and striped muslin skirt, perches on a bench next to me, and I have yet to decide how to take her constant attentions. She's looking up at a window—a window from which we once sat behind on a pair of chairs at a table strewn with letters written in Latin and Greek. The nuns told us to transcribe them, and when I showed little aspiration, Charlotte transcribed all of them, the ambitious thing.

"I need to tell you something," Charlotte says as a burly man bumbles about, setting up a produce stand of cherries.

Only now do I spot the red rings from crying round her eyes. I am not the only one who has lost much lately. "Sister Josephine founded the Girondins, Tempeste."

"No, that isn't her." I cannot think of the true founders, but they're rattling around somewhere inside my brain."

"She's a cofounder." Charlotte insists, leaning closer. "Anonymously."

But what she says doesn't make sense. The clergy are not concerned with politics the way most citizens are in this city. Of course, Sister Josephine was on alert ever since the Jacobins started pressuring her to denounce what she believes, but Sister Josephine is—*was*—concerned with helping the beggars, *the least of these.* Not the public workings of the Assembly.

From the other side of the latticed window, a pair of girls traipse by, and when I see their dark robes in the middle of day, I realize they are in the perfect place for being tutored, for becoming whatever their leaders want them to be. But isn't it a stretch, to think that children can make a difference in this city?

Holding out a child-sized apple, Charlotte says, "Sister Josephine would want you to eat."

I do not know what to think of what Charlotte's saying to me, but her offer of food only reminds me of the porridge Sister Josephine gave me when she was forbidden to do so. And her subsequent lashings, but Charlotte is remorseful for spilling that secret, so I forgive her, I think.

Even so, my stomach scrapes for the apple. For rotten pears, eggplant, juicy meat. But I do not deserve these dishes. Sister Josephine is dead because of me.

"We've converted several others to join us," Charlotte says, nodding toward the girls through the window again.

"We go from door to door, proselyting our message of peace. Most do not wish to hear it, but you'd be surprised by some of the headway we're making. Aristocrats, homeless, bourgeois. Though peaceable, we believe in defending ourselves. Our message knows no social hierarchy."

Her words of "peace" and "messages" has me sitting uneasily. "How many members do you have?"

"Several hundred."

Not too shabby, though that's only a drop in the water— we have half a million souls in this city.

"You have seen what the Guillotine does," she adds. "The people use it as a weapon now to kill *more,* not lessen pain."

I grab the edge of the splintery bench beneath. How Maman would roll in her grave.

"It makes death quick and painless enough, but you've seen the growing lines in the executioner's square. Jacobins are sending more aristocrats. Trials are becoming less and less a matter of innocence and guilt, and more of a nicety. It's why we need you, Tempeste."

But this Girondin faction isn't as perfect as Charlotte claims. I once woke up in a pool of my own blood after being struck by one of her darts. Before falling unconscious, I'd swung for my attacker, accidentally slicing my own wrist with my paring knife. My wrist had been bandaged, but not tightly, and I had nearly died from the loss of blood. I'd been so weak that I had to crawl my way out of that abandoned alleyway. Charlotte doesn't know, probably.

Is that how they recruit their other Girondin members? With wounds and treachery? No, they go *door* to *door.* I've never felt so exploited for my supposed "gifts."

Besides, Sister Josephine never wanted them to treat me that way. I am soiled. A ruined attempt to stabilize a prodigy.

I examine Charlotte's prim and proper posture, the way she effortlessly sits with her legs crossed. She's a silent, commanding queen. Why is she bothering with my sullied ways? "Why don't you lead?"

Charlotte's stoic face crumbles slightly. "I do not possess your leadership qualities." She pulls a bone-made ring from her skirt pocket. "The girls require someone with passion, someone they don't get bored observing. I've—" her voice hitches, "—attempted to run a few meetings, but they do not feel any great urgency to listen to me. Besides..." She holds out the ring. "Sister Josephine wanted you to lead."

The last time I accepted that white piece of jewelry, I ended up throwing it to the ground in the warehouse while dozens of priests and nuns were murdered outside. I can still hear their wails when I walk down the dark alleyways. Papa wanted me to stay with him. He even tempted me with those muffins with the lemony zing, but I am not ready. Charlotte must have doubled back to retrieve the ring just for me.

I want to thank her, but am not convinced yet I will accept this jewelry. Doing so would mean for good. And I am not sure if I'm ready to take that step. I am so flawed. So cruel and angry.

"Liberty means boundaries," Charlotte says, and I know she's trying to convince me to accept the ring, but need she be so condescending *all the time*? I'll give her a boundary or two—all the way from the top of her curled head down to those quaint white pumps housing her feet.

But my threat sticks like candy. I'm a waterlogged grizzly bear trying to swim for fish on the opposite side of the *quais* when I manage, "The National Guardsmen locked Saint-Just away?"

Charlotte watches the convent's window, where a pair of

girls are exchanging books. I wonder what they could be reading. Her voice cracks as she murmurs, "The Hospice de la Salpêtrière."

The hospital for the criminally insane. There was said to be quite the epidemic of smallpox there last week.

The cherry vendor is just hanging his final bunch of cherries when Charlotte digs her fingers into her pocket, paper rustling.

"I have something you need to read." Surreptitiously, she wipes a tear from her cheek.

I hadn't realized that she, in fact, was crying. I am deplorable at mourning with those who mourn and weeping with those who weep, but in spite of this, I ask, "Charlotte, are you okay?"

"You *have* to know," she chokes out. "Louis is not the sort of person I thought he was. I met him when he was a budding poet, before he even joined the army."

I stare at the letter in her hands. Perhaps she was thinking with her eyes instead of her brains. No, that is not fair. I had been fond of Saint-Just as well—until I realized the wool he'd pulled over my eyes.

"He told me he wanted a better France." She wipes her splotched face with her shoulder, which is so uncharacteristically Charlotte, I nearly pat her knee. "He wanted *Liberté, Equalité, Fraternité*. He actually—" she hiccups "—once told me he wanted to marry me. He wanted to have *children*, Tempeste. He never hinted that Sister Josephine was his *mère* or that he would do—" she glances down at my legs.

My voice is as flat as a lake. "He stole my virtue."

Tears fall from her typically mechanical eyes. "No one is sorrier than me."

I watch the cherry vendor's canvas roof flap its skinny, pale fabric in the breeze. The way a terrace, full of ladders, should be painted, and cleaned up some day. Ivy crawls like a hungry parasite over one side of the convent just like the Jacobins and *sans-culottes* are overcoming this city.

Glancing down at the letter in her skinny fingers, I succumb to a question. "What is it you want me to read?"

She lowers the letter to her pleated lap as if it is heavy, because she is right—she *should* be sorry, but she also shared her cloak with me when I hadn't bothered to bring mine in after I left it outside the convent in the rain. She took the blame for talking during lessons when it had been me.

The things regarding our friendship I had conveniently forgotten are many.

The letters scribbled on the paper's surface are the pained, shaky scrawl of Sister Josephine, and I am hit by a warship, rowing.

My heart twitches. My hand slips, for I do not know the context of what I read. I scan the long, cramped page, feeling my heart lodge sideways. "When did she write this?"

Charlotte's gaze falters from the apple on her knees. "She didn't say."

I swallow the knot in my throat, unable to comprehend what she would want to tell me. Did Sister Josephine know her end? Saint-Just said something about her "believing him" finally. Did he always promise to kill her?

In response, Charlotte gently sets the ivory, bone-made ring on her side of the bench and stands up to leave. I should say something to her, but do not know what to say.

So I curl up over my letter, tucking it under my chin as I pull my feet from my wooden shoes and brace my stockinged feet on the ledge of the bench. I am tight *tight*. Ready to read.

My dearest Tempeste,

If you are reading this, then I have gone to our Lord in Heaven, but do not mourn for me. I am at peace. My concern is for you, *for by now you know my greatest sorrow. My son does not understand liberty.*

Even when young, Louis struggled with listening to me. He wanted to be allowed to do anything he wished, and when I objected, he grew violent. Hurt others. Held a fascination with fire. Any object capable of harm.

I do not believe one is born devoid of conscience, but some spirits have a greater affinity for darkness. These spirits wrongfully believe it will make them happy. It pains me to say it, but such is the case with my Louis.

I thought if I looked to God more in my life, Louis might eventually come around. Be like his père, *who died before he was three. But the more I taught my son, the more resistant he became. He did terrible things to animals, to children. I felt overwhelmed, so I sent him to a reformatory. I followed him there to be nearby. I know the nature of God's plan is to allow every soul to choose for themselves the choices they make, but how is it that my son could be so devoid of conscience? Actually* enjoy *pain?*

From the shadows, I helped Monsieur Brissot and the Rolands found the Girondins, because I quickly saw that Louis wasn't the only one in our country suffering from this fever of bloodlust. Paris needed a faction, unlike the Jacobins, that understood the true *nature of freedom. Many believe locking up or killing the nobles and clergy is the only way to go about this. But if we harm anyone dissenting from our views, we are as guilty as our enemies.*

I was careful to hide the fact that I began the Girondins, but Louis eventually discovered me. I didn't know about his and Charlotte's attraction until they'd long been courting. Naively, I hoped Charlotte had succeeded in doing what I had tried all along—instilling a goodness in Louis. I had my doubts, including terrible night terrors, and if you are reading this, I was right to fear all along.

I still remember the day you wandered into the Madelonnettes Convent. With that wild black hair of yours, you even looked like him. I do not know the particulars of what happened when you returned to us the second time, but I could surmise with the way you held your knees. May your attacker pay a thousand times for what he did to you. Please tell me it wasn't my son.

As our time together grew longer, I saw how you could be one of our greatest sources of inspiration. People look to you, Tempeste. They cannot help it. I know you try not to draw attention to yourself, but you are hard to forget. You do not play by society's games. After you ran away, Charlotte and Louis told me you were one of their projects. When you returned, I knew I had been foolish to allow them to commence your training. I believed they were teaching you how to dress, how to hone the manners one should have to gain the favor of high-ranking Jacobins, but they were cutting you; tricking you. This was never my intention. Louis used his charms and charisma to convince Charlotte this is what we needed for our city, but this was his deep-rooted Jacobin extremism. I wasn't certain of this until one of my Girondin daughters caught wind of Saint-Just's intentions outside Marat's factory. I shall conclude this letter before facing my son for, what I suspect to be, the final time.

Charlotte must be mortified that she fell for his antics. She thought she was serving the better good, but she let her adoration for him blind her vision of what is right. I believe I am speaking for the both of us when I say that we are so, so sorry.

You are a natural leader, my lamb. You have this iron stamina unlike any I have ever known. You believe your independence somehow makes you mad, but I've seen how you feed the beggars when you believe no one is looking. You pressed eucalyptus into my wounds. You care nothing for monies nor treasures, and how refreshing it is!

Now, though, it seems that I am gone. Louis has ridden this world of me just like he always promised. Please do not think you are like him. You are nothing like him. You are capable of turning the other cheek.

Charlotte is there when you are ready for her friendship. I know the two of you have a past, but you must forgive her for her mistakes. You and I both know we all make plenty.

We are on the winning side, for we fight for our country, our kindness, our liberty. Remember the Lord's scripture, when he said "Inasmuch as ye have done it unto one of the least of these, ye have done it unto me" and "Feed my sheep"? Think on it, my daughter.

Yours,

Sister Josephine

Tears splotch the ink. She didn't know it was Saint-Just who did that to me. But reading this letter, she would have me let him do it again because she said *turn, turn, turn the other cheek.*

No, that isn't right. She would never have him do that to me. So what does that command, her command—*God's* command?—really mean?

26

GABRIEL

WITH HIS NAVY-BLUE GREATCOAT, brass buttons, and musket swung over one shoulder, my brother's never been more fetching. He pulls the musket over his head while Père and I gape.

"You came!" Père's raspy voice curls past his music stand, oval portraits, and a hurdy-gurdy.

"You *knew*?" I cry.

Père holds up a meaty finger. "I thought you abandoned me."

To this, Henri, in his half high-pitched, half throaty voice laughs, carefree. And his laugh is so loud, so utterly absurd, I'm laughing, too. It's all a bit sudden coming.

With a clatter, I attempt to set my violin on the maroon carpet (or the much nearer wooden floor shall do nicely) before bounding for my brother, whom I haven't seen in months. I trip over a chest that's somehow hopped in the way, and I'm very nearly crashing through a supplemental table when Henri stretches out his wide arms to catch me.

Grasping me by the collar, he chuckles. "I see not much has changed."

Blood warms my face. Still, he knows little of my journey with Tempeste—of the other people I've harmed along the way.

Regardless, my brother and I throw our arms around each other's wide shoulders and slap the way men do when they come of age. Henri's hair's a little longer than mine, and a slight tear breaks open the back of his blue uniform's seam. His military-issued belt buckle jabs me in the waist, so I flick the whimsical plume of his bicorn hat.

He clubs my hand out of the way. "You *know* you want one of these."

His blow was sure, but not unkind. In truth, I might want one of those military hats, for then I would stand for something besides the badge of executing.

The hinges of Père's chair squeak as he strides toward us, wrapping my brother and me up in a hug not unlike the one he gave me when we were outside. He pulls us so close, his powerful chest crushes mine. What a sight the Master Executioner of Paris and his sons must be.

Eventually, Père releases us, and taking Henri by the yellow caps of his shoulders, he says, "They let you come because of my tumbrel injury?"

Henri respectfully bows his head as he pulls off his bicorn hat. "Seeing you up and about is such a relief."

I search Henri's rounder cheekbones, the fair hair he inherited from Mère's side of the family. His soft slouch of the shoulders, which aren't really even slouching anymore.

"You've toughened up." I slap the yellow tassels adorning his shoulders. Graze.

He wrinkles his regal nose. "*You* smell like you've bloody well bathed in a latrine." His muddy eyes shine with laughter, though, and I should have known that months on a battlefield would never steal my brother's joy. Mère and

Grandmère always said Henri has the sort of smile that brightens the gallows and pillory. Even with my bandages and exhaustion, his very presence makes me stand a little lighter on the balls of my feet.

"Come. Sit!" Père gestures to the pair of chairs where we had been sitting. He strides to the far side of the room for a tall wing-backed chair and drags it to our grouping.

Henri beams before clomping over to the chair Père recently vacated. I do not move at first, because the sight of him, well, it bloody well makes things go blurry. He is *here*. In fair shape. The both of them are. They never were nor will be locked up in the Conciergerie.

"How did you get away?" I trot after him, grazing my wound on the corner of the writing desk. *Bon sang!*

Henri grabs the snifter of brandy and pours himself the glass Père had been using, but Père simply sits back in his chair as contentment erodes his face.

After taking a long drink, Henri shrivels up his pale, cheerful face. "That brandy's bloody awful." He smacks his lips three times before shrugging his tasseled shoulders and downing the entire glass.

Slamming down his glass like a veritable Viking, Henri appraises Père, who's gone silent, observing things. "You've healed, then?"

Père straightens his shoulders, looking down on my brother in mock disdain. He lowers his voice so that it's never been gravellier. "Never underestimate a Sanson, boy."

It's all I can do not to reach for my violin and play a rift of Nardini. With Père and Henri here, and the brandy warming us, it's heaven—or how I imagine it would be. But Henri's eyes are skirting to Père's, and the silence lulling between them tells me something's going on. Are they hiding something from me?

Père's grandfather clock chimes twelve times as Henri's glass clinks. He pours himself another generous glassful as my leg twitches. What I would give to find a stick that could itch my wound, which, no doubt would garner a lecture from Père.

Henri eases back in his chair with a great flourish and says, "There is something I would like to say." He chuckles, and his hidden amusement is quite lost on me.

He swishes the amber liquid in his glass, purposely building the tension. He looks to Père, who nods, and at long last, Henri takes a deep breath before saying, "I have a proposition to make."

I lean forward in my chair. Perhaps he has other ideas for appeasing the people? Twin Guillotines? He's found safe passage for exporting the king: The people *will* wish to execute him, but perhaps he's found a safe place.

Wordlessly, though, Père pulls out his pipe, and I have an inkling that this has little to do with the king.

"I have a few stores of money," Henri says, and I do not know why he's boasting of this to me.

His eyes twinkle in pleasure, and I'm just beginning to frown when he says, "I mean to give them to you, Gabriel." He purses his lips and pins me with his eyes as if in a tease, only the murky depth residing in them proves he is not teasing. *Non*, he is serious, *oui*! He actually means to utter these things. Père, too, is puffing on his pipe, and this is the unspoken matter I had foreseen.

"But it is yours," I blubber, accidentally kicking my violin, which slips to the floor with a screech. "You went to battle. It is *your* money."

Henri chuckles now, and, *mon dieu,* he's a bloody Père Noël, threatening to bring an embarrassing number of gifts on Christmas Day. Casually, he crosses his cream pantaloons. Seeing as I've just about gone numb in the brain, he mutters, "Why else do you believe I bloody well decided to join the French army?"

The fire crackles and spits and none of this is right. Everything is too warm, too perfect, too cozy. Henri and Père are here. I, as of yet, am still in one piece. Tempeste wanted to slice me apart. She should have, really, but maybe I still am passed out in that decrepit doctor's house where Antoine nursed me back to health. Maybe I'm having a reaction to the medicine he gave me.

"You are not real." I'm lurching from my chair. Landing, somewhat landing, on wobbly feet.

Père shakes his head, black curls flopping. "You have nothing to fear, Henri—Gabriel. We have long known that you do not have the stomach for killing, so Henri proposed an escape."

"But the Conciergerie!"

Henri rises to his well-measured feet. "Will you stop blubbering about the Conciergerie? I have a plan." He glances to Père, who is just about as somber as when he told me about the impending Killing Machine. "But it is not without risks. Now." Henri shoves me back into my chair. "Sit for a while and listen to me."

27

TEMPESTE

THE BOWL in my hands is full of porridge like little mashed up larvae. My stomach twinges, but this is precisely what I mean to bring.

Papa and I trample past a shopkeeper sweeping bits of glass, a broken bust of an old king, and it isn't until we pass an old ottoman littered with blood that I mutter something about the deserter, but I'm not really even paying attention to my own muttering.

Papa looks like he wishes to ask me what I mean, but a wildebeest twists apart everything I'm seeing. Everywhere I look is blood and it's Sister Josephine.

Papa's fingers tighten round the gold-plated hilt of his cane—I'm sure it pains him to see me even more insane—but he must be here. Be my support—if I am to survive this folly.

My little gargoyles, Maximilien, Claude, and Philippe greet me from atop my favorite tower, and I wink at them because they are here to witness my escapade.

Papa clears his throat like he's long considered sending

me to a hospital for brain softening, but he manages in his low, polite way to say, "How do you know this prisoner, exactly?"

I stare down to the lumps of porridge as an old woman slops the contents of her chamber pot out a window, narrowly missing me. "He killed Sister Josephine."

Papa's wonder is as palpable as the tree bark I resorted to chewing when I couldn't find something to eat. He searches my face, but I have washed it, scrubbed it clean. I am as presentable as he could hope, in my silly tiered frock and gloves that are surprisingly velvety.

My taffeta skirt rustles as we drift past a cemetery, and Marat spoke of Maman being the cause of that heap of bodies. But I shut my eyes against the gravediggers currently exhuming bodies to make room in the overcrowded cemetery. They dig past the headstones and ferns, only to dump them in the catacombs where the bourreau helped me.

I scrape my boot on the edge of a hay cart after accidentally stepping in a pile of horse droppings, and I'm reminded all over again of why I plucked up that Girondin ring.

I've been a mite too careless. A portion of porridge slops down the front of my skirt's pleats, and the image is *most* settling, so I smile like I've just taken a lick of sugared plums. "That's better." I sigh. And lick the lumpy substance from my gloved fingers, feeling much more at home—*almost* like me.

Shaking his white-wigged head, Papa reaches to take the bowl, but I bat his hand away. Steady the mess in my hands with poise.

"Did you know Maman was a noble, Papa?" I say.

Papa's step falters as he turns to face me. Tears prick his

eyes, and I think I may have given him chest pains. He settles his gaze upon a nearby street bench, hobbling over to sit in his exhausted, proper way.

Papa opens his mouth as I saunter over to join him, but clamps it closed once again. His face is tired. Dry. I wish I had Marat's balm to smooth that worried face, for I am the only one who's supposed to suffer now in our family.

Papa watches a flock of pigeons settle on a street lamp nearby. He studies them as they peck the corpse of a rodent before looking away. "She made me promise never to tell you." Avoiding eye contact, he adjusts his cane.

A rosebush hugs our park bench, thorns reaching precariously close to the knee-breeches of his feeble legs. I think he might make a simple complaint, but he reaches past the menacing thorns and pets one of the petals like it's a human being. "She was so beautiful, Tempeste."

Because I've often stood and looked at her portrait—even stealing in at night at times—I proudly contend, "She looked like me."

Papa nods, and I am pleased he sees me this way. "Did I ever tell you of the time I took her to a greenhouse and she identified every last plant, down to the genome and species?"

I scoot closer to Papa just to feel his body heat, the warmth from his shining waist jacket, his knee breeches, which perfectly house his limber legs. Gabriel—the bourreau— held a fascination, too—for music. Probably other things. "Maman was obsessed with plants."

Papa chuckles.

"Do you think love should always make you happy?" I blurt. I do not know why I am asking.

Papa raises his en-humbled gaze to look upon me, and

the sorrow I find lurking there makes me feel guilty for once spreading the seat of his carriage with horse feces. For the nights he begged me to come home. For the hours he wasted attempting to deliver my favorite books to me.

That is to say, he *must* be startled that I should bring up the topic of love, indeed!

"Your relationship with Maman was troubled." I lift a shoulder, proving I am not thinking of me. And, thinking on my horrid stepmother, I add, "You always get along with Élise."

Papa chuckles. "That is not true." He pats my hand— once—and I do not jerk back, because he is *mon papa* and he loves me. "We have our spats at times. In fact, when she prattles on about the failings of the cook, I get quite angry."

"That is not what I mean."

The timbre of his voice trembles. "But that is love, *mon cherie*. Wonderful and overprotective—" He glances down at his cane, embarrassed, and I know he's referring to the way he loves me. "Full of faults and holes, too." A bee whisks so close to him that he leans away from it to allow it to roam free. Softly, he adds, "You should experiment with that kind of love sometime."

I stiffen, because I have felt *love*. How else would he describe my love for Maman and Sister Josephine? And, the bourreau—well—he cares for me and I do not know *how* or what that specifically means, but I have felt that glimmer of emotion when the bourreau looked at me. When the world grew still while the *sans-culottes* danced round us in the cave.

I've felt the protective regard from Papa, too, and most keenly.

While I am not, by nature, a sentimental being, there is

no denying Papa's love for me. Once, at the Palais de l'Égalité, he purchased for me a parasol I didn't like, and I stomped on it, claiming he should have used the coin to purchase a coat for a starving boy.

Parisian onlookers stopped and stared—looked at me.

That child is out of control. What a tantrum. Detain her, s'il vous plaît!

Because Maman had been jailed that day, I did not know how to deal with the anger building inside me. All I knew was that *mon papa* was already courting someone else. Even though he once begged Maman to marry him, and she would never entertain the idea. And then, all of a sudden, he was courting a proud, snippety woman named Élise, while Maman—*Maman*—was in a dungeon in a location I could not ascertain.

I snapped each and every one of the umbrella's boning. Smeared it in the dirt, because it might make Papa cry.

Instead of winning the approval of the other shopping Parisians, Papa plucked a flower—one of the fine lilies in the garden borders of the Palais de l'Égalité—and because he had never done anything so improper, I quieted my antics immediately.

Shoppers stared. One of the women whispered behind her hand that *mon père* was a terrible parent, indeed. A policeman frowned at the stolen flower Papa gave, so I closed it in my young fist and held it like a dying birdie. Dragged that broken parasol home, suddenly pleased with it, the entire way.

Bowl laying treacherously on my lap, I reach past Papa's fancy knee breeches and snap off a rose head and thrust it on Papa's proper lap, because this bowl is evidence of a very different thing. Still, a flower for Papa is the only proof I have for showing I finally understand his infuriating need to protect me.

"I am one-half Colette de la Croix," I whisper, thinking of his lily, which I pressed in the pages of Rousseau down in the caves. "But I am also exactly one-half Joseph-Ignace Guillotine."

28

GABRIEL

"Bottoms up." Henri hands me a vial of thick green sludge, and he is real, but at this point in time, I'm not entirely sure I want him to be.

Tentatively, I take the thin glass tube beneath my fingers, relieved I do not drop it to the stones outside the Pillory. The Patients are getting restless inside the tumbrel, grappling for hands and moaning as if the Place du Carrousel, now the Place de Révolution, will give them a reprieve.

Still, Henri has offered me an escape, and I am loathe to overthink matters, so I throw back the thick green liquid as it coats the back of my teeth. It tastes like piss and mold all rolled up in a cow patty.

My stomach clenches. "You are a grub-shite," I say, because the reality of Henri's little concoction is not any better from what I imagined I drank. Ground human intestines mashed up with who knows what Henri has chosen to poison me. For science, Henri's dabbled about with human tissue that shouldn't be his or mine.

I am still fighting the urge to vomit when Henri checks the locks on the tumbrel's gate, though I properly fastened the chains. The latch itself is bent—from landing on Père the other day—but it shall work well enough until they can get it replaced. We've chosen a different horse, though. Justice has been moved to the fields for a little reprieve, and it's a miracle Père's already waiting for us at the square, like he was never injured in the first place.

"When you lose consciousness," Henri says, taking the filmy green vial from me, "your pulse will be so indiscernible that no one will believe you could still be alive."

"I'll drop, dead center, on the scaffold." I cannot believe I'm saying such things.

"After you hold up the head, *oui*. No one will doubt that you've suddenly been overcome with a fit of Falling Sickness —especially considering all the heads you've raised."

I loosen the cravat round my neck. It's getting a little bit hard to breathe.

"Just be careful, brother, not to fall until *after* you move away from the edge of the scaffold. Last thing we need is for you to actually die today."

I blush, for I do not know if he's heard that I nearly fell from the stairs while accompanying a Patient. That I may have died at Tempeste's own hands for what I did in earlier years to assist this family.

"Do I dare ask?" I nod toward the vial he just tucked in his breast pocket, my throat still chalky. "Where you first tested this monstrous remedy?"

A Patient's hand reaches through the tumbrel rail for Henri's pistol, which is currently lodged in the front of his belt. Henri swats at it, happily. "You may not." He gets this faraway look in his eyes. "*But—*" he holds up a meaty finger, like Père, but decades younger "—suffice it to say that it works." He pats my head like I'm a child of three. "Don't you worry your pretty head about such things."

It rather frightens me to think of my brother, traveling abroad with his contraband of potions—snippets of liver, large intestines—with the whole of the Prussian, Austrian, and French armies at his back, asking questions regarding what he's doing. But, then again, Henri has a way of warding off curious looks or stares. He cracks a joke, tells a story. He performs, per the Sanson way.

Still, a modern-day Savior, he is willing to shear his profession out there for *me*. He's willing to fake my death and take my place.

My throat's all tight again, and last thing I need is for him to see me curled up and crying, so I stomp around the horse to take up the reins.

"They'll think I'm dead." I say this to myself as I climb to my seat, thinking of the loud, fearless shriek of Tempeste. Of her tiny, powerful body. Henri tromps after me, too, so I imagine the dirt under my fingernails as I sow lettuce and pumpkin seeds. Water dribbling from the well Carvell just finished digging . . .

My brother's muddy eyes scour me, like even now he might outsmart me. He needn't say what he told me last night—how he worked hard to obtain an officer's income to saddle me up properly. And again, how Père always hoped I would stay, but allowed Henri to follow his dream to indulge me. It's a wonder that Père's fine with faking my death, but as he put it before tucking away his pipe, *Better for one of my sons to escape our trade.*

He once dabbled in Henri's macabre sciences, too. As did an entire line of my ancestors, a topic which makes me want to hurl the contents of my breakfast on the street.

Even so, I trust Père, and I trust Henri. It shall be an adjustment to live apart, but they are giving me a life I never thought I would have. Carvell's land is only a few miles away.

So, I snap the reins, and I expect Henri to watch me roll away, but he jumps up and joins me on my wooden bench. I haven't "died" yet, though, so he should be riding out to rejoin his regiment, strictly speaking.

"I'll jump off before anyone sees me." He rolls his muddy eyes. "Now." He interlocks his fingers and dramatically cradles the back of his blond head like we're off for a Sunday drive. "Tell me about this girl you're mooning over."

I shoot him a suspicious glance, for I've never said anything about Tempeste.

"Oh, don't pretend that I'm not right." He swats me with a glove. "Only a devastatingly handsome young woman could be responsible for such a long face."

I shoot him a look that's somewhere between helplessness and sheer and utter loathing.

He barrels out a laugh that's long and hardy. "Oh, this shall be good." He chuckles some more. "This shall be good, indeed!"

29

TEMPESTE

TEN THOUSAND PRISONERS are housed in the Hospice de la Salpëtrière. Ten thousand of Paris' scariest beings. When I was a girl, Maman used to tease me that I'd get locked up there if I didn't listen to Papa better. *You'll have nothing to eat but rats.*

Maman could be humorous in her own way. She never lived with us, but Papa always encouraged our weekly walks —far away from where she worked. He used to come along, too, until she threw a watermelon at him and called him names.

A long time ago, an escapee from this place traipsed past me in the market while I was pilfering some cheese. She grunted and swung her arms like a monkey. At first, I believed she was doing this for attention, but then the guards found her and prodded her with bayonets and she squawked loudly. She foamed at the mouth and writhed on the ground. I felt sorry for her madness. Sorry that she had to return to this place.

Now, though, arms snatch at us through iron bars as our footsteps echo in the narrow stairway. Stone walls provide little heat. Someone sweeps the floor, and dust floats like miniature faeries.

When an arm grapples for *mon papa*'s cane, I shove it back so fast, the prisoner shrieks. Papa's eyes stretch wide at my response, and I find myself changing the subject.

"This won't take long," I say.

Someone's barking, chains somewhere *clang*, and perhaps I shouldn't have brought him with me in the first place. I didn't want to go alone, but Papa shouldn't have to see the foulness of this place.

The bowl is brittle and cold in my hands as a guard examines shackles hanging from a wall like bones of a ghost. Beneath my caraco jacket, bruises mark my wrists from when Saint-Just chained me, but that isn't something Papa should see.

Wiping the sweat from his brow with a laced handkerchief, he opens his mouth to say something when a rat scurries beneath the shallow bars of a cell and over his feet. He sucks in a breath, and I think of Maman's warning. *You'll have nothing to eat but rats if you get locked up in that place.* So I drop a spoonful of porridge for the rat just in case Maman is watching. Papa's gentle eyes strain with worry, but he wouldn't understand if I tried to explain.

We enter a gallery of wooden boxes clustering together, each large enough to fill a body. I think of coffins standing, but that's not what they are. They're wooden boxes for living people—for solitary confinement.

Coils of rope drape over bloodied tables, and a low-hanging cobweb marks our hallway. I'm just ducking beneath when a shrill voice cries, "*Give* me!"

A shadow of a woman half my size tries snatching up my spoon, and I jerk it away as I spot sores covering her body. Smallpox. We shouldn't be here; we should hurry. I would love to share, but the guard who let us in clubs her fingers with the back of his musket. She squeals and backs away.

"Make your visit quick," the guard says. Coins jangle in his pocket from Papa's and my bribery. It's the only way we could convince him to let us inside. If another guard doesn't like the sight of us here, they will make us leave.

More arms writhe like worms through the bars, and I think of sailors on a ship, the ocean *swallowing.*

The stench is as vile as any chamber pot; worse than any opened cemetery. I press my gloved hand to my nose when I see a lone man watching me.

The filthy window behind him barely shines enough light to see, but I can just make out his dark hair, and his face—sneering and mud-streaked.

I could say I'm looking in a mirror. Someone feral reflects back at me, but that is not how I look anymore. My skin, my hands, though clammy, are clean.

What would it be like to visit my rapist? I asked myself before coming. *Offer food to the man who murdered my one true ally?* I contemplated grabbing him by the hair and, with my favorite paring knife, splattering apart his brains. *Sometimes one needs to make people pay.*

I thought about doing what the Sansons do and find a mechanism for smashing apart his feet, but the Sansons do not do that anymore. An odd irony.

Saint-Just's dark eyes seem to devour me.

> *his fingers poke and prod my neck*
> *my hips*
> *other tender parts of me*

He ran his tongue down my neck. Like cockroaches crawling down my body. I tried grabbing his fingers and bending them backwards, but he was too agile; controlled everything.

I felt the whimper of my own womb. Felt the loss ringing inside of me.

I still feel it, and I cannot believe I've come here with nothing but porridge and *mon papa* to assist me.

Saint-Just moves away from the wall, and my tongue is a rock. I've grown lame. Papa, unaware of the full extent of what Saint-Just has done, fidgets with his cane. "Is this the young man, Tempeste?"

The bowl in my hands is an arrow I'll plant in his brain. A cannon I'll stuff down his blouse ka-*booming!*

I grip the bowl's porcelain edges. "You probably haven't eaten today."

Saint-Just tilts his head to the side just like when he wore the mask over his face. "If *this* is your solution to Paris' problems, we're even more doomed than I believed."

I hear the Guillotine blade *falling,* Sister Josephine's blood smattering across the wooden beams. I close my eyes to push away the image.

Turn the other cheek.

Papa clears his throat like he'll rid himself of the dank air and disease. "My daughter has brought you food, young man. I believe she deserves a *merci.*"

Heart thuds. *Thud-thud-thudding.*

My voice, a breeze.

Saint-Just opens his arms just like he did on the scaffold that day. He tilts his head. "By all means, then."

It's the *exact same words* he used when I wanted his approval for destroying Marat's printing press. I'll smear the porridge in his face.

He prowls closer, like he means to pull the bowl away. I

know he must be hungry, but this is harder than I ever dreamed.

Moans echo from an adjoining cell. Across the hall, something is scratching, and Papa raises his cane like he means to defend himself and me.

My fingers are petrified pieces of wood. Icicles too frozen for moving. He is foul. Deserves to die more than anybody.

I'm just about to tuck tail and run when this calm washes over me. A tiny wave of comfort, the smallest whisper of peace. The hairs on my arm stand on end. Papa is watching, and I do not do it for Saint-Just, or Papa, or even me. I do it for *them*. Maman and Sister Josephine.

I bend down. My hands, like they're not even my own, cooperate.

I set the bowl on the stony floor like I want to share with the man who took from me. And, shoving it beneath the metal bars of the cage, I know I shall be vastly different from this day.

Half the porridge slops to the ground. Doesn't matter, though, for he prowls, is down on bended knee, and tears into it much like a wild boar might tear into a baby.

30

GABRIEL

I MOUNT the scaffold for the final time.

I'll write of this in my journal. Of how the blood splatters like water down the stairs of the scaffold, all the way down to my shoed feet. Of the raw eggs smashed into the twin posts of the Guillotine. I'll write of this day, that is, as long as our plan turns out properly.

There's a million things that could go wrong. My pulse could still be detected. They'll know I'm really awake. What if, because of my incompetence, the Assembly decides to give our vocation to another family?

Non. With the people, Henri is even more popular than me. If I'm gone, they'll never be happier.

Lurking near a font twenty or so paces from the garden of the Tuileries, Henri winks. Ever the ample source of optimism, the bastard means everything to me. I try not to think of the holes, with shovels, he'll soon be digging. I force myself to not think of what a pair of extra hands could do to lighten his chores, but he is doing this for me.

My head spins sort of like a nearby child is spinning,

and now Henri's waving a gloved hand to an old friend like he's the bloody queen.

I shake my head. Things had better go as planned, or Henri's in for a whipping for not immediately rejoining his brigade.

The Patient, an articulate woman with spectacles, clutches my arm as we mount the scaffold as if I'm accompanying her to a soiree.

"I don't quite know myself without the length of my hair," she says in a schooled voice. Her short outcrop of auburn hair bristles in the breeze.

Père chopped her hair as he always does—before the execution, back at the Pillory—though I am a bit surprised that he didn't ask her to remove her spectacles. Perhaps he doesn't want two blind fools traversing the stairs of the Guillotine.

My arms already feel as though they've been imbued with salt. My head—well, my vision's even worse than it is typically. Banners and towers and ropes and birds spin dangerously fast. So instead, I look past my bandaged leg, which twinges with pain, to my black pumps while the Patient sinks her brittle nails into my arm.

We reach the top of the stairs of the Guillotine.

My leg smarts, but I cannot send her off without knowing her final story.

"What is your crime?"

Her ribboned skirt slaps her stockinged legs. "Teaching the rightful place of the king."

I look down to the banners and blue, red, and white flags, which boast of our grand rise to liberty. But this is not the way it should be done. Liberty does not mean harming those who do not believe as the majority believes.

"You believe our king should reign?"

The woman nods, the loose skin beneath her chin doubling in size. "There shall be a return to the monarchy." For myself, I might agree with her, but what of those souls like Tempeste? Who live in squalor because the aristocrats do not share the bare necessities?

The Jacobins get away with killing priests and nuns, so I shouldn't be surprised that they're putting targets on governesses and tutors who teach the old ways.

On the street below, maybe fifteen souls stroll between squashed bales of hay. A pile of burning armchairs and curtains suggests there might have been a greater ruckus last evening. National Guardsmen surround the scaffold in their spritely uniforms, bayonets pointed like readied fireworks to the sky. No doubt they're here to ensure the people don't interfere. That Père and I faithfully discharge our duties.

A baker, his money pouch bouncing too freely about his waist, balances a full tray of lumpy loaves, though no one buys a thing. The people may have locked up the king and queen, but the vast majority of France is still poor. Would that I lived in America, where there are foodstuffs and land enough for everyone. Where social status means nothing.

The wind rustles the woman's chopped hair round her spectacles, which have the King's initials inscribed on the frames. I imagine a fan in one hand, a gooseberry tart in the other, offering treats to her pupils who answer her questions the proper way. Now, though, she's looking down on the crowd with an overwhelming sadness, but she's accepted her fate.

"*Vive la révolution!*" someone cries, pelting the woman's matronly chest with a rock the size of my fist. The woman buckles, but I help her again find her feet.

With shaking hands, she carefully removes her spectacles before placing them in her pocket's silk lining. She lays down on the platform, unaccompanied. I watch with a sweeping sadness at the lace of her petticoats mingling with the blood and rose petals of yesterday's festivity.

A bird caws. It's my conscience struggling against my rib cage. But this is the last time I must do this.

The woman starts to sing a song—a simple one she must have taught the youngest of her pupils—just as Père pulls the rope, and the blade falls.

The singing ceases.

I'm a mechanical windup toy, stooping down to collect her head, which blurs to look like seven—three. But I must show the whole of France what they expect to see. Her head's as slimy as the gills of a fish. Blood drips like tomato sauce down my knuckles and wrist, so I pretend I'm holding my hurdy-gurdy.

I'm on a carousel of children's horses, spinning amidst red and blue and swirled candy. As I lift the head high, a few people clap happily. I stumble toward the edge. I must do this before I collapse in the middle of the scaffold, in a heap.

My shoes, as if bound together by a rope, manage to comb the distance. The scaffold's wood creaks, and I lift the head so high, I'm practically connected to sunbeams.

The dead woman's neck still drizzles like honey, and I look up because, my, she is bleeding profusely.

She blinks as if in surprise, as if she's awake, and I jerk.

Off the scaffold, to the bayonets pointed straight at my face.

31

TEMPESTE

CHARLOTTE TAKES MY HAND, which is warm and slick with perspiration, for this is new territory. Not just because we stand high atop the Paris Observatory with its octagonal towers and precarious stairway, but because the Girondins are *here,* and they're looking at me.

"This is Claire," Charlotte says, introducing me to a squatty girl with square cheeks. A bandage clutches one side of her face, and I know she must have been there when Saint-Just took Sister Josephine. "She has several contacts," Charlotte adds, "through her parents to the Assembly."

She pauses in front of a girl so small, so dark, I doubt she's much older than thirteen. "And this is Cécile."

The girl's dark skittish eyes nestle into mine, and I've seen her before. Huddled over a fire? Roasting chestnuts?

A pair of girls hover together toward the back, each of them wearing slings. Another props herself up with a crutch that used to be a cane.

"Bernice and Sébastienne should be on their way," Charlotte says, assessing the girls, and I know Charlotte's avoiding the fact that some of her Girondins are attending an execution down below, but she needn't avoid the topic of "the bourreau" with me. I'm healing from what he did to Maman.

Not entirely.

I detest the fact that I've been unable to purge the image of his beautiful, lying face. When we stood before the lake in the catacombs, my favorite place in the world, in that smart greatcoat of his, he earnestly said, *Tue es belle.*

Can I believe him? *I want to believe.*

I'll take a forgetting serum. Commit myself to the Hospice de la Salpêtrière, because these tangential thoughts of mine are nightmares. The worst kind of plague.

I peruse the black-robed girls who look to be in number about four and twenty. I recognize most of them from Saint-Just's charade.

Ravens flap round cathedrals, settling on little alcoves and a crucifix the *sans-culottes* haven't managed to dismantle as of yet. "All of these girls," I murmur, "were welcomed by Sister Josephine?"

Charlotte lowers her dimpled chin to her kerchief. As of now, she looks to be quite capable and ordinary in her mob cap simply embellished by her blue, red, and white cockade. But what no one realizes is Charlotte tucks her emotions inside—does not wear them on her sleeve.

"All of us have taken oaths," she explains. "To protect our city."

I look down to the ring I finally managed to slip on my finger, which is too heavy and shiny. No longer do I smell of cow dung or the dank of the cave, but of soap and the shiny new tendrils of hope Papa won't stop lavishing on me.

I twirl the too-big ring on my middle finger before settling it back on my thumb, where it fits almost perfectly.

Still, I do not understand the hard, crude edges. "It's such an odd shape."

A raven flutters not a foot from our grouping. "It is in the shape of a compass," Charlotte explains.

I squint in the growing darkness, trying to make sense of the jagged edges, but the symmetrical outline jutting to the north, south, east, and west proves she knows what she's saying.

"We have members in the Assembly." She strolls through her girls, which are a bit worse for wear, but quiet, at least. "We are the younger faction. We support, eavesdrop, and provide supplies to our more experienced side."

I nod, though I'm tempted to complain. She lathers me with platitudes that I am meant to lead, only to reveal that this is the step-child to the *real* Girondin faction. If I have learned anything, though, it is to trust Sister Josephine. "The compass reminds us that north is the way?"

"It is easier to be less vengeful when you're living for others, Tempeste."

I bristle, but she is a testament to the fact that she has a point.

Charlotte whisks her long robe to the telescope on the outermost edge of the roof of the building, where one edge of the octagonal tower comes to a point. The sun dips below the horizon, shooting out hues of bright oranges and pinks. "Look through the telescope, please."

I'd like to tell *her* where she can look—domineering, Charlotte, *bossy*—but I didn't come here to argue nor complain. So instead, I think on the scrawled note left by Sister Josephine, and the bourreau and his winsome, clumsy ways. Might we have had a future—of cleaning fish? of gathering birdseed?—if he hadn't stolen Maman from me?

I peer through the telescope, a telescope not unlike the smudged, dusty one in Papa's office. But this one is bigger and points to brighter things. I absorb the shiny balls of gas. Yellow and white and gray.

"We are the stars," Charlotte whispers, "fighting through the clouds to soothe our wounded city."

Through the lens, a white one's so close, I could snatch the front of its face.

"As Girondins, we fight past the scorching sun and depressive clouds that persecute the innocent. Do what we can to provide mercy. And peace."

Charlotte's speaking of the relief we can provide from the Jacobins, and the starving, repressed *sans-culottes*, who would kill anyone standing in their way.

The girl I noticed before, the short, young one, Cécile, pulls out a multi-barreled pistol, a dagger, and what might be fifteen quills, along with a roll of parchment, which dramatically unfurls at her feet.

The girls on either side of her inadvertently giggle, but when the girl crouches to retrieve her supplies, a flash of a vision washes over me. I *remember* where I saw her. She robbed the unconscious National Guardsmen who I clocked on the head weeks ago, because he was about to wake. Before that, she held out tins—any way to support herself— to find a way to eat.

She's just standing again, rising to her feet when her gaze flicks to mine, and I stare past her hood, which is torn down the center and frayed. Threads hang in her charcoal eyes, and she hunches like with one wrong word, she might stab me in the mandible with hidden knives.

I quite like this newfound protégé.

Footsteps clatter up the stairwell, so I tense for my favorite paring knife in my sleeve, when a duo of girls in black robes present themselves atop the roof. I must say I approve of everyone's dark clothing.

"Something is wrong," one of them, the taller one, says, and I doubt whatever they have to say can be all that life-altering.

But the shorter one steps up to Charlotte and whispers into her ear as one of the ravens' ragged feathers swoops nearly into my face.

Charlotte's typically even eyes startle as she covers her mouth with her gloved hand. "Your executioner," she cries as my stomach pitches. "He died."

~

J'm one of those ravens—flying, swooping down the curved staircase—past broken rubble and smashed apart carriages. I plow, headfirst, into a line strewn for washing and snatch a tunic out of the way. Shove it to the ground. Keep flying.

Wind and rain clog, pelting my eyes. I had been perfectly groomed, but hair whips its angry tendrils round my face. Nose runs. I make a noise.

I must see where he fell. Must *see* for myself. The bourreau falls off the scaffold and a bayonet slices apart his brains like two stretched pieces of clay?

I *refuse* to believe.

My movements are loud and, like him, clumsy. My raven's feathers pump and sway. I wipe a string of snot from my nose, and run, glide. I *did not* give him permission to leave!

I was supposed to kill him. Squeeze his lovely face. Tell him, *Tu es beau,* in return, because he was beautiful in so many ways. I have spent these last four long years working to avenge Maman—to protect my family—and I've hated him for doing the same thing.

I am a hypocrite, the *worst* attribute of the aristocracy.

He did not die. He did not die. He let that mangy old woman in the catacombs cup his butt-cheeks!

I duck under drooping banners torn from the Tuileries, remembering how he touched my hand and arm and face and coals sparked inside me. And when I reach a row of stately hollies, all I can think of how he also wanted to loom, to hover near me. This is something no sane man should ever crave.

My wings break. I fall to my knees. The rope he threw over Maman was what he needed to do to feed, to support his family. The rope's corded fibers asphyxiate.

He cinched it tight.

the devil's hammers tap the gallows

I cannot breathe.

the devil's hammers tap the gallows

I shouldn't care that he left me.

the devil's hammers tap the gallows

He is gone. And I detested him for his love, even though he retrieved that axe. Even though he sang for me down in the caves. When he saw my painting, my rudimentary Dans Macabre, he said, "*C'est bien,*" like he believed it. Lies should never be so sweet.

No. *No.* The bourreau never loved me.

∾

*T*wo things I know of a surety:

I am a Girondin. And the bourreau loved me. He is gone. *Gone.* We were supposed to go to the opera— once!—after I smashed apart his brains.

I stare at the ruined rose petals smeared into the mud at the mighty scaffold's feet. Abandoned gloves and scarfs swirl between mud and sand and there's *too much* going on in this city.

Raindrops *splish-splash* my robe as I bend and sniff a circle of blood like a blood-hound would do. I stick my barren fingers in a faint pool of blood. *His* burgundy.

A rush of wind ripples over my cheek as a figure approaches, crunching dead leaves. He's a man—*the bourr!* —not the bourreau. For he is of stalky build and fair coloring.

He wears the sharp lines of the military dressing, and I consider ducking and flying away, when two eyes the color of dirt find me.

"Are you Tempeste?"

32

GABRIEL

TOAST CRINKLES as I swipe it with the butter blade. My head bloody well hurts, but at least I survived. Thirty-two stitches and a barrel's worth of laudanum later, I would not recommend dive-bombing off a scaffold of fifteen feet.

"And THEN—" Henri feigns surprise, flexing his neck muscles at the table where we eat "—I bloody well threw the trout in the bear's face!"

Père laughs as Henri imitates the bear, catching a fish with his teeth.

"Never again," Henri pledges, "will I fish alone in my skivvies."

I have missed the gist of the story, but it is a pleasure to hear Père and Henri getting along so famously. They'll garner enthusiasm and respect from France, the *sans-culottes,* everybody.

I am not feeling sorry for myself, *non, non*, indeed. With the old, broken chandelier curling toward us from the ceiling, and the hardboiled eggs, scones, and preserves—it's a wonder the cook was able to cook at all, considering the wretched condition of this place.

The remainder of Henri's generous gift still jingles in my pocket, and I'm reminded for the tenth time that I am able to sow cabbage and potato crops in the spring.

Henri's moved on to recount another, slightly more rakish story when I am able to contain my gratitude no longer. "I shall never forget what you've done for me."

Henri stabs a hunk of pork before sticking it between his teeth. "Just don't grow radishes. I *detest* radishes." He burps, then laughs a little at Père's chiding eyes. "*Excuse moi!*" He taps his lips with a folded napkin, ever the contradiction of refinement, Henri. "What I don't understand is why you felt like you needed to take a bloody head-dive!"

I glance up, a little more than embarrassed. "It turned out all right." Still, I stare at the folded napkin on my lap. "When did you know? That I wanted to delve into farming?"

"When *you* wouldn't take interest in my fine potions from the deceased!"

I glance from him to Père, not fully grasping his meaning.

"I would be dissecting a perfectly good spleen, and you'd be over there—" he waggles his fingers in dismissal, "—counting out pumpkin seeds."

"Or carrots." Père nods. "I knew you wanted to leave, but timing, son. Timing. All that sneaking around with Carvell before Henri had settled everything?"

Henri raises his large arms in agreement. "You may have *thought* you were discreet, brother, but we've been planning this for half a decade."

My heart squeezes as I avoid my brother's gaze, because he's done too much for me. Through the filmy window, I survey the swampy lot Carvell sold Henri in my name. The plum trees, the blackberries that grow here without any need for cultivating. With its perpetually murky soil and nearness to the coal factories, the land may not be *quite* what Carvell promised, but the fact that I own it is far more than I had ever hoped. Still, I will miss Père and Henri. "You know I am only a few kilometers away."

Père holds out a newspaper for Henri. "Are we certain we shouldn't have purchased this place?" His wide fingers tap a block of letters, and I recognize the advertisement— land covered with trees, which the owner suggests will be ideal for the lumber trade.

Henri bats a paw. "Too close to a Jacobin Club. Besides," he says, jabbing another wad of pork with his fork, "Carvell had another buyer and was good enough to sell this one to me."

Ah, the other buyer the prostitute warned me of weeks ago. I raise my glass in a toast, which I very nearly spill, but secure my fingers round the brittle glass surely. "To Père." My voice hitches. "To Henri."

Père raises his glass to meet mine as Henri breaks into a grin that could clobber a Jacobin and clinks his glass into mine.

The sound of galloping horses has me lowering my glass.

Père leans forward in his chair to look through the window, spindles groaning. "Did Carvell convince you to buy his broken-down plow, as well?"

Henri scoots his chair back. "Perhaps he's brought one of his daughters—the one with the pegged leg."

I have no clue who could be approaching, but Père strides to the window, his long, green greatcoat flapping as he strides. Henri snatches up his bicorn hat.

"Might it be—" he leans across the top spindles of his chair "—Tempeste?"

He—did? *Non.* Absolutely *non.* "You told her I'm alive?"

He does this obnoxious head bop he does when he slaughters me in cards. "I *may* have mentioned where you might happen to be."

I clamber to my feet, and my head-dressing nearly plummets to my plate. I look up at him as he smiles like the twin of Bonaparte. *Dieu, aide-moi.*

Henri waggles his eyebrows before grabbing his gloves and exiting through the back door.

So I glance to Père. If it is her, she might have come here to murder me, and I haven't exactly told them everything.

"You are a louse," I cry after my brother as a well-built maroon carriage slows on our drive.

A door swings open, and a tall, white-haired man angles his long legs to the driveway. He's clutching a cane. I've seen him before in the Place de Greve when he comforted his daughter. Joseph-Ignace Guillotine.

I stumble to my feet as my chair crashes unceremoniously to the floor. It takes me a few tries, but I settle the chair back on its legs. "Don't let her in, Père. She's come here to kill me."

Père chuckles, oblivious to just how truthful I'm being. I told him of her fighting skills, true, and her recent loss of Sister Josephine, but as for my leg injury, Père only knows I got that when we were with the *sans-culottes* down in the cave.

I adjust my head wrap and am patting down my pockets in case they're turned the wrong way when Père says with utter amusement, "My, my, my. She *must* be something."

Through the window, Monsieur Guillotine reaches up to help a young woman from the carriage. My heart's in my throat as a feminine figure emerges. Her curls are a little unkempt. She's meticulously dressed in a plumed hat, tight-fitting caraco jacket, and printed cotton kerchief. Though she looks an awful lot like Charlotte—I might not recognize her on the street—I spot the scowl and cynicism perpetually covering her eyes. Tempeste.

Monsieur Guillotine reaches behind her to shut the carriage door, but she rounds on him and slams it closed before he has the chance to say "mincemeat."

Père laughs round the rasp in his voice. Settling his top hat on his curls, he says, "I can see the appeal."

I nod, already feeling filleted.

The old family Bible, which *mon père* offered to me before leaving, lies open on a table in the adjoining shoddy parlor, and I would reread a passage I read yesterday—about trusting in the Lord with all my heart and not leaning unto my own understanding. But the only thing I understand is she is here, and last time she saw me, she wanted to murder me. Not that I blame her, but Père's here, and it could get messy.

Before I can stop him, Père strides to the front door, and I could kill Henri. Perhaps I should have mentioned to him how she very nearly sliced me in half with our family heirloom, but I didn't want to prejudice him against her that way. All either of them knows is that I executed her maman, and we had a falling out. Père appreciates simplicity.

The back-door rattles closed as birds flutter about our visitors; pots of ruined flowers line the pathway. I might change my shirt, properly shave, but Père's already opening the door with interest.

"Joseph-Ignace, you brought your daughter for visiting."

I would crawl in a hole, mess with the tea. But she is here, skirts rustling, and Père's extending a hand.

Monsieur Guillotine shakes it wordlessly.

Père looks Tempeste up and down the exact same way *mères* do to scrutinize potential brides for the family.

Though my *mère* has long shut herself away. Gaunt Tempeste lifts her chin as if a relative of the queen, and Père's eyes twinkle. I told him she had a little more spunk than your average dame, and the gleam in her eye backs up my story. Her shoulders are not so much regal as tight, though—like she'll always be ready to strike.

Père must find the way she carries herself altogether endearing, for he smiles, opening the door wider for the family.

"Come in," he says. "Please."

Monsieur Guillotine steps forward with the tap of his cane, and Père squeezes the base of my neck, pushing down my collar. "No doubt you've seen my son, Gabriel, performing his duties."

Tempeste's eyes are so round and amazed that I'm a little uncertain whether she wants to slice me in half or smother me with her monstrous kerchief.

Monsieur Guillotine loosens his cravat as his gray eyes flounder over me. Ah, yes, he's seen me many more times than once in the Place de Greve. "Quite often," his low voice pitches, "actually."

Bourreaus aren't typically considered a fine catch for any bourgeois young lady, but I doubt Tempeste's had many suitors, so I hold out a hand, wondering if he'll insult me the way Saint-Just did that day when I offered to shake.

"It's a pleasure to meet you," I say.

Monsieur Guillotine's cold fingers find their way in my hand, and I almost feel sorry for the man, for most respectable households do everything in their power to avoid the Sanson family.

"What has brought you to this neck of the woods?" Père asks, a bit too jovially. With the garden tools still piled up outside, we're obviously not ready for visitors, and no one in France is really supposed to know I'm alive.

Monsieur Guillotine, however, seems to be at a loss for words. In truth, he did propose our Killing Machine, but it has not gone as he has expected. Everyone knows how he pleaded with the Assembly to allow the creation of the machine in order to offer softer blows to the criminally charged. To lessen pain.

Père examines Monsieur Guillotine's tight shoulders, his shaking fingers as he grips the arm of Tempeste. Lacing his voice with as much care as he's ever used with me, Père says, "Perhaps you'd like to see the topiaries."

While I am quite certain Tempeste's *père* has little interest in seeing the clipped and pruned perennials in this marshy land, the white-haired man bows his head as if this is just what he had been hoping. "That would be lovely."

Still, he does not loosen his grip on his daughter's arm. Knuckles whiten as he gives a squeeze, but Tempeste rolls her eyes. "I'll chop off both his hands if he tries anything."

Monsieur Guillotine chortles like he's trying to swallow a piece of squid that he never wanted to eat. Père lifts his head and laughs hard—I don't believe he's laughed that hard since Henri first returned from the front to share his war stories.

The bumpy floor groans as our *pères* leave, and Tempeste looks at me with this tortured, muddied gaze. And I don't know why, but I find it hard to look back, for it is rather hard to know what she's thinking. An oily stain marks the front of her gown and I state the obvious, because I am a rake. "You mussed that up rather quickly."

She glances down at her gown. "I have talents for embellishing things."

It is a reminder of what she did to Marat's office—how

she felt splattering the walls with piss and ink made the decor "lovely." My chest swells in pride, because I'm a madman falling for a girl who detests me.

Has she come to testify that I took her *maman* for my own personal gain? We already went over that. *Oui,* I did. For my family. Perhaps she's here to lament the fact that I'm not dead, and promises to tell the Assembly.

It matters little, though, for I have long decided to take upon myself whatever cross she extends to me. "How did you find us?" Then, because I'm an idiot, I add, "It is nice to see you, Tempeste."

She stabs me with her eyes. If I but knew why she was here today. As *mon père* and Monsieur Guillotine converse over a mostly fallen over holly, Monsieur Guillotine glances up just in time. He traps me with his practiced physician's eyes, and I cannot help wondering if he can see the stains on my soul. Every life I have taken. But he ducks his head like he has no business judging me.

I warm a little to the old man. Is this what France has done to the doctor-made politician who once tried to abolish the death penalty? He would not smile on the name-calling of my schoolmates.

"You are not dead," Tempeste says, as if admitting this is in and of itself a defeat. She adds, "Your brother told me."

I laugh this silly laugh where I sound like I'm far too young and much too deranged, because my brother's gone a little too far this time. Still, I am thankful for his desire to help, as always.

Tempeste surveys the lone painting I brought to bring a bit of cheer to this cramped, musty place. La Magdalena. Tempeste studies the woman's pale skin and naked shoulders, touching her throat where it indents in the same place.

Spotting the family Bible near my violin which rests in

its velvet case, she raises her palms, brows furrowing. It's an act of supplication, but there must be some misunderstanding. The sun's bleached the tip of her nose. The wind ruffles her hair, and my heart pitches, as she's never looked more lovely.

Outside, our *pères* laugh round a misshapen log, and everything is so utterly bizarre, it is as if I'm in a dream.

Her wooden shoes clomp as she crosses the warped wooden floor, and I do not know what to do, so I close the front door. Because *pères*, as well as *mères*, are capable of eavesdropping.

My mind's as blank as the foliage that should be stuck in pots around the periphery, and I scratch my head, causing my head wrap to shift precariously. I secure the rags back in place. "So. You have come here to kill me."

She studies the maroon carpet—another gift from Père, and before that, the king. I would tell her about the history, but as a girl yearning for a republic, I doubt that would instill fondness for me.

Half-melted candles crouch on the wall, their flames highlighting the open Bible beneath. She leafs through the pages like she'll find what to say.

She pauses on a gilded page—of cherubim and a flaming tree—before smoothing her hands on her skirt. I can just make out the outline of a dagger hidden in one of her pleats. "I have come here to apologize."

Before she stabs me. But I do not wish to tell her that she'll need a better hiding place for her knife, so I offer, "We have a few knives in the cellar if you'd like to get started."

She stares into my pupils like she's a seeress, about to prophecy in some way. She can see inside my soul and knows every terrible choice I've made. I dare her to find something that I haven't already tried to mend. She knows the worst of the worst, unfortunately.

She runs her skinny fingers along my mahogany desk—where I've placed every letter from Henri. Her eyes scan my brother's latest letter and his cramped writing. He spoke of needing reinforcements and how the Duke threatens to storm France if we do not release the king. He asked about the usefulness of the Killing Machine and said he already spotted visiting wives of soldiers wearing the contraption as miniature earrings.

If he hadn't helped me fake my death, he would be there even still. Père could be locked up. Henri could be dishonorably discharged from the army.

Tempeste still hasn't looked up, and her long lashes veil how she's feeling. "The king's men murdered Charlotte's family."

I know little of Charlotte, but I know she was as aghast as we were at Saint-Just's betrayal. Henri even heard from one of his friends that she burned all his poetry and political writings. I could ask Tempeste to share their story, but that dagger of hers imprints again, so I murmur, "*Oui.*"

"She forgave them," she says, tracing the ink quilled by Henri. "Chose to run a political faction with Sister Josephine."

She told me that the Club thought she was too much like an animal to let her join. She needn't think on their snobbery, so I tell her, "You didn't need them anyway."

She blinks her long lashes, her impossibly large eyes staring up at me. "I've decided to lead."

I survey her slim figure. Those wiry arms that smashed Marat's printing press to smithereens. How she quoted Rousseau in her sleep. She doesn't boast of her accomplishments, but she doesn't apologize for them either. "I hope they are deserving."

She runs her fingers along the desk like a spider, creeping. "They've a few hundred followers, these Girondins. We must convert more across the country."

I clench my fingers round the side of the desk three—nine?—inches from where her hand lays. If this Club is part of the Girondin faction, indeed, I'm impressed she wants to share the message of moderation with other French cities. It is what France needs. A leader who will fearlessly tell the truth about the tyranny the Jacobins, together with the *sans-culottes* and Assembly, are inflicting.

Further, I would take her hand in my own, tell her of a thought that occurred to me this morning while penning a list for supplies, but I do not want to be slapped like when we were in the caves.

There are daytime thoughts and nighttime thoughts. Daytime ones, wrought with cunning and hope. Nighttime ones of hopelessness and fatigue. And it's like Tempeste's previously forgotten about her daytime ones—her belief in goodness, kindness, charity. I do not blame her for these former lines of thinking. I imagine if I were in her shoes, I would have done the same thing. But if I aim to take upon myself the charge of helping her find those daytime ones again, like leading this Club for Young Ladies, I must shed the final layer. Tell her one last deplorable fact about me.

"I have something for you," I say, throat splitting.

Her eyes narrow. She's unable to believe that I could have anything she would desire. I hardly believe it myself, but I pull open a drawer, reaching past Henri's stack of papers. I pluck up a box—a box I whittled one night when the guilt was too much for me.

Mistrust twists apart her gaze, so I lift the lid. It's right there, and her hand's flying to her mouth, gasping.

When she told me on the hammock that she wanted something to remember her *maman* by, I knew I had the very thing, but it's wrong. Unthinkable that I should have it in my possession still this day.

It is black. Like hers. Gnarled. Her *maman's* braid.

I do not know how to tell her I kept it for myself—my object, my singular trophy—but as soon as I snaked the fibers inside the box, guilt churned to disgust, and I wanted to burn the thing.

I set the open box on the table as my voice shakes. "When you screamed during her hanging, I didn't know whether to burn it, bury it, or throw it away." I knew it was her when I saw her in the Place de Greve those weeks ago, though I tried to squash my memory.

I point at the drawer of the table. "So I hid it."

She snatches it up, running her fingers along the coarse strands of the braid. And I know how it feels—like rope. Like Tempeste's would feel.

She runs her fingers over the strands of hair before taking the lid and settling it closed. "May I have it?"

I nod, unable to speak.

She steps closer. Her gnarled curls brush my shoulder, and I cannot breathe. I would run my fingers through those curls, but I'd rather not be thrown to the sky. Perspiration trickles down my hairline, and my heart slams like a battle-ax clubbing me. A tree branch scratches a window, our *pères* out of sight.

Why has she come, really and truly?

33

TEMPESTE

It is like I can still hear him singing in the cave.

I *remember* how he sang for me. The girls draped them-selves over him like itty-bitty bits of browned up gravy, but I do not care. *Do not care.* Only care about this—possibility.

His shoulders, half a foot higher than mine, are but inches away, and instead of being repulsed I want to know what those shoulders would like feel pressed into me. To touch and not be trapped. To dissolve any final embers of hate.

His lithe arm reaches out for mine, but it's like he doesn't really believe I'll accept him. His head bandage slips again, and his shoulders sag. He reaches a full foot wide, anyway.

I grab his bandage and carefully pat it in place. Snatch his fingers, his calloused fingers, because I must see. But I need control. Need to know beforehand where these calloused fingers will touch me.

He blanches nearly as white as his head-wrap at my grip —I'm tightening—and it feels good to fight back in some small way, but then I see the fear splitting open his eyes.

And I soften.

"I am so sorry." His voice breaks.

He did not kill Sister Josephine. That was the man with the sack over his face.

"Sometimes—" My throat shifts beneath its dust in-lay. "Love is full of faults and holes." *It's hole-y.*

I lift his hand, remembering the time he fought the *sans-culottes* with nothing but candles when he couldn't even see, and stare down at the scars covering his hands from the hot tallow.

What if he touched me in the most platonic place? Where even Papa wouldn't blanch to see?

I lift his hand to my face, graze the edge of my ear, and the touch is so light—

—like dandelions in a breeze.

But it's probably a fluke, so I need to know what happens when he touches other parts of me.

Concentrating, I jerk his hand to the bottom half of my face and close my eyes to absorb the sense of his knuckles bumping into my chin. I know there will be nothing but bones knocking skin, but it comes softer than I imagined. Like river water depositing pebbles on the *quais*.

I open my eyes, and he's smiling like there's some sort of victory, so I slap his palm to the side of my face.

I mean to drop it, but he lingers there. I do not dare to move my hand. Heat emblazons my cheek, and embers of fire shiver up my neck.

I whimper because even my breath has grown smokey.

This is wrong. I am not supposed to *feel* things. I'm supposed to twist his arm, shove his head into a latrine— but I want him to be close to me.

I squeeze his fingers, telling him to do something.

As I wait, I'm placed in a choke-hold of feathers, of itty-bitty bones and wings. Like a bird, I am again stuffed in Medici's cage. Only I care what happens now, ears ring.

Sweat trickles from my brow. The ticks of a pocket watch have me. The portrait of the praying woman swarms about my head, and his boot smacks, crowding my shoe—a black one Papa purchased for me—and I bite my lip, because I could see myself yanking off my stocking and wrapping my foot round his feet.

He grazes the fringe of my dress—fingers a-twist in lace —and I want to kiss, *be* kissed, which is the bloody opposite of all I should be feeling.

I'm black matter smeared in the hardwood. Stubble left on the maroon carpeting, for he traces the pleats of my dress, and all traces of oxygen evaporate from me.

I grab him by the shoulders. Strong shoulders, as the heady smell of the leather from his boots washes over me. My palms are two hot coals, scalding.

He raises an arm. His fingers miss, so I grab his strong, lean hand and slam it against my waist. I would be good and proper, but all I can do is growl, "Kiss me before I scramble apart your brains."

He flinches before lowering his head and aiming to kiss me.

We're two different civilizations, too far away. He's about to kiss my ear, possibly graze my cheek.

So I grab his face and direct his mouth to my lips, hungry.

As our lips connect, our kiss is sweeter than sap from a tree. Tangier than the juice from a nectarine. I want to cover his skin with my mouth, but I'm ashamed, because I did not want this before. He always wanted me. I grip the back of his hair, and it's smoother and tougher than I expected. I twist my fingers in the long strands, because it makes me feel complete.

He grips my hair, pulling it from my scalp, and I may or may not have let out a little shriek.

We're hunting wild boar. He's holding the knife. His boots crackle leaves. He's a blacksmith, forging a sword. *I am the sword. Sparks flay.*

Fingers trip across pleats.

Palms secure round my hips and he is my scaffolding.

Hot breath.

Singes cheek.

I clutch his forearm, fingernails knead.

His blouse bleeds into the stomacher of my caraco jacket, and he's not close enough. We wade in a hot spring. I clutch his cravat; he, my kerchief. His jagged breath is made of madness, and I know he's about to ask me something. Perhaps he wants to talk. Discuss the itty-bitty part of my former desire for killing, but I am a Girondin now, which stands for love, forgiveness, mercy. Perhaps I'll show the girls not as I am, but as I am trying to be.

The bourr—Gabriel's—tone wraps round me like a blanket—warm, snug, sweet. His hooded eyes are round. Doe eyes. Two pools of empathy. My chest bursts apart with sunbeams.

He asks, "Stroll the meadow with me?"

I laugh, because that swamp of his isn't quite fit for strolling, but I thought he was going to ask me something risky. Make vows or promises I'm not ready to make. I clutch the linen of his shirt, though, hungry to stay with him a while longer—as long as Papa will wait.

I expect him to take me by the arm, stroll through the front door, but instead he grabs my hand and tugs me to the back of the room like a boy eager to show off his brand-new pony.

He pulls me, limping, round the family Bible. Past that oval portrait, a music stand, hurdy-gurdies. My plumed hat catches air, flies backward like a sail catching wind. His head-dressing falls, but he lets it slip away.

Our shoes *pitter-patter* across the blanched parquet flooring. My nose twitches at the heady scent of strong, warm coffee. The dining table is a portrait of serviettes, knives, plates, toast, eggs. A fire's aglow in the fireplace.

My arm's just clipping a harp's sharp, slender strings —*brrring!*—as we reach double French doors. Gabriel stops, and I stumble into his strong shoulders, which do not budge nor sway.

When he releases my hand, my heart trips a little, because he's smiling moonbeams. I never thought I wanted him to smile at me that way. But he's building a bridge for us of stone and wood which is surprisingly sturdy.

His cheek boasts a new vertical scar—from the cata-combs, from fighting—and I fight the urge to trace this latest badge of bravery.

When his eyes drift to the wooden French doors, I'm reminded of another time—when we stood at a different door—Marat's office—with a locked chain.

Gabriel—*the bourreau! one and the same!*—must be having the same memory, for he holds his breath for one, two heartbeats. There's a swift rise and fall of his chest before his eyes skirt back to mine, and they shouldn't feel like a warm, sudsy bar of soap running over each and every inch of my already scrubbed body.

He's anxious, which I cannot help but find a little darling. He scratches the back of his pony-tail. Shifts his feet. "Promise not to claw me?"

I laugh, because I'm proud that he knows I'm rather talented at scratching. And then I'm frowning a little, because it's rather unfair of him to ask for promises already.

He waits. When I don't say anything in return, he gruffly grabs the muslin of my skirt and jacket's stiff sleeves and hoists me up to his warm chest, cradling me like an overgrown baby.

My lead-filled heart may have just sprung a leak.

He clutches me. I'm a bird—*not!*—in a cage. I do not kick nor scratch nor bray. For once in my God-given life, I'm content to keep my razor-sharp claws to myself. When he sets me down, eventually I'll teach him how to hunt quail, elk, deer. Use his ears instead of his eyes. I'll show him the bows and arrows I've hidden in the swamps, much like this one, west of the city.

He shoves open the door where sunlight bursts like confetti. My chest glows with tulips and humidity.

We leave behind those holes and faults that stopped me. And I wrap my arms around his neck as he carries me past lavender bushes and finches and cherry trees.

ACKNOWLEDGMENTS

I began this book after Googling "guillotine" and learning it was created for a quick, painless death. To me, it was the image of barbarism. To think how far off I was—in a historical context.

I want to thank my husband for creating the perfect chapter heading images and for putting up with my insufferable dream to publish this book. Thank you, my children, for your questions regarding the guillotine and reminding me that this is a horrific topic! Most especially, thank you, Heavenly Father, for parsing out the way for me to go with this colossal undertaking. You were probably shaking your head when I embarked on this treacherous one.

Muchas Gracias to my partner in crime, Cammie, who stands by me no matter what. *Merci beaucoup* to Vanessa, my fairy godmother and dear friend I'm pretty sure I made up. Thank you also, Cammie for our latest cover for reaching our readers! It's breathtaking! And Tamara Heiner, who line and copy edits like a boss. A tremendous thank you to those friends who agreed to letting me watch your kids, and for you watching mine, so that when it was my turn to be child-free, I could research and write earlier drafts.

Thank you, my early readers, who were willing to take the time and risk to read and review this story. Your faith and support means the world to me. I shall try, but may never be able to repay you for that.

And thank you, dear reader, for completing my effort to share a treasured yet twisty book. Please leave a review if you enjoyed reading.

AUTHOR'S NOTE

The people did, in fact, scream for the wooden gallows to be returned when they saw the efficiency of the guillotine. It was not horrific enough for them. Beheadings were only for the nobility.

Gabriel Sanson, son of Charles Henri Sanson, did hold up heads for the crowd after a beheading. I'm not sure how the real Gabriel felt about it, but I personally can't imagine performing that duty. One day, while holding up one of those heads, he fell to his death—one of the very first facts I learned while researching this story. Henri, his brother, resumed his work. Suppose Henri really did use one of his family's homemade "remedies" to assist his brother in faking his death so he could get away?

Louis Saint-Just was the youngest Jacobin to be elected to the Assembly. He eventually worked (and died) alongside Robespierre. The fact that we hear so little about this young, handsome, bloodthirsty politician baffles me.

Joseph-Ignace Guillotin (back then, the name didn't have an "e") proposed the invention of a painless killing machine when the Assembly refused to abolish the death penalty. The guillotine did spoil his family's reputation which forced many of his kin to change their name.

Charlotte Corday was a devout Girondin who ended up killing the infamous Jacobin, Jean-Paul Marat, by stabbing him to death in the bathtub. (Looks like she spent a little too much time with fictional Tempeste.) Corday claimed that she "killed one man to save a hundred thousand." This was following the fall and execution of all the Girondin leaders. Corday was executed the very next day.

Hundreds of clergy were slaughtered in what later became known as the September Massacres. Saint-Just's little performance was a fictional precursor to what really happened.

"La Carmagnole" was a song the *sans-culottes* sang about the short jacket they wore, or "carmagnole" to celebrate their growing liberty. They sang many songs. Johnny Hallyday sings a fine rendition of "La Carmagnole," which can be viewed on YouTube for anyone interested in watching. His performance inspired Gabriel's song in the caves.

The Jacobins and Girondins were true factions that warred during the Revolution. While the Girondins believed in helping the working class gain more freedoms, they were far more moderate. During the Reign of Terror of 1793-1794, the Jacobins were responsible for murdering approximately 40,000 people they considered "enemies" to liberty, all via guillotine

For a detailed account of the Sanson family history, including their macabre interest in concocting remedies, I highly recommend both volumes of *Memoirs of the Sansons*, which have been archived on Google books in their entirety.

RECOMMENDED READING

Alleyn, Susanne. *Palace of Justice: an Aristide Ravel Mystery.* New York: Spyderwort Press, 2014. Print.

Alleyn, Susanne. *The Executioner's Heir: A Novel of Eighteenth-Century France.* New York: Spyderwort Press, 2013. Print.

Davies, Paul. *The Art of Assassin's Creed Unity.* London: Titan Books, 2014. Print.

Dickens, Charles. *A Tale of Two Cities.* London: Chapman and Hall, 1859. Print.

Donnelly, Jennifer. *Revolution.* New York: Delacorte Books, 2010. Print.

Fletcher, Susan E. *A Little in Love.* Frome: The Chicken House. 2015. Print.

Garrioch, David. *The Making of Revolutionary Paris.* Los Angeles: University of California Press, 2002. Print.

Hibbert, Christopher. *The French Revolution.* London: Penguin Books, 1980. Print.

Kreis, Steven. *The History Guide: Lectures on Modern European Intellectual History. Lecture 13: The French Revolution: The Radical Stage, 1792-1794.* 5 Mar. 2017.

May, Gita. *Madame Roland & the Age of Revolution.* New York: Columbia University Press, 1970. Print.

Ribeiro, Aileen. *Fashion in the French Revolution.* London: B.T. Batsford Ltd, 1988. Print.

Rousseau, Jean-Jacques. *Emile: Or, On Education.* New York, Basic Books, 1979. Print.

Sanson, Clément, Henri. *Memoirs of the Sansons, from private notes and documents, 1688-1847.* London: Google books. Full Text of "Memoirs of the Sansons." 5 Mar. 2017.

Scurr, Ruth. *Fatal Purity: Robespierre and the French Revolution.* New York: Metropolitan Books, 2006. Print.

Voltaire. *Candide.* New York: Random House Publishing Group, 2003. Print.

ABOUT THE AUTHOR

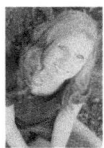

Mary Gray balances dark and twisty plots with faith-based messages. Some of her best ideas come when she's lurking in the woods, experimenting with frightening foods, or pushing her kids on the tire swing. She is a contributor to The Faithful Creative Magazine and is the membership chair of Indie Author Hub.

If you enjoyed reading this, will you please consider leaving even a tiny review? It would mean the world to me. If you'd like to join my mailing list or street team, shoot me an email.

marygraybooks.com
marycgray@icloud.com

ALSO BY MARY GRAY

HER DARK FANTASY: A PREQUEL TO OUR SWEET GUILLOTINE - A short story prequel to French Revolution-era novel, OUR SWEET GUILLOTINE. Young Tempeste witnesses an executioner break apart her mother's feet in an attempt to extract a confession.

THE DOLLHOUSE ASYLUM - a group of teenagers are granted asylum from the apocalypse, only to be forced to reenact some of the most famous, tragic literary couples... or die.

HOW TO WRITE FAITH-BASED MESSAGES FOR A SECULAR MARKET - for secular writers who hope to incorporate messages of hope and faith.

HUSH, NOW FORGET - in the vein of the CW's Supernatural, two somewhat cloistered sisters team up with a pair of hottie hunters to unmask what the Blurred Ones really are.

THE DEVILS YOU MEET ON CHRISTMAS DAY - a short story anthology about the outliers, the murderers, the misunderstood, and the forgotten, all penned by editors of Monster Ivy Publishing.